THE HUSBAND HUNT

"Jillian Hunter serves up a story that is greatly enhanced by unique, smart characters."

—The Romance Reader

"The characters are a delight. . . . Readers who relish a humorous offbeat novel need hunt no further than this charming book."

—AllReaders.com

ABANDON

"Charming characters and perky dialogue."

—*Publishers Weekly*

"A delight to read."

—All About Romance

INDISCRETION

"Ms. Hunter has the perfect touch for adding wit and passion to tempt a reader to forget the clock and read all night."

—*Romantic Times*

"A rousing, madcap tale with scintillating passion, humor, and a cast of quirky characters. Ms. Hunter pens unique, fascinating stories that draw the reader right in. Impossible to put down."

—*Rendezvous*

Books by Jillian Hunter

Fairy Tale
Daring
Delight
Indiscretion
Abandon
The Husband Hunt

JILLIAN HUNTER

DELIGHT

POCKET BOOKS
New York   London   Toronto   Sydney

This book is a work of fiction. Names, characters, places and incidents are products of the author's imagination or are used fictitiously. Any resemblance to actual events or locales or persons living or dead is entirely coincidental.

An *Original* Publication of POCKET BOOKS

 POCKET BOOKS, a division of Simon & Schuster, Inc. 1230 Avenue of the Americas, New York, NY 10020

ISBN-13: 978-0-671-02682-0
ISBN-10:   0-671-02682-8

First Pocket Books printing January 1999

10 9 8 7 6 5 4 3

POCKET and colophon are trademarks of Simon & Schuster, Inc.

Front cover: Lettering by David Gatti. Illustration by Jon Paul.

Manufactured in the United States of America

For information regarding special discounts for bulk purchases, please contact Simon & Schuster Special Sales at 1-800-456-6798 or business@simonandschuster.com.

For my three princesses—
Jacqueline
Julie
Jennifer
May all your dreams come true.

DELIGHT

Chapter 1

The Scottish Highlands
1662

CAPTURING THE PRINCESS WOULD BE HIS LAST CON-
quest.

The pirate planned to win this woman just as
he had won countless past prizes—with outright
deception.

Flying false colors had worked well enough for
him before. Hoist a Spanish merchant flag and
sneak past the galleon's guard. Steal the treasure
without wasting a single pistol ball. He'd always
preferred a battle of wits to one of weapons, and,
after all, he was dealing with a woman.

The woman was innocent. She had been protected from scoundrels like him all her life. Accustomed to easy victories, he did not anticipate
'twould take him long to win her.

Assuming he did not make an utter ass of
himself.

Yet deception could be a dangerous game. He knew this too from experience. The princess was to be his personal victory, but he did not wish to hurt her as he had hurt others. Too many black marks had been tallied against his soul as it was.

Clouds passed over the moon. A wind blew up across the battlements. The breeze shredded the layer of mist that enveloped the stalwart towers of Castle Dunmoral. A deep sigh built in his massive chest.

He was an impostor, and he felt it to the very marrow.

Four solemn figures watched him. They waited for his deep baritone voice to issue orders. They were as uncomfortable as he, venturing into these hazardous waters of social convention. They did not know the primary rules of play.

"She should have been here by now," he said to no one in particular. "Why did I not ride out earlier to escort her? She could be lost. *We* got lost our first time here. The roads are impossible to follow."

"The reivers, Douglas," a young feminine voice said behind him. "They ruined everything. It couldn't be helped. We'd have been able to meet her if we hadn't wasted the day chasing cows."

His face darkened at the reminder. Early that same day, in the wee small hours, a band of outlaws had struck the defenseless village of Dunmoral again. They had stolen cattle needed to see the clansmen through the cruel winter months ahead. They had assaulted a young woman. The impoverished king could not afford to maintain armies in these distant Highlands. The feuds and raiding begun two centuries ago had flared up again.

Douglas had spent seven hours futilely pursuing cows into the hills when he should have been planning a reception for the princess.

The raiders had fled, promising to return. Their leader, Neacail of Glengalda, deerstalker and unsuccessful claimant to Castle Dunmoral, had declared open war on the new earl. Douglas had galloped back to the castle, frustrated that he had been unable to prevent or avenge the attack.

The biggest of the three other pirates on the battlement approached him. He was a bald-headed mountain of a man who acted as Douglas's bodyservant and man-at-arms. Actually, Dainty hadn't held either position until a month ago, when word reached them of the princess's imminent arrival. Before then he had served as first mate on the pirate ship *Delight*.

But the Cornish giant had looked so misplaced in the castle that Douglas had been forced to give him an official title.

"Aidan and I could ride out to find her, sir," Dainty said.

Douglas's gaze flickered to the austere face of the second man leaning against the wall. "I don't think that's a good idea," he said with grim humor. "The pair of you are enough to give anyone nightmares, let alone a princess. We'll wait until Willie and Roy come back from their patrol."

Aidan shifted, his hand moving to his sword. His hair stirred in the wind, restless, unable to hold still like the man himself. Shadows obscured his expression, but Douglas believed there was a gentleness deep within the young pirate's heart. "The reivers are still out there, sir."

"I am aware of that." Douglas's contemplative gaze lifted to the outline of hills above the land he had been entrusted to protect. "I shall go after the princess myself. Someone has to stay here in case there's more trouble."

Which there would be. The promise of it hung in the air. His men sensed it too; Douglas had never met a pirate who didn't possess the devil's instinct for disaster.

"Disaster," he said under his breath. "And here we are courting it in spades, pirates masquerading as gentlemen. Dear God, why did I think this would work? 'Twould be easier to civilize a pack of wolves."

Dainty shook his bald head. "We don't need to be civilized, sir. Nothing wrong with our manners to begin with."

"Not a blessed thing," Douglas said. "Baldwin spits on his hair to give it shine. Willie cracks walnuts under his armpit. Roy puts a peeled grape in his empty eye socket to scare children." He paused with an ironic smile. "And you, Dainty, well, who could ever overlook your ability to consume one-hundred and eight pickled onions in a row, followed by a rendition of 'Greensleeves' belched in perfect pitch? How could the princess fail to be impressed by such spectacles of human refinement?"

" 'Tis a hundred and ten," Dainty said, unperturbed by the criticism.

Another sigh escaped Douglas. Concern emphasized the creases that bracketed his finely molded mouth. He pivoted on the walkway of the watchtower. He seemed immune to the cold air that chafed his hard-lined face, the rugged planes carved into sharp relief by moonlight. How *did* a pirate go about pleasing a princess?

In truth, he was not even supposed to be a pirate anymore. To his shame, however, stealing what belonged to another had become a habit he could not easily break.

As of seven months ago, Douglas Moncrieff, the Dragon of Darien and Scourge of the Spanish Main, had been rendered null and void by royal decree. Soon he would be lost and forgotten in the mists of folklore and infamy. His days of sailing under a letter of marque from an exiled king had fizzled to an unremarkable end.

May the Dragon rest in peace. Douglas wouldn't miss him at all. In fact, he was appalled by the monstrous deeds attributed to his brutal alter ego. Unfortunately, however, more than a few of those monstrous deeds could be well and truly laid at his door.

The Stuart king had regained his throne. Douglas's reward for his rich contributions to the royal coffers was an earldom with an obscure castle buried in the Scottish Highlands. The golden age of piracy had taken on a tarnish. Freebooting had become an embarrassment to the British Crown. He had been asked by his sovereign to behave.

This might prove easier said than done.

The short Scotsman named Baldwin, with crimped reddish-gray hair and protruding ears, stepped forward. A worried frown wrinkled his sun-blistered forehead. The middle-aged man had been Douglas's quartermaster from the very beginning, and he wasn't happy about his demotion to castle steward.

"I dinna know why we need a hokery-pokery princess anyway," Baldwin said. "Not unless we're going to hold the lass fer ransom. Women are always more trouble than they're worth."

"We are not holding Princess Rowena for ransom," Douglas exclaimed. "Have I not made myself clear? Earls do not hold women hostage. Where would you get such a ungodly idea?"

"From yerself." Baldwin scratched his scraggly whiskers. "Are ye forgettin' we ransomed Doña Maria in Cartagena? Her papa paid a pretty penny to get her back, and we didna have to go to all this bother."

"Those days are gone." Douglas drew his hand

over his eyes, deliberately keeping his expression stern. "We are not holding the princess prisoner. She is to be our honored guest."

"What if the princess is as homely as hell?" Baldwin wondered aloud.

Douglas frowned. "My brother would not court an unattractive woman."

"But what if she is just plain ugly, sir?" Dainty asked, glancing around to wink at Aidan.

"I'll cross that bridge when I come to it," Douglas said. "Now cease your stupid questions, and do as you are told."

"We'll do whatever you want us to do, Douglas." His sister Gemma spoke up again, but the girl was only seventeen; she'd spent half of her life in a brothel, the other on a pirate island. She knew no more about royal protocol than Douglas.

The three men behind her subsided into silence, their weather-beaten faces mirroring Douglas's own uncertainty. They were the thorn in his side, the crew members of the *Delight* who'd shadowed him like a malodorous smell to the Highlands because they couldn't find gainful employment elsewhere.

Douglas didn't know how to get rid of them so he'd given them various jobs in the castle. They still held hopes of getting him back on a ship. They still dreamed of gold and adventure.

He said, "God willing the princess will be safely arrived within the hour. Remember there are to be no references to the past. No mention of pirating, ransoms, or stolen booty. Is that understood?"

"Aye, aye captain," Baldwin said.

"Not 'Aye, aye, captain.'" Douglas glowered at the man from beneath his heavy black eyebrows. "'Tis to be 'Yes, my lord,' from now on. I am the third Viscount Strathkeld, and ninth Earl of Dunmoral—"

"Eighth," Gemma said. "You're the eighth earl."

"A little polish, sir, and she'll never notice that we're the dregs of society," Dainty said with another grin.

"Mary MacVittie, the doctor's sister, has been giving us all little lessons in proper behavior," Gemma said proudly. "She was a seamstress's assistant at court a year ago. She sewed for the Duke of Buckingham's nursemaid."

Douglas glanced down at his own costume, tartan trews and a dark blue-green belted Highland plaid that fastened at the shoulder with a silver stag's-head brooch. Buckled shoes, a dirk and *sgian-duth*, a short knife, completed the image. His shoulder-length black hair was tied back in a leather thong. Mrs. MacVittie had assured him that this was the correct attire for a castle laird to greet a foreign princess.

Now he was a nobleman dressed by a nursemaid's assistant.

The woman wanted to help him because Douglas had promised to help the people of Dunmoral. Her quavering voice echoed in his ear.

"The plaid was made for men built like warriors such as you, my lord. You canna wear those garish waistcoats and tight black leather breeches to greet a princess. She'll appreciate a touch of tradition for a first impression."

A touch of tradition to hide the uncouth scoundrel beneath.

His scowl deepened. It amazed him that he'd sunk Spanish galleons with less forethought than he had put into impressing this Rowena of Hartzburg, who, by the way, wasn't traveling day and night to meet a disgraced pirate, but rather the pirate's respectable half-brother, Sir Matthew Delacourt, a former Grenadier Guard.

"She probably won't even spend a single night when she finds out her Sir Galahad isn't here," he said darkly. "She'll scamper home like a frightened squirrel the moment she realizes I am the black knight on the chessboard."

"Perhaps not," Gemma said encouragingly. "We still don't know why Matthew arranged to meet her in Dunmoral when they both have lodgings in London at their disposal."

But Douglas knew. Matthew had been boasting of his personal relationship with Rowena for years. He had described her in great detail, her warmth, her charm, her wealth. He was proud to have fought for Rowena's family when rebels threatened to attack her palace.

Saint Matthew, the dragonslayer and polished courtier.

Douglas, the dragon and social outcast.

"Do you think he was hoping to woo her?" Gemma asked curiously.

Douglas arched his brow. "I would bet my astrolabe on it. I think he means to use this castle as a stage for his seduction. He knows I am in no position to pass judgment."

"Shame he's stuck in Sweden with a broken leg," Aidan said from the shadows.

"Isn't it though?" Douglas's voice was softly mordant.

Gemma sighed, too innocent to understand the undercurrent of sarcasm. "Matthew probably meant to marry her in the Highlands."

Not if I have my way. Douglas straightened his wide shoulders as if preparing for the challenge. He had accepted this earldom in the hope of finding an antidote to his inner pain. He'd wanted to forget the lives he had ruined in his blind passion for power and riches. Instead, he had stumbled upon a village of people more in need than he, ravaged by civil wars, famine and raiders. The princess would help him accomplish this.

"Poor Sir Matthew." Dainty gave a tragic sigh. "And him so brave, trying to rescue an injured horse from a ravine."

Douglas laid his hand over his heart. "A hero in the truest sense of the word."

"Only a pirate would take advantage of another's misfortune," Aidan murmured.

"A pity we aren't pirates anymore." Douglas's voice was solemn, but devilish lights danced in his obsidian eyes. "As subjects of the Crown, we are expected to welcome the princess in my brother's place with open arms."

"If you say so, Douglas," Gemma said, shaking her head. "But don't forget we lost everything except our garters when the *Delight* was wrecked. We're paupers living in a grand castle. I still think you should swallow your pride and accept Matthew's offer of a loan."

"A loan, Gemma." He reached down to ruffle her glossy black curls. He flashed her a smile of sheer wickedness. "I think we can do even better than that, lass—if our honored guest ever arrives."

"Dinna fret, sir," Baldwin said. "Someday yer princess will come."

Chapter 2

ROWENA LOWERED HER LONGBOW AND RETREATED into the cave as the two horsemen thundered back toward the hills. A badger-skin quiver slid off her shoulder. The men had searched the woods with weapons drawn.

"They were definitely looking for someone." Her low smoky voice echoed against the cavern walls. "I wonder where they came from. There were no lights in the distance."

"They came from the depths of Hades by the look of them," her older companion replied with a shiver. "Who but scoundrels would attack two women lost and alone in this inhospitable land?"

"They hardly attacked us," Rowena said. "They never even saw us. For all we know, Matthew might have sent them as our escort, and we, like spineless ninnies, hid so they could not help us."

"Sir Matthew—send men like that? Never."

Rowena sighed. "While we may be lost, we are no longer alone. That's Frederic coming through the woods."

The princess, as straight and strong as one of the arrows she could shoot with such deadly accuracy, motioned to the rider with her sable muff. Her thick chestnut-brown hair tumbled in tangles to her hips. The November chill had turned the tip of her nose pink. Her temper was frayed from traveling all the way from London to meet her old friend.

'Twasn't like Matthew to send such a summons and then forget an escort, but Rowena did not want to agree with Hildegarde aloud.

They had been following a haphazard road for three days, relying on Rowena's instincts. Now those instincts warned her something was amiss.

A tall man with a goatee dismounted to approach the cave. He bowed from habit before he spoke, the gold epaulets of his blue velvet jacket covered in dust. Frederic was her personal advisor and bodyguard, dependable if dour. He too showed the strain of traveling under such dangerous circumstances.

Hartzburg was a tiny principality beneath the Vosges mountains in the Rhine basin. France was her neighbor and friend. Yet even France had pretended not to notice that the rocky enclave was on the verge of collapse with rebels threatening to seize control.

Rowena's brother, Prince Erich, the heir of
Hartzburg, had mysteriously disappeared while
hunting. No one knew whether foul play was
involved. But fearing Rowena would be abducted
and used as a political pawn, her father Prince
Randolph had packed her off to London.

Shortly after her arrival, Sir Matthew Delacourt had contacted her. His letter haunted her
on this bitterly cold Scottish night.

> Dearest Rowena,
>   I have learned of your plight. You must be
> protected. Meet me at Castle Dunmoral in
> Scotland. Should I fail to make our meeting
> on time, place your trust in my brother the
> Earl of Dunmoral.
>
>   Your servant,
>   Matthew

"There was trouble?" Frederic frowned in suspicion at the bow lying against Rowena's tapestry
valise.

Hildegarde answered for her. "Two horsemen
were hunting down someone. They had the look
of cutthroats about them."

Rowena shrugged. "They could have simply
been two husbands who had been out hunting
and were now hurrying home to supper. What did
you find out? You've been gone all day."

His thin face tightened. "For lack of encountering a single human being who could speak a civilized language, I was forced to return to the crossroads where we abandoned our carriage. There I met a minister of the kirk who begged me not to let you go any farther."

Hildegarde smothered a gasp of alarm. She was younger than she appeared, not yet fifty, but grief had taken its toll, graying her hair, destroying her faith. "The rebels from Hartzburg have sent men here to ambush us?"

Frederic scowled. "Woman, you have an imagination like a windmill, always going at full tilt. I did not say anything about rebels."

Hildegarde's chin trembled at the rebuke. Rowena patted her hand, remembering the times when the woman had not been so afraid, before her husband and three strapping sons had been slaughtered by the robber barons who haunted the mountains of Hartzburg.

"Everything will be fine," she said calmly, studying Frederic's face. "What did this man say? Is all not well with Sir Matthew?"

"The minister I met had never heard of Sir Matthew." Frederic paused for effect. "The Earl of Dunmoral is another matter. A rumor is circulating that he is in no way related to the ancient family whose title he claims. The castle may well be under the command, and I use the term loosely, of the nefarious pirate once known as the Dragon of Darien."

Rowena's temples began to throb. "But I thought—the London broadsheets said that the Dragon was dead."

"Apparently, he is very much alive." Frederic's frown deepened. "According to rumor the Crown has insisted he take on a new identity and play a more productive role in society than a brutal sea robber. How is it *you* know of such a miscreant, Highness?"

Rowena suppressed a smile. "He was part of history, was he not? And history was my favorite subject at the convent school. But I never dreamed he was Matthew's half-brother. Matthew mentioned him but never went into any detail."

Frederic said, "One usually does not discuss the black sheep of the family, and from what I understand, they do not come any blacker. The earl is said to hold orgies in his hall. Village women have entered his keep never to return home."

"Then perhaps they were enjoying themselves too much to bother," Rowena said. "Besides, Matthew once risked his life for us, and if he says I am to trust the earl, then that is the end of it. Anyway, Frederic, you know better than to listen to gossip."

"He might be a pirate!" Frederic exclaimed.

"And he might not," Rowena said. "What matters is that he is Matthew's brother—oh, goodness, what a wonderful combination, Matthew's military skills and the Dragon's daring."

Frederic drew an outraged breath. "To lead you into a pirate's lair—well, my imagination does wicked things."

So did Rowena's.

Any sensible princess would have hastened back to the safety of her London-based friends. She would have sniffed into her scented hanky, lamenting her papa's fate as she dressed for a masked ball. She would have flirted with King Charles, who, famous for his roving eye, had already sent her a patch box along with condolences for her plight.

But Rowena had a mind of her own, and for the first time ever, she was on her own. Freedom shimmered before her like an unexplored map of mysterious avenues and shadowed pathways leading to endless little adventures. Or misadventures.

Cosseted, sheltered, trained, she chafed like a filly against the bridle of her upbringing. Besides, no one else had a plan to help her papa. A fortnight should be long enough to persuade the Dragon to take on another crusade. She would enlist Matthew's help.

Rowena had nothing to lose.

She also believed in fate.

Even in her obscure European principality, known mostly for its arrogant rulers and truffles, the Dragon of Darien had been discussed at the dinner table, his exploits admired or abhorred depending on one's political viewpoint.

"Is he married?" she asked matter-of-factly.

"Highness," Frederic cried, "what could you be thinking?"

Hildegarde smirked at him. "If the princess has a premonition, it must be obeyed."

"Premonition about a pirate? This rogue has killed people for gold. He is tainted, with no regard for human life—"

"The barons who threaten to hold Papa hostage in his own home are barbarians," Rowena said. "They have burned hamlets and slaughtered entire families. They killed my poor Hildegarde's family. Who better to conquer them than a pirate who has perfected the art of plunder?"

Frederic studied her with grudging respect. "The nuns may not have tamed that stubborn will, but they did teach you to think."

"Thank you, Frederic."

"I am not sure thinking is a good thing in a woman," he added.

"But you will do as I ask?" Rowena said, crossing her fingers inside her muff.

His jaw tightened. "Your father gave me funds to assemble an army of mercenaries to send back home. He believed that these Highlands breed fierce fighting men."

"Even an army of mercenaries needs a leader," Rowena said.

Frederic let that remark go unchallenged. "I suppose I could allow you a fortnight or so in the castle while I visit General Crichton in Dunbrodie. The man is retired but he has offered to help me recruit some decent soldiers."

"Is it far from here?" Hildegarde asked.

"A three-day ride each way," he said.

"I will watch over the princess," Hildegarde said.

Rowena felt a sense of relief sweep over her. "My grandmother always said that one's true destiny leads to unimagined delight."

"Or disaster," Frederic muttered.

Hildegarde snorted. "Destiny, I don't know. I'd settle for a warm fire and bowl of tasty mutton soup. These Highland winds cut straight to the bone, not to mention giving one an appetite."

Rowena brushed around her. "Help me dress—the ermine-trimmed purple, I think. Find my perfumed gloves and pearls. And Mama's tiara."

"Tiara?" Frederic shouted.

Rowena stifled a giggle. "I want to make a good impression."

"Impression?" He clapped his hands over his eyes. "On a pirate? God in heaven!"

Rowena started to laugh in earnest then. She just couldn't help herself. She couldn't wait to kick up her damask slippers and link up with a man who had dared to live out his most dangerous dreams. She had been led to Scotland for a reason, after all.

It was time, at long last, for the princess to raise royal hell.

* * *

"After all," Gemma was saying, "you and Matthew are flesh and blood."

"Indeed, we are," Douglas said, his smile vanishing at the thought.

Flesh and blood who had nothing in common. Matthew had made something fine of his life. Douglas had made a scandalous mess of his. Matthew wore a sash of honor and white satin. Douglas wore a gold earring and galley-slave scars.

Half-brothers with nothing in common except Princess Rowena of Hartzburg, one of Europe's great heiresses and eligible maidens, though on this point Douglas privately had his doubts. How innocent could the young woman be if she was using his castle as a rendezvous with Matthew? It was a scandalous age. The nobility was infamous for its affairs.

The echo of footsteps within the stairtower drew Douglas from his post. He turned, recognizing the pigeon-breasted figure of the *Delight*'s former sailmaker, a short young Devon sailor who had run away from an orphanage at thirteen.

"I've been searchin' all over this accursed castle for you, sir," Willie said sourly. "What the hell is everyone doin' up on the poop in this weather?"

"This isn't the poop, Willie," Gemma said. "They're called the parapets."

"Pair o' what?"

"Parapets, moron," she said, her hands planted on her hips. "And if you use that foul language in front of the princess, I'll be throwing you off them on your witless head."

"Did you sight the princess's entourage?" Douglas demanded.

Willie pulled off his woolen cap. His blond hair stood up on end like patches of straw. "Aye, sighted it and lost it. They left their coach miles and miles back when the road ended. I figure they'll be comin' the rest of the way on horseback."

"I told you to stay with the women," Douglas said in a clipped voice. "How could you lose a royal entourage?"

"They flew by us like bats out o' hell and that scared my horse. The animal threw me onto my back. I ain't much of a rider, sir. By the time I caught my wind and got the guts to get back on that bad-tempered beast, the princess's party had vanished." He blinked at the memory. "Weren't much of a party to speak of neither. Could've been a family of gypsies on the way to a fair for that matter. Coach looked like an old wagon."

Baldwin grinned at him. "Willie, were you chasin' after the wrong princess?"

"I was not," he said indignantly. "I got me a good look at the princess's face. Like a fairy angel she was, all tiny with curly yellow hair and teeth like pearls and a crown of gemstones—" He hesitated. "At least I think I saw her."

Gemma snorted. "I thought she flew by like a bat out of you-know-where."

"He *was* chasin' after the wrong princess." Baldwin slapped himself on the knee. "What a blockhead."

Douglas advanced on Willie until the shorter man backed into the stout wall of Dainty's chest. "If the princess is lost, we're going to have to find her, aren't we?" he said in that deadly quiet voice his men had learned to dread. Douglas didn't shout a lot or hit anyone unless he meant it. He was usually just so frightening with his silences and unnerving stares that some sailors had jumped overboard to escape the evil discipline they feared was coming.

"I cannot imagine a young noblewoman traveling an unmarked Highland cattle track on a November night," he said between his teeth. "Dainty, have two horses saddled. Aidan, go with him but keep that wicked sword in its sheath."

Before either man could move, a flickering light in the black hills beyond the castle caught Douglas's eye. It floated closer, taunting, then went out like a will-o-the-wisp.

Apprehension tightened his scalp. Some of the Highlanders in Dunmoral practiced Celtic magic. There were raiders hiding in those hills, outlaws who had declared war on Douglas and all he protected. And there was Rowena of Hartzburg, with curly brown hair and a crown of gemstones, a royal princess in a savage land.

The light reappeared. He touched the golden earring he wore in his left ear like a talisman.

"Someone's coming," he said in his deep lyrical voice, as calmly as if he were announcing the time of the day. "Gemma, go downstairs and make sure everything is in order. I don't want her tripping over a tankard of ale or Simon's wooden leg on the stairs."

Gemma stood unmoving, black curls blowing around her white face.

"What is it, lass?" Douglas said.

"I don't know what to say to her," she whispered with a look of panic.

"Just remember Mrs. MacVittie's advice," he said sternly. "When in doubt quote Shakespeare."

"Shakespeare." Gemma nodded, taking a deep breath.

A smile of cynical amusement crossed Douglas's face. In his deep actor's voice that could have graced Drury Lane he said: "Twelfth Night: 'Go, hang yourselves all! You are idle shallow things—'"

The clatter of wheels on the other side of the loch rose in the distance. Douglas turned, his lean face suddenly serious. "She's coming. Remember everything I've told you, and we'll all be the richer for it."

Dead silence.

Then all six of them rushed to the edge of the merlons and stared down. It seemed to take forever before the wheels rumbled over the wooden bridge to the castle.

Even Aidan, that most aloof and skeptical of souls, leaned down fractionally for a better look.

"She's almost at the drawbridge now," Baldwin said in excitement, all plots of ransom and troublesome women forgotten. "I've never seen a real princess in her coach before."

"I don't think we're seeing one now," Gemma said in confusion. "If my eyes don't deceive me, that's no carriage."

"'Tis a peat cart." Douglas looked up. "Willie, you didn't mention a peat cart on your way."

A flush crept across Willie's freckled face. "I did not pass that cart, sir. I swear it."

The peat cart, led by two ponies, and missing a driver, rolled to an uneventful stop in the bailey. Gold splotches of torchlight from burning pitch illuminated the eerie arrival. As their mentor Mrs. MacVittie had suggested, two serving girls danced forward to strew dried heather buds in the princess's path.

The buds drifted to the dirt. The ponies nuzzled them, shifting a few steps forward. But no princess alit from the cart to place her dainty foot on the flowered path.

"I do not know much about ancient history," Douglas said. "But that cart brings to mind a certain Trojan Horse. Dainty, get those two girls inside to safety and fetch my sword and pistols."

The giant melted away with the grace of a man half his size. Douglas glanced back down in the bailey with anger burning in his eyes.

"Pistols?" Baldwin studied Douglas in horror. "Ye canna greet a princess with a pistol. 'Tisn't seemly."

"We could greet her with a gun salute," Willie said. "She might like that."

"There's no princess in that cart," Douglas said in contempt. "Did you not see that tarpaulin move when the girls came toward it? Something very much alive lies beneath, and I'll wager it doesn't have curly yellow hair and a crown."

"A trick, sir." Aidan searched Douglas's face. "Let Dainty and me take care of it so you won't get powder burns on that fine plaid."

Douglas sighed. "I wish everyone would stop worrying about how I look."

"We only want to help, sir," Aidan said. "You can't very well greet the princess if you're killing villains."

"What sort of fool would challenge ye on yer own ground, sir?" Baldwin asked.

Douglas didn't answer, moving to catch the weapons Dainty threw him from the watchtower stairs. Moonlight sculpted his sun-burnished face into a grim mask as he buckled on his sword belt. "Gather the men from the hall, Gemma. Quietly, lass."

She backed into the stone watchman's seat, shivering in her pretty green silk gown. "But what about the princess?"

"Raise the drawbridge." He strapped a bandoleer of pistols over his powerful shoulders. The ebony barrels gleamed against the rich hues of his plaid. "Send out two men to keep her away. The last thing I want is for a helpless woman like Princess Rowena to ride into the middle of a battle."

Baldwin shook his head in sorrow. "I canna bear to think of it, sir. That poor wee princess lost in the hills amongst them villains and thieves. What will become of her?"

"Villains and thieves indeed," Douglas murmured, his men falling in step as he moved to the stairs. "What has the world come to?"

Chapter 3

DOUGLAS HEFTED THE BASKET-HILTED CLAYMORE
IN both hands above the cart. The Scottish weapon was heavier than his cutlass, but he could
handle it. His shoulder muscles flexed in anticipation. His pistol would offer better protection,
but there might be gunpowder hidden in the cart,
and he wouldn't be surprised to see a barrage of
flaming arrows come flying out of the dark.

He knew every evil trick in the book. He had no
desire to become a human bonfire.

Had Neacail of Glengalda sent one of his outlaws on a suicide mission to blow up the castle he
coveted for himself?

"There are at least twenty armed men surrounding this cart," Douglas said with a deliberate calm. "Lay down your weapons, and come out
slowly, or I'll cleave you in half."

The tarpaulin rippled. A low muffled groan sounded beneath it. Douglas felt a bead of sweat slide down his throat, absorbed into the rough wool of his plaid. He wet his wind-chapped lips, and waited.

He half-expected a small army of outlaws to burst out at him in a killing frenzy. His hands tightened around the hilt of the claymore.

Every nerve and muscle in his body stretched, tightened, poised for action. Every breath he took burned. He was prepared for anything.

He was prepared for anything except the convulsive sob that he barely heard above the sound of his own harsh breathing. A cry that bespoke so much pain and desperation he dropped the claymore to tear the tarpaulin from the cart.

Dainty and Aidan flanked him like twin shadows, dark angels willing to follow him into any danger.

"Could that be the princess?" Dainty said in disbelief. "Could the bastards have caught her on the road?"

Douglas said nothing, his mouth flattening into a line of fury at the thought of a woman being used against him in a game of revenge.

The victim was not a woman at all, but a boy, twelve or thirteen, bound, beaten, and gagged with a filthy rag. His naked body shook convulsively. His eyes were bruised slits, his face a swollen mass of cuts. He curled into himself on a bed of peat, the mossy turf his people used for their fires.

Dainty lifted the injured child from the cart and cradled him to his chest. Aidan gently removed the gag. One of the serving girls covered his unclothed back with her shawl.

"There, lad," Douglas said, smoothing the boy's hair back from his face. "You're safe now. Who did this—"

The boy shied away from him, hiding his head in Dainty's chest. "H—hurt." His body quaked, the words burst from him like gunfire. "D—did bad things . . ."

"Neacail and his followers?" Douglas asked softly.

The boy jerked his head into a nod. Douglas glanced at Dainty. "Get him into the keep. Willie, fetch Frances from the kitchen. She'll know what to do."

Gemma fought back tears as she pulled on Douglas's arm. "I know who the boy is. I heard him begging his father to let him bring peat to the castle by himself. He wanted to prove he was big enough to be trusted."

Douglas stared at the cart. Peat to warm the cavernous hall where he had planned to welcome the princess. Charm, seduce and befriend her. He wasn't certain which. He'd worried about it for a week, obsessing over every angle, the possibilities endless but pleasurable to contemplate.

Yet one possibility he had never entertained in his darkest fantasies was that Princess Rowena might not reach the castle alive.

"Aidan." Their eyes met. The man was at his side. "Ride with me. I'll take the obvious roads, you take the moor. I want that woman found."

Aidan found them on the moor. The sight stopped him cold. A royal princess with a tiara, riding a tavern nag. A scowling old goat of a man, and a blonde woman built like a Valkyrie giving the old goat orders in no uncertain terms.

Aidan shook his head in wonder. Angels must be watching over this entertaining trio. Neacail of Glengalda could have kept his outlaws alive for twenty years selling the stones in the princess's tiara one by one.

He kicked his horse into a canter, his mouth stretching into a wicked smile. He wouldn't want to miss the look on Douglas's face when this entourage arrived at the castle.

Rowena held her breath as the dark horseman thundered down the hill. She wondered if this could be the infamous Dragon of Darien. He looked like a pirate from the distance. Then again he looked like a Highlander too, his black hair hanging to his shoulders, his face aloof and hard.

"You are the Princess Rowena?" he asked without expression as he reigned in alongside her, ignoring the pistol Frederic held pointed at his chest.

"Yes."

She studied him in silence, aware of disappointment slowly settling in. Handsome, strong, unsmiling. He was all these things and more. A man to break hearts and fight battles, but not her heart. Well, what had she expected?

That anticipated sense of destiny, that hoped-for *ping* of rightness, the inner voice that affirmed her hunch, did not come. Rowena trusted her intuition. It rarely failed her.

She sighed in resignation. "I am she."

"I am Aidan of Dunmoral," he said, wheeling his horse in a wide arc. "Come. The earl has just returned to the castle to organize a search party to find you. If we hurry, we will be able to stop him before he goes out again."

This young man looks like my middle son, Hildegarde thought as she followed Aidan over the hill, and her throat closed with unshed tears, her arms ached with the grief of not having held her beloved boy one last time before he died.

Still, her Stephan had never been a pirate. He'd never hurt anyone in his life. This man had stolen for a living. Could they trust him, despite his courteous demeanor and comely face?

And what was his master like? Hildegarde wondered. *Have I made a mistake letting my lady come to this place?*

Pirates! Frederic thought. *Prince Randolph will have my head on a pikestaff when he learns what I have allowed. Well, better that than have Rowena and the old woman haranguing me night and day. Reasoning with these females is worse than fighting a war.*

As Aidan rode behind them, he thought, *I ought to play a joke on Douglas. The son-of-a-bitch deserves it. He'll kill me, of course, but at least I'll die laughing. I never paid him back for putting that turtle in my bed last summer. Douglas is so serious of late with all his talk of reform. I am not ready to settle down myself.*

The boy would live, but only because Neacail had wanted the child's battered body to carry a graphic message to the castle. The message was meant to warn Douglas that his enemies had no scruples. A child's life meant nothing to the men who hid in the wild hills beyond the castle.

Frances Jagger was an Englishwoman who had run a bawdyhouse on the pirate island of Tortuga. She now ran Douglas's kitchen. She calmed the boy and got him cleaned up. He fell asleep in her lap beside the fire. She'd never had children of her own. Her husband had deserted her when she was pregnant, and she had lost that child. But she knew how to nurse a wounded man.

Douglas watched her from the arched doorway. He didn't say anything. Neither did she.

But when he left, she touched the boy's unsightly face and said in a certain voice, "Neacail is a dead man now, little one. Don't you worry. This evil will be avenged."

Chapter 4

THE FIRST WOMAN, IN FACT, THE ONLY WOMAN Douglas saw in the bailey, wore a black bombazine dress and laced-up black leather boots. Gray-blonde braids dangled from either side of her lynx-skin trimmed bonnet. A squirrel-lined cloak covered her wide shoulders. She carried a tapestry valise, and a heavy casket. She looked as if she should have been carrying a spear.

Dainty whistled low. "Now that's what I call one warship of a woman."

"She's a full-rigged ship if I ever saw one," said Gunther, *Delight*'s carpenter. "Look at her high poop. 'Twould be a job to man that pump."

"Is that the princess?" Gemma whispered, straining to see around Douglas's back.

"For a princess, she's plain as porridge," Baldwin said in disappointment.

"Plain?" Willie hooted derisively. "Hell, she's just plain ugly."

"Be silent," Douglas said. "Show the woman some respect." He glanced at Aidan, standing apart from the others with his arms folded across his chest. "Is that the princess?" he demanded.

Aidan didn't utter a word. He just lifted his shoulders in a little shrug as if to say, "I'm sorry. 'Tisn't my fault."

Dainty gave Douglas a sly grin. "You said you'd cross the bridge of the princess's homeliness when you came to it, sir."

Douglas hesitated. A faint smile touched his firm mouth. "If that's the princess, I won't be crossing that bridge. I'll be jumping off it."

His men laughed in appreciation as he stepped forward to greet the woman. He bowed gracefully. "Your Highness—"

Hildegarde dropped the casket at his feet. "God in heaven, that thing is heavy!"

Douglas straightened abruptly. "You—"

"Are you the earl?" Hildegarde asked, clamping his jaw in her powerful hand. "Well, let me have a good look at you. Old Hildegarde has a touch of the Sight, as they say in Scotland. Not that it's done any good. Let me see your face."

She examined him thoroughly while Douglas stood there, dumbfounded, the truth slowly sinking in. "Hildegarde, you called yourself?" he said, easing his aching jaw free. "Then you are not Princess Rowena?"

Hildegarde burst into a loud storm of laughter. "Me—the princess? Why, aren't you the flatterer? As if a mountain peasant such as myself could pass for a princess."

Douglas glanced over his shoulder at Aidan, whose shoulders shook with silent laughter. "Madam," he said gravely, "I apologize from the bottom of my heart for the mistake."

"What for?" Hildegarde said in astonishment. "I haven't had such a good laugh in ages. Frederic!" she shouted to the gaunt-faced figure approaching the small crowd. "Wait until you hear this—"

Then suddenly Douglas wasn't listening. He wasn't paying any attention to the tall man who regarded him in scowling silence. He was busy studying the second woman walking across the bailey. Willowy, from what he could see, lithe with flowing brown hair and a very compelling profile, at least from this distance. Relief pounded through his veins along with a surge of potent male interest.

He wanted the princess's fortune, yes, he admitted it. Perhaps, too, she was all the more attractive because she was the only woman his sainted half-brother had gone to such intriguing lengths to seduce, and there was a lifelong rivalry between the two of them.

But for a moment he couldn't decide if Rowena represented more than revenge or rivalry or even redemption. For a moment he wondered if she could restore a portion of the purity stolen from him so long ago that he couldn't remember the day when sinning hadn't been second nature. For a moment she was merely a woman unlike any other he had met.

They met in the middle of the moon-washed courtyard like two figures in a formal dance. His men were strangely silent, never having seen their Dragon behave in such a way.

He bowed low, his chest tightening at the smile of sweet curiosity she gave him. No breath-taking beauty this, he thought in surprise. Not the winter-cool blonde with guileless blue eyes that Matthew seemed to prefer but rather a vivid brunette with a bright pink nose and chiseled cheekbones that lent elegance to a face one might easily pass in a crowd.

What did Matthew see in her? He didn't need her wealth.

He didn't need her as Douglas did. Douglas, who had perfected the art of claiming what belonged to others. Still, for the first time he could honestly claim he was motivated by an unselfish cause. He refused to let another child under his protection die for lack of food. He would help his people.

Yet oddly he had never felt more like Mephistopheles than at this moment. Predator that he was, he was about to take advantage of his brother's misfortune for his own personal gain.

The Dragon of Darien, accustomed to the rough sport of wenches and whores, would devour this girl in a few tasty bites.

'Twas almost unfair. Assuming he committed no atrocious blunder in protocol, he'd capture her with more ease than a Spanish galleon in a bathtub.

The Earl of Dunmoral, however, would proceed with more restraint.

"Your Highness," he said, hiding a smile of remorse as he straightened to stare down into her brown eyes—and found himself the subject of a cool penetrating scrutiny that caught him broadside. And challenged him. Excited him.

Had he thought her less than beautiful? Then he hadn't been paying attention. She was more dangerous than beautiful. She was intelligent. The princess had an edge.

"I am Douglas Moncrieff, the Earl of Dunmoral," he said, recovering with only a moment's hesitation. "I trust you had an uneventful journey."

Before the princess could reply, Gemma came forward to execute a perfect curtsy; Mrs. MacVittie had made the girl practice until she was blue in the face. "Welcome to Dunmoral, Your Highness. I am the earl's sister, Gemma."

Gemma looked expectantly at Baldwin, who, forgetting Douglas's order to stay out of the way, pushed next in line to greet Rowena. Confusion clouded his weathered face. Everyone was staring at him.

Hell's bells, Baldwin thought. The princess was so pretty, he was going all fool-tongit. He couldn't remember whether he was supposed to bow or curtsy. He knew bowing had something to do with boys and curtsying with girls. But did you curtsy to a girl because she was a girl? Or did you bow?

He curtsied. "Please to meet ye, princess," he said, limp with relief that the ordeal was over, and Douglas hadn't killed him. In fact, Douglas probably hadn't seen the curtsy at all because he had his hand clapped over his eyes the entire time. "The name is Baldwin McGee."

"The honor is mine, Mr. McGee," Rowena said with a smile.

Baldwin's mouth dropped open. " 'Tis? Well, I'll be—"

"—seeing to your duties," Douglas said in a lethal tone. "I know you'll want to make sure Her Highness's rooms are ready."

"I hope I have not put you to any trouble," Rowena said, her voice sweet and low-throated.

Douglas turned toward her.

She was gazing up into his face, searching for things, he suspected, that he had hoped to keep hidden. Then she said, "The journey was tedious but not dangerous until a few miles back when we abandoned our carriage at the crossroads."

"There was no road to follow," Hildegarde said.

"So we followed our instincts," Rowena added.

"We were pursued by brigands," Hildegarde said. "We took refuge in a cave."

Douglas frowned at his men. "Brigands?"

"That was not proven," Rowena said, peering around Douglas to the dark bulk of the castle keep. "Has Sir Matthew gone out to look for us?"

"Ah. Sir Matthew." Douglas allowed several moments of mournful silence to elapse. His men bowed their heads in respect, some of them sighing. Then, with the utmost gentleness, he took her gloved hand in his and looked deeply into her eyes. "Perhaps 'twould be better if we went inside for me to deliver the unhappy news."

The deception was about to begin.

Chapter 5

"WELL, WHAT DO YOU THINK?" ROWENA MURmured to Hildegarde as they accompanied the earl to the keep.

"I think they are a strange lot, Highness," the woman whispered. "That little troll of a man *curtsied* to you."

Rowena grinned. "Perhaps 'tis a Highland custom."

Hildegarde stared at Douglas's darkly sculptured face, shaking her head. "A pirate is a pirate," she whispered. "Do not forget that."

Rowena didn't intend to. In fact, she was hoping against hope that he *was* a pirate, and that ruthlessness was the cornerstone of his character. She stole a glance at him from the edge of her eye. Tall, broad-shouldered frame, starkly arrogant profile, he did indeed appear to be the proverbial black sheep of the family. His brooding eyes held little of Matthew's warmth and whimsy. His hard chiseled mouth suggested forbidden pleasures and a restrained sensuality.

Both of which fascinated Rowena to no end.

She glanced down at his big hand, clasping hers in a masterful hold. His grasp was confident, possessive, making her feel strangely feminine and fragile. Rowena had never felt feminine in her life. Gangly, awkward, stronger than the sons of the palace guards she played with. Rare was the man who did not make her conscious of her height.

Annoyed, she realized she rather liked the feeling.

The Highland plaid of raw wool the earl wore surprised her. Yet it did suit his dark rugged looks and made no secret of his strength. Rowena's father would probably approve of such a costume, respecting tradition. But in her mind she'd pictured the pirate in tight leather breeches and billowing shirt, cutlass in hand, swinging from a yardarm to snatch her from the jaws of danger, bellowing out swear words in one breath, declarations of undying love in another.

She would be waiting for him in his cabin while he went off doing whatever it was pirates did. Possibly he would tie her with silken bands to his bedposts—*Good Lord!* Rowena thought, staring ahead with a grin. What imp of Satan sneaked these naughty images into her brain?

She suppressed a wry smile at her silliness.

There was an awkward moment as they reached the steep outer stairs to the keep.

The earl seemed to hesitate. For an intensely pleasurable instant Rowena fancied he was tempted to carry her up the narrow steps in his muscular arms. Which of course was more sheer fantasy on her part.

"After you, Your Highness," he said.

Rowena sighed. The climb proved a trifle difficult due to the voluminous bulk of her velvet skirt, silk underskirts, and quilted petticoats. Still, she was glad she had changed from her rumpled garments in the cave.

She hoped her tiara was still on straight.

The earl called out only once. The black oak doors to the keep swung open as if by magic to admit them. Perfect, she thought. He was born to command whether in a castle or on a pirate ship.

She had to convince him to help her. After she convinced herself he was entirely trustworthy, of course.

His low melodious voice sent a shiver down her neck. "My castle, as humble as it is, is at your disposal."

They climbed another flight of stairs and paused in a narrow torchlit passageway of the keep. The rough stone walls smelled of moisture and spilled wax. The earl fit the dark atmosphere,

master of his surroundings, his shadow filling the
small space. He turned toward her. His broad
chest pressed against her forearm. Rowena's
breath caught in her throat. Hildegarde and the
others were still lumbering up the stairs behind
them.

He withdrew his hand.

Rowena looked up slowly into his face, the
black eyes, the rough-hewn features. She noticed
the gold earring that glittered in his left ear. All
the beaux at court wore earrings now. It could
mean he claimed ties to his illicit past, or it could
simply mean he followed current fashion.

Frederic would soon be gone, hunting for warriors in the Highlands to take back to Hartzburg.
She and Hildegarde would remain alone in this
castle. Their wits, sharp as they were, would be
their only weapon for the next fortnight.

Against what? Was the Dragon a danger to her?
Or was the minister's information false?

"Well," Douglas said, and then he waited, leaving her to imagine a wealth of meaning in the
single word.

Her heart gave an erratic flutter. Her whalebone corset threatened to squeeze the air from
her ribcage. She seemed to shrink in the silence.
He seemed to grow. Well, he'd said, as if to add,
"You are at my mercy now . . ."

Rowena had been a dutiful daughter all of her
life. She had done whatever her papa had wanted.

And now, to save him, she was about to embark

on a mission so scandalous it would have sent the poor man to his grave.

Douglas stayed at the princess's side like a shadow, determined to ward off any trouble before it started. His men kept staring at her in awe. They stared at Hildegarde too, but for entirely different reasons. They were probably afraid she was going to hurt them.

Besides, he liked standing beside the princess. He was amused at how obediently she followed him while the look in her eyes hinted of a woman who had a definite mind of her own. He felt a rare urge to protect her. Yet in truth it was him she most needed to be protected from.

"You must be tired after your journey," he said politely. "Perhaps after a glass of warm milk and evening prayers, my servants can show you to your chambers."

"Milk and evening prayers?" Rowena repeated as if she hadn't heard him correctly.

Douglas frowned. He was sure his suggestion was what Mrs. MacVittie had advised him would be proper, propriety being his weak point. Did the princess look disappointed? Should he have planned a poetry recital or village tribute in her honor? Would Matthew have greeted her with pomp and ceremony?

He hid a wry grin. Hell, if the woman wanted entertainment she should have been here four hours ago when Willie dropped his false teeth down the garderobe chutes. And had to retrieve them.

He cleared his throat. "What I meant," he said suavely, "is that you will no doubt need both material and spiritual replenishment after I deliver the news about Sir Matthew."

Rowena absorbed this in silence. Then, "News?" she said at last, her voice troubled.

He drew a breath through his nostrils. The suspense, the uncertainty of success or failure, strangely appealed to him. He inclined his dark head. "My poor brother has met with an unfortunate accident—"

"An accident?" She paused. Douglas watched her in concern. "Not Matthew," she said. "Oh, no."

"He took a fall in Sweden and broke his leg," he said in a tragic undertone.

"He was rescuing his commander's horse from a ravine," Gemma added from the background.

Douglas shot his sister a look. He saw no need to be enhancing Matthew's reputation of epic heroism. He returned his gaze to Rowena, wondering if she might faint. She seemed quite steady on her feet so he continued in the same remorseful tone. "My brother sends his deepest regrets that he cannot meet with you."

Rowena bit her lip. Douglas stared, distracted, by the ripe contours of her mouth. A mouth made for lingering kisses and shared pleasures.

Now the lie.

"Matthew has asked me to take his place and offer my services."

Rowena's silence gave him no clue to the precise meaning of her rendezvous with Matthew. Douglas burned with curiosity to know the depth of her involvement with his brother.

"Not meet with me?" Rowena said. "But this is dreadful. I've come over a hundred miles—"

"Closer to a thousand," Hildegarde corrected her.

"Over hills," Rowena said.

"They were mountains, Highness."

Rowena smiled tightly. "Mountains. Hills. Is there a difference in the dark?"

"There is if ye fall off one," Baldwin said in a shy voice from the end of the passageway. "We wouldna want ye to hurt yerself, princess, so it might be a good idea to learn the difference."

"I don't think we need to alarm Her Highness about such improbable dangers," Douglas said in a sharp tone.

"It never hurts to be cautious," Hildegarde said.

Douglas nodded politely. "True."

"I fell off a mountain once," Baldwin said.

"Why doesn't that surprise me?" Gemma muttered.

Douglas frowned. "The princess will not fall off a mountain. This I promise."

"That is kind of you," Rowena said in a gracious voice.

There was a faint commotion behind them.

Dainty had just poked his bald head through the iron-hinged doors of the great hall and was whispering furtively to Gemma. Then Gemma whispered to Willie, who whispered to Baldwin, who pushed a path forward to tap Douglas on the shoulder.

"We have a wee problem, my lord," he said hesitantly.

Douglas frowned. "Later, Mr. McGee. Her Highness's comfort must come first. I suspect the princess would appreciate resting in front of the fire we have readied in the hall."

"We are chilled to the bone," Hildegarde said heartily. "Hungry too. And the princess's personal advisor must leave early on the morrow. He needs food and rest."

Baldwin pursed his lips. "Canna take the princess in there, sir," he said under his breath. "The boys have been misbehavin' again."

The hackles rose on Douglas's neck. He raised his broad shoulders in a shrug of apology to the princess. "Pardon me a moment, Your Highness," he murmured, dragging Baldwin to the doors. "Now what the devil is the meaning of this, you dimwit?"

Dainty poked his head into the hall again. " 'Tis Shandy and Phelps, sir. They got into an argument over whether to serve the princess rum or beer. Shandy broke the whole damned keg of rum over Phelps's head. Then Phelps broke a chair over Shandy's head. Then they made up and got drunk to celebrate."

Douglas's face darkened. His voice was deadly soft. "Rum or beer? They planned to serve the princess rum or beer?"

"Those idiots wouldna listen to me," Baldwin said indignantly. "Rum is far too powerful fer that nice lassie, I told them. Beer is too common. I said we should give her a keg of good grog punch."

Douglas's upper lip curled at the corner. "What would we do without your wisdom?"

"Shandy and Phelps won't be causing any more trouble tonight, sir," Dainty said. "They're passed out. Which would have been the end of our woes."

Douglas frowned. "Except?"

"Except Simon bet Gunther he could jump off the minstrel's gallery and land on Martin's shoulders."

Douglas passed his hand over his face. "He missed?"

"No." Dainty chuckled. "He didn't. But Martin took exception to being jumped on seeing that he was fixing the wobbly plank on the dais and had no idea what hit him. The place is a shocking mess."

Douglas lowered his hand. "Take all five of them down the inside stairs to the dungeon. Let them spend a night in that pleasant atmosphere. Then get the scullions to clean up the hall. Again."

Dainty grinned, disappearing a split-second before Rowena herself marched up to the doors, trying to peer inside. "Is that a fire I see in there?" she asked hopefully.

"Fire?" Douglas planted his feet apart to prevent her slipping past him. "Yes, 'tis. But I cannot allow you in there, Your Highness. The hall is a disgrace. Dust and cobwebs everywhere. Crumbs all over the table. I'm—I'm ashamed."

"I promise not to judge you by your housekeeping standards, my lord," Rowena said in amusement, trying to squeeze around him. "And I won't fall off a mountain either. All I ask is a little warmth to thaw out my toes."

He threw down his arm like a barricade. "Impossible. Some miscreant is burning peat in the fireplace. I expressly forbade the burning of peat in your presence."

Rowena gave him a strained smile, studying him like a soldier about to storm a citadel. "Pray do not put yourself to so much trouble, my lord."

"Why, 'tis no trouble at all." He flung down his other arm just as she shifted direction. For a ludicrous moment he feared he would be forced to engage the princess in a wrestling match. 'Twould not bode well for the future, pinning her to the floor with his forearm. In all his bragging, Matthew had never mentioned the woman had a will of iron.

"The royal health must be guarded," he stated. "The rough conditions of Hartzburg give rise to hearty rulers," Rowena said tightly, looking as if she might just throttle him.

"Her Highness is as strong as an ox," Hildegarde added.

"Thank you for that, Hildegarde," Rowena said.

Douglas forced a smile. Lord, what a lie could lead to. "Strong or not, I will not jeopardize her physical well-being. Peat is a bog material. 'Tis used as a cheap source of fuel in the Highlands. The smoke can make you ill if you are not accustomed to it."

"It can?" Baldwin said in alarm. "Well, I wish someone had told me this before. Here I've been sleepin' by that accursed fire in the kitchen every night. I could've woke up dead."

Gemma snorted. "I'd like to see that."

Douglas stepped away from them, gently forcing Rowena into the corner. "The castle is in an uproar over your arrival," he said by way of an apology. "The servants insist that everything be just so."

Princess that she was, Rowena took the peculiar refusal in stride. "Goodness, I'm really not that difficult to please. Perhaps my companion and I could retire to the solar and have a cup of hot chocolate."

Douglas looked blank. He nudged Gemma with his elbow. "Where is the solar?" he whispered from the side of his mouth.

"Right above the hall, ninny," she whispered back. "Turn left off the spiral stairs."

Rowena watched their exchange with a puzzled smile. "If it isn't too much bother, I would also like our bedsheets warmed."

Douglas's expression did not change, which was probably a good thing. Her words had electrified him, evoking the sensuous image of lying with her in his roomy four-poster bed, sharing the heat of their bodies as he tenderly took her innocence. Unless Matthew had already claimed that honor, although Douglas doubted this. There was a purity in her eyes he could not mistake. Still, 'twas the woman's gold he required, not her maidenhead, as tempting a conquest as it was.

And if the wheel of fortune didn't turn in his favor, well, he knew plenty of ways to force it.

Chapter 6

ROWENA WOULD HAVE GIVEN HER TIARA TO KNOW what the pirate had hidden in that hall. She wondered if a past lover had shown up unannounced at his door, a child in tow. Or if one of his infamous orgies was coming to a close. Surely the man did not expect her to believe that nonsense about unhealthful smoke.

Yet where there was smoke, was there not a dragon at its source?

She wished she could tell him outright she had been told of his disreputable past. But of course such frankness was unthinkable, dangerous even, considering the fact that the Crown had demanded he assume a new identity. Wiser to pretend to accept him at face value. After all, she had nothing more substantial than a rumor to act upon.

She would have to wait for such a confrontation until he trusted her, and she knew she could trust him. She suspected he was a pirate, but the man's inner nature had yet to be proven. Never would she enlist the help of a man who might betray her. Her homeland and father's life were at stake.

Yes, he was hiding something. Hildegarde clearly thought so too, peeping over her shoulder in distrust as if she expected a spy or evil spirit to suddenly appear from behind a tapestried alcove.

Hildegarde had devoted most of the past two decades to protecting Rowena from the traitors she feared would abduct her precious charge, and from the bad fairies who coveted the princess's unblemished soul.

The woman thrived on battling these imagined threats. Castle Dunmoral apparently would provide both.

Rowena sneaked a yawn behind her knuckles. Perhaps a good night's sleep would bring perspective. Perhaps sunlight would dispel the air of secrecy that overclouded this medieval castle. Whatever happened on the morrow, she would have to proceed without poor Matthew's help. She would have to tame her dragon alone.

"Mayhap we should not be so hasty to dismiss Frederic," Hildegarde grumbled in Rowena's ear. Then, "Heavens, what is this on the floor?"

Rowena glanced down at the damp splotches on the uneven stones. "What do you suspect?"

she whispered mischievously. "Bloodstains from the last princess the Dragon dragged in for supper?"

Hildegarde glanced down the passageway at Douglas's dark countenance where he stood giving orders to his small cluster of retainers. "If he is indeed the Dragon of Darien, then he has killed before. The man is known for his cruelty."

Rowena knelt surreptitiously to examine the floor. "It smells like spirits. Perhaps the last princess he lured here drank herself into oblivion. Or, more plausibly, perhaps his lordship has his distillery in the dungeon like Uncle Carl."

"Spirits do not concern me," Hildegarde admitted. "However, one does not expect a wild creature to become tame simply because he is put in a cage." She gathered her cloak around her ample figure. "Or castle."

Before Rowena could respond, Douglas returned to her side. His even white teeth glinted in a disarming smile that banished Hildegarde's warning from Rowena's mind. He offered her the support of his arm again.

"Let me show you to the solar." He was the essence of solicitous charm. "The servants will bring up your bread and chocolate in a few minutes. Unfortunately, a minor problem has arisen that will require my absence."

"May I be of any help, my lord?" Rowena asked.

"You?" he said in astonishment. "Good heavens, Your Highness, I should not dream of your lifting a finger. In fact, I am merely going to drive a village boy to his home—the same boy who delivered that dreadful peat to the castle. The lad was injured in an unfortunate accident on his way here."

"How kind of you, my lord, to pay that much personal attention to a child. Few men of your rank would care."

The flickering glow of the torches told her nothing of his thoughts. His black eyes absorbed the light. He said, "I want your stay at Dunmoral to be as pleasant as possible."

Dragons in their pleasant palaces. The Biblical verse flashed through Rowena's mind, but she could not remember what words followed as she laid her hand on his arm again. She seemed to recall something about wickedness and the day of destruction being at hand, and women being ravished—

I am as foolish as old Hildegarde, she scolded herself, restraining the urge to laugh. *Would this man hurt me when he frets over the crumbs on his table? Or is that a masquerade?*

Certainly when she felt his muscles flex beneath her fingers, strength contained in the subtle movement, she did not envision a man obsessed with domestic standards.

His aura of power aroused powerful feelings inside the princess. Perhaps Hildegarde had good reason to be afraid.

Pirates were by nature unpredictable. They

stole, murdered, and destroyed as did the barons who threatened her father's life.

Matthew was an effective warrior, but he did not think like a barbarian.

She needed this man.

Dangerous shivers danced over her skin as he moved his hand to her shoulder, guiding her up the unlit stairwell, into the very heart of his lair.

"Forgive me for being so bold." His voice enveloped her like velvet in the darkness. The richness of it raised gooseflesh on her arms. "But the torches have gone out, and I would not want you to slip. The castle poses many hidden hazards. It has a violent history. Some have said it should be destroyed."

She felt her heart accelerate. Should she read a warning in his words? "Perhaps its history adds character," she said quickly.

"Perhaps," he said at last. "But I would still advise you to be on guard. I would never forgive myself if you were harmed."

The air seemed to thicken, to sweeten like the fumes of an exotic incense. Was this desire? she wondered distantly. His heavy-lidded gaze drifted over her. It marked her like a brand. Heat seeped into her skin. His fingers tightened imperceptibly around her arm.

Rowena scarcely dared to breathe. No male except her brothers, who thought nothing of rendering her black and blue, had ever laid a hand on her royal person. Sensations unfurled deep within her, disturbing yet oddly pleasant. Before the rebellion, her papa had been in the process of arranging a marriage for her.

Rowena frowned at her reaction to this man.

She had been in the presence of big burly soldiers all her life, her father, her brothers, the hardened mercenaries Papa paid to defend Hartzburg, the intimidating palace guards.

But none of these men had affected her as did the earl. None of them sent this bolt of curious longing to lodge so deeply inside her. They had not touched her on such an elemental level.

He was unabashedly male. She could sense the dark passions and power that simmered beneath his off-handed charm. She could sense something very animal and untamed in him that he kept under control.

And she responded to it.

She sighed, chastising herself.

She needed this man for his fighting skills, not for his masculine prowess, as impressive as she suspected he would prove in that arena. Was she going to lose her head just because she was alone with a sinfully attractive man for the first time in her life?

He took the final step to guide her up into another passageway where low-burning torches threw shadows on the wall. His size enhanced that foolish illusion of fragility she had felt a few moments ago.

She was a little unbalanced by the rush of blood

through her veins, which made her feel reckless and lightheaded.

"Follow me," he said, his voice polite yet imperious as if he knew exactly what effect he had on her and was waiting for her to compose herself.

And Rowena did as he asked, suddenly afraid she had answered her own question.

She followed him with the eagerness of a woman compelled by her own curiosity to explore and experience life to the fullest.

She was definitely going to lose her head.

Douglas swore to himself in three different languages. Here he was alone with one of the world's most eligible heiresses. His bedchamber was only a stone's throw away. She followed him with virginal innocence, unaware of her precarious situation.

Was he nuzzling her neck and whispering love words in her ear? Was he peeling off her gloves, blowing kisses on her wrist, as he learned what pleased the lady? No. He was serving her hot chocolate in the solar and fussing over her like a great-aunt. This princess wielded a strange power indeed.

Douglas didn't think he would enjoy behaving himself. Such self-denial went against his true nature. It caused him physical discomfort to pretend he hadn't noticed the tempting curves beneath her gown, to pretend he was unaware of her feminine appeal. He had to restrain himself from backing her into the wall and kissing her until she dissolved into a puddle of helpless passion at his feet.

He had to be satisfied with holding her hand.

Hell, he couldn't even impress her with a Shakespearean sonnet because he had to run back downstairs and help tidy the hall before the princess realized she had stumbled into a den of salty old sea dogs.

His princess.

A smile twisted his mouth.

He could smell her light floral scent, some delicious type of French-milled soap like lilies or violets. He wondered how she'd react if he treated her as he had his other women. Would she like gentle wooing? It seemed unlikely that a princess would enjoy being tossed over his shoulder like a barmaid. He'd bet his jack-boots that sensuous flames smoldered beneath her self-possession, waiting for the man with the magic spark.

Well, if everything went as planned, if he actually managed to convince her he wasn't the Devil incarnate, he might just be the one to light her candle.

He steered her toward an arched doorway. "The solar, Your Highness. While you make yourself comfortable, I'll go downstairs and see what's taking those oafs so long."

Rowena glanced up at him in amusement. "Did you just refer to your servants as oafs, my lord?"

"What?" He looked down at her in astonishment. "I believe I said loafs. As in loafs of bread."

"Loaves." She bit the edge of her lip. "*Loaves* of bread."

"Quite so."

She stared past him with a puzzled smile. "Oh, dear, if I'm not mistaken, this isn't the solar at all. It appears to be the chapel."

Douglas swung around. Altar, candles, holy water-stoop, moonlight piercing the lancet windows. What the hell had he done now? Turned right instead of left? He felt like a complete moron.

"I've prayed so often of late that I came here without thinking," he said, shaking his head. "Of course 'tis the chapel. Silly me. The solar is to the left."

"I see." Rowena looked a little embarrassed for him. "May I ask what it is that you need pray about with such passion, or is it a private matter?"

"I pray for my brother's recovery." he said. *That it may be long.*

"As I will," Rowena said sincerely.

An unfamiliar envy overcame him. She would pray for his brother. An intimacy with a woman beyond sex that Douglas had never experienced. Nor desired to. Why, a year ago he would have fallen overboard laughing his head off at the notion.

How naive they were, Sir Matthew and his princess. Douglas couldn't remember a day in his life when he'd felt even a twinge of faith, when he had thought of himself as innocent. He had been bone-deep bad from the beginning.

He studied her oval-shaped face, seeking darker motives. "You and Matthew are more than friends?"

Her swift response stung. "I trust him with my life."

And her heart? He could not ask. A pall of awkwardness settled around the unsettled question.

"He speaks of *you* with great affection," Rowena said stoutly, as if she sensed the lack of fraternal loyalty on his part, and disapproved.

"Matthew?"

"You sound surprised, my lord."

"Well, he and I did not grow up together," he said evasively.

"I see." But clearly she did not. "Surely you come here to pray for other matters beside Matthew?"

She had changed the subject in the apparent hope that spirituality would bring them back to common ground. A praying pirate. If only she knew. Douglas suppressed a grin of irony at the preposterous image.

"I pray for my soul, naturally," he said, feeling a surprising twinge of guilt as his gaze drifted to the unlit candles on the altar. "And I pray that my village will be spared further raids and suffering."

That part at least was true. Douglas might not have come to Dunmoral with any personal attachment to the handful of Highlanders who depended on him, but he had always protected what was his.

"Raids?" Rowena said in dismay. "But I thought your civil war was over."

"'Tis over." Douglas turned his back on the altar and the pangs of conscience it stirred in him. "But since the war ended, the English soldiers stationed here to keep the peace have been withdrawn. Often in the aftermath of war, there are wolves who prey on the weak and wounded."

"Wolves?"

"The human kind, Your Highness, although we still have a few genuine wolves and wildcats in our uninhabited hills."

"The human kind are the worst," Rowena said with understanding. "However, I don't imagine 'twill take a man like you long to subdue them."

Douglas controlled an unholy urge to pull her into his arms and kiss her for that compliment. Her faith in him was touching if unfounded.

"'Tis my goal," he said soberly.

"I will add your beleaguered village to my prayers," Rowena murmured as they left the chapel. "And you, of course, my lord."

Douglas said nothing.

Let the princess pray.

Perhaps her innocent intercession would move the Almighty where the prayers of a young neglected boy had failed. Hell, it couldn't hurt, even if Douglas knew in his heart of hearts that heaven had given him up as a lost cause the day he was born.

Chapter 7

DOUGLAS SLOWED THE PONIES, CRANING HIS NECK to see beyond the utter darkness of the hills. A pipistrelle bat fluttered from the thin stand of trees that edged the precariously carved track. The cart leaned around a curve. Several rocks scattered down an unseen ravine. The princess was sipping hot chocolate at this very moment.

"What happened to the damn light?" he demanded.

"Baldwin dropped the lantern," Gemma said from the tail of the cart.

"I couldna help it," Baldwin said unhappily, walking ahead as a guide. "I tripped like a rigwiddie-nag right over a boulder. The men who made this path were half-brained as well as damned inconsiderate."

"They were smugglers." Douglas scowled as a bitter gust of wind whipped his black cape from his broad shoulders. The ponies balked.

"Well, I didna sign on for this sort of thing, Captain."

"You didn't sign on at all," Douglas said without sympathy. "You're free to go whenever you want. In fact, I wish you would."

"Your arguing is disturbing the lad," Dainty said from the bed of the cart. He was cradling the bundled boy in his enormous lap. "I don't want him to fret until he's safe in his own home."

By sheer determination, Douglas drove the cart down into the glen, wheels crunching on the gravel-strewn lochside path. Crisp whitecaps churned on the loch's surface. He stared at the small tidal island in the middle of the water.

"A good place for a few men to hide out," Dainty said quietly from the cart. "They could sneak out to attack from there without being seen."

Douglas studied the island with a scowl. "Possibly. We'll check tomorrow. For now let us get this lad back to his family. He's been asking for his mother since he awakened."

The castle loomed over them, its dark contours stark against the blue-black sky.

"I hope the princess isna watching us from her window," Baldwin said. "She'll think we're up to no good."

Douglas grinned. "The princess is a woman, and there's no telling what a woman thinks. Now step to it. I want the boy carried up to his hut with as little fanfare as possible."

Mary MacVittie laughed in delight from her window. Her spyglass was focused on the loch below the stone cottage which sat at a snug angle in the hillside.

"The pirates are smuggling something," she said to her brother, seated on the oak settle behind her. "I wonder how the welcome with the princess went. I should have been there to help."

"You were helping me," he said. "I daresay that tending the sick is more important than teaching a scoundrel how to impress a princess."

"Not if the scoundrel convinces the princess to help Dunmoral."

"Ha. Is that what he told you?"

"Yes." She returned to the settle, lifting a well-worn book into her lap. "I've been reading up on local superstitions. I've found out just what we need to save the village."

He got up to take her place at the window. "This village is beyond saving. Bad enough it must tolerate me, a drunken physician who was banished from court for allowing one of His Majesty's mistresses to die. But to boast a pirate, a *pirate*, for its laird."

"A reformed pirate, Norman," she murmured.

"Not that the former laird was any better," he said, "carrying on conversations with his marigolds while a war was being waged right outside his own castle."

" 'Tis called Needfire, in case you're interested," Mary said.

He adjusted the spyglass. "Dear God. The pirates are carrying something wrapped in plaid up to the huts."

"Did you hear me, Norman? I said that the only way to save Dunmoral is with a touch of Needfire."

"I just lit a fire," he said. "I wonder if the rogues are burying treasure in the hills. Or a body. You don't suppose they've killed someone already? Pirates are famous for drunken brawls."

Mary's mouth tightened. "I wasn't talking about *our* fire. Needfire is an ancient Celtic fire ritual that is still done secretly in this part of the Highlands. The Druids used it when they wanted a blessing. The practice is very powerful."

He lowered the spyglass. "Not that pagan nonsense again. Fairies and mermaids and Druids. The intelligent mind cannot bear it."

Mary tapped her book. "The ritual requires two sticks twirled against each other until a spark catches. I gather that it helps to use virgin wood. All the other fires in the village must be put out first and then relit from the sacred flame." She hesitated. "I shall help the pirate become a gentleman if 'tis the last thing I do."

"A gentleman pirate?" He gave her a scornful look. "Then perhaps you had better ask the old gods for help after all. 'Tisn't a gentleman we need in that castle. 'Tis a man with the courage to take control, and to care."

Chapter 8

AN HOUR AFTER RETURNING TO THE CASTLE, Douglas stood at his arched bedchamber window, his goblet of Bordeaux untouched. He could see Rowena's candlelit silhouette in the window of the east tower where he had placed her, removed from the rest of the castle. She beckoned him to stare at her like a solitary star in the dark sky of his life. An iron grille reminded him she was a treasure not to be touched—at least not yet.

Yet it pleased him to look upon her.

She appeared to be pacing—the princess kept late hours. He wondered whether her mind was so burdened with worries that she couldn't sleep. Or was she distraught over Matthew's failure to make their meeting?

Why?

Why had Matthew lured her here without warning her that his half-brother Douglas was a wolf in nobleman's clothing? God knew she wouldn't have strolled down those shadowed passageways holding Douglas's hand if she'd had a clue to his true identity.

He raised the goblet in a mock toast. "One brother's loss is another's gain."

"Why are you quoting Shakespeare to that goblet of wine, Douglas?" a puzzled voice asked behind him. "Are you that drunk?"

"'Twasn't Shakespeare, lass," he said, half-turning to see Gemma in the door, her young face creased in concern. "And no, I am not drunk."

She glanced past him to the window. "You weren't watching the princess, were you? 'Tisn't decent to be watching someone undress."

"And I am such a pillar of decency."

"She seemed to like you well enough," she said grudgingly as she slipped into the room. "Did you count the stones in that tiara?"

"What tiara?"

She stared up at him with a look of worry crossing her face. "How could you not notice such a thing?"

"I don't know. I suppose I was a little taken aback. She is a charming woman."

"She isn't yours. She's Matthew's."

"That remains to be seen." He took a deep gulp of wine, frowning in irritation.

"Never expose your beam, Douglas. No matter what fancy title they give you, you're still a pirate at heart."

"Go to bed, Gemma. It must be two o'clock in the morning."

"Do you think you could fall in love with her?" she persisted, perching on the foot of his bed.

"If I'm a pirate at heart, then you'll remember I have no heart. I cannot fall in love."

"Dainty said that Henry Morgan had been elected Admiral of the Black," Gemma said conversationally. "He's looking for men to help him find Maracaibo."

Douglas showed no reaction, but something of his conqueror's spirit, that wildness he'd hoped to subdue, stirred inside him. Maracaibo was the city built of gold, passage to the legendary El Dorado. Was there a pirate alive who had not dreamed of discovering it? Could he really reform when that magical chimera still eluded him?

Gemma curled her knees into her chest. "He said that Morgan wants to name you Vice Admiral. The entire fleet would be at your disposal."

Douglas smiled, setting his goblet down on the nightstand. "'What profiteth a man if he gains the whole world but loses his own soul?'"

She gazed down at her ragged slippers. "From where I sit, a little profitething wouldn't be unwelcome."

He laughed quietly. "Aye, lass."

"Will she help us?" Gemma asked anxiously.

"Not if she finds out what rotten scoundrels we are."

Gemma giggled.

"'Tisn't a laughing matter, lass. We are the veritable scum of the earth. 'Tis only a matter of time before we betray what bastards we've been by our behavior. All we need is for the Princess Rowena to walk into the hall to have a pirate with a braided beard and wooden leg jumping onto her shoulders from the gallery."

"She's quite lovely, isn't she?" Gemma said, chin propped on her knees. "I can see why Matthew wants to keep her all to himself."

Matthew, who had braved enemy cannonfire to save his commander's beloved horse during battle. Defender of the innocent and protector of helpless animals.

And Douglas, seducer of innocence and, at times, a helpless animal himself.

She chattered on. Douglas removed a gold doubloon from his pocket, tossing it from palm to palm. He resisted the urge to look out the window again. Gazing upon that woman roused peculiar feelings inside him. Was it possible for a man to be beguiled by a gentle spirit and a clever mind?

"Leave me now," he said abruptly, interrupting Gemma's flow of talk. "I have plans for the night to find this Neacail who begs to be killed."

"I pleased the princess, didn't I?" she asked. "I said the right things?"

"Aye, lass."

"Baldwin curtsied at her. She didn't even tell him what a moron he was."

"She is an unusual person," Douglas said thoughtfully.

"Are you going to wed her?" she asked.

"'Tis ludicrous to think of such a thing."

She stood, glancing suspiciously at the unshuttered window. "What about bedding her?"

"That," he said, pushing her toward the door, "is none of your business."

"Why do you hate Matthew so?" she whispered.

Douglas sighed. "I do not wish to speak of it."

"Please, Douglas. It has to do with Mama, doesn't it?"

"Mama was very ill for a long time, and you were a wee scrap of nothing," he said after a long pause. "I tried to take care of you both. I had stolen and worked to be able to afford a simple stone cross in a Highland kirk when she died." His face hardened. "Then Matthew appeared in his fine clothes and lacquered carriage while I was pleading for a cart. He had her body taken to a private graveyard in England for a burial."

"'Tis not the worst sin in the world, is it?" she said softly.

"He deprived me of my last chance to prove to

her that I loved her—and that I had some goodness in me."

"She must have known," she said with fierce loyalty.

He lifted her up and deposited her in the hallway as if she were an annoying kitten. " 'Tis past. I want to change my clothing now, Gemma, and as you said yourself, 'tisn't decent to watch someone undress."

The single knock had a distinctly familiar echo. Aidan. And it meant trouble.

Douglas crossed the bedchamber in silence, opening the door on the man who more resembled him, inside and out, than his half-brother.

Black hair, black eyes, black temperament. Aye, Douglas and Aidan might have been spawned by the same ungodly source.

Aidan wore his hunting clothes and heavy jackboots. He looked austere and anxious.

"I've come to ask your permission, sir."

Douglas lifted his brow. He rarely inquired into the private lives of his men, their loves, their past. Long ago Aidan had confessed that his young wife had died in a coaching accident, that he had taken the blame, that he came from a noble family who had disowned him. Certainly the aloof pirate had his secrets. But he obeyed, and he was loyal and brilliant. Douglas demanded nothing more.

"Permission for what?" he asked, glancing beyond him into the passageway.

"To murder a man," Aidan answered.

"Hell's bloody bells!" Douglas dragged him into the chamber. "Have you taken leave of your senses? Did you hear nothing I said? How could you have already made an enemy in the short time we were here?"

Aidan stared at him in stone-faced silence.

"Answer me, Aidan." Douglas shook his head in disappointment. "I hope you have told no one else of this folly. What hapless soul do you wish to murder?"

"The reiver who raped the village girl earlier today and left her for dead. 'Tis the same man who beat that boy senseless on his way here. I know you, Douglas. You're going to seek vengeance tonight, and I would help you. This castle . . . well, it reminds me of things that are painful."

Douglas turned slowly, assessing the stoic composure of Aidan's face. "That is the first time I have known you to speak of the past since we met."

Aidan shrugged, changing the subject. "The villagers plan to ambush him on the moor. They'll get themselves killed. We must move now, sir."

If there was more to the strange request, Aidan's eyes did not reveal it, and Douglas would not ask. "As you wish then. You may accompany me. I wish for an hour's sleep before we leave."

Aidan gave a stiff nod. "We'll be done before dawn. With a little luck we will find that pig Neacail."

"Does Dainty know of this?" Douglas asked.

"I haven't told him."

Rowena's face rose in Douglas's mind, an image of innocence, but also of temptation. Neacail's pack of mongrels would never have seen anything as fine as her in their worthless lives. Douglas did not wish for word of this to reach her ears.

"Tell Dainty to stay here," he said. "Tell him to stand watch over the princess."

Sleep eluded Douglas.

He paced in the darkness of his room, refusing to yield to the temptation that burned in his blood. He would not return to that window to stare at that woman again. He would not prowl the parapets like an animal, hoping she would acknowledge him.

"I want her," he said in a rough whisper. "I did not plan on this. Yet for once in my life I want something pure and fine that no man has ever had. I want a woman who belongs to me alone. Someone I don't have to steal or pay for."

She isn't yours. She's Matthew's.

He swallowed, his face a mask of suffering as

he lifted it to the window. He wasn't the prince in this fairy tale. He was the dragon. How long would it take Rowena to see through the masquerade?

He closed his eyes, but the past would not be blotted out. The castle walls dissolved. The candles that burned beside him became the blistering sun of Hispaniola. Images seared his mind, as fresh and painful as the day he had struggled to forget.

A Spanish merchantman drifted toward him on the sea. A small cluster of women crowded on deck, bonnets fluttering in the wind, pale faces lifted like flowers to the sun. One of them held a young child in her arms.

'Twas a trick.

He was so sure it had been a trick.

The Spaniards had used this ploy before, disguised a hostile ship as a merchantman. They had dressed their sailors as women. The child was a convincing touch.

But the Dragon of Darien was young and ruthless, out to prove his prowess. No one would deceive him. Sweat trickled down his lean brown face as he raised his hand to order the attack. He hesitated a moment. Why had he ignored the prickle of unease that shot down his spine?

"God," he whispered, forcing his eyes open, his voice raw. "God forgive me."

He had attacked a ship whose precious cargo

was a handful of women to be sold as slaves. Two of them had died, and the child, left an orphan.

He had taken the battered ship to Tortuga and given the dead a funeral worthy of a king. The Spanish priest he had dragged along thought him mad. His friends had laughed at him. No one had mourned at the shallow graves of his victims. No one had cared that he'd killed a few slaves, which made his shame all the deeper.

He was determined in those days to become the best of the worst, a blackguard, and guilt was not an emotion he could afford if he expected his men to respect him. He did not realize, in those days, that the time would come when it would matter more that he respect himself.

Rowena sat in bed braiding her hair while Hildegarde examined the room for spy-holes and secret passages. "He isn't quite what I expected."

"Frederic tried to warn you." Hildegarde tested the bolt on the heavy door, *tsk*ing in dissatisfaction. "I should not have allowed you to dismiss the old fool. Sour he may be, but I do not doubt he would die to protect you."

Rowena grinned. "Protect me from what? A pirate who spends all his spare time in prayer? Perhaps I should go to the chapel and pray the Dragon hasn't retired if indeed that minister's rumor is true."

"A minister would not lie," Hildegarde said.

"But a minister could be mistaken."

Hildegarde shook her head as she lumbered down on her knees to peer under the bed. "One can hardly ask the Almighty to make a man sinful."

"'Tis useless if he's reformed," Rowena said thoughtfully. "Hartzburg needs a man wicked enough to conquer my adversaries." She scowled, setting down her silver-chased brush. "How many spies do you think are hiding under my mattress, Hildegarde?"

"No spies." The governess snatched a poker from the stone hearth and skewered a dustball. "Look at the size of this. And Sir Matthew is not wicked, although you were willing enough to ask his help until this pirate lore filled your head."

"True," Rowena murmured. "Compared to the Dragon of Darien, Sir Matthew is entirely tame."

The older woman took the dustball to the window. "Sir Matthew would make a fine mate."

Rowena's delicate fingers tightened on her heavy coil of hair. "Better than the Duke of Vandever, or my cousin, I'd agree. But Matthew is too much a friend, I fear. If it weren't for his bravery on the battlefield—"

She fell silent in frustration. Hildegarde, as usual, was not listening. Something—some imagined act of intrigue below in the bailey had caught her attention.

"'Tis the quiet man named Aidan—and the

earl," Hildegarde whispered. "Where could they ride this late at night?"

Rowena rose, sighing in resignation. Her reflection in the yellowed pier glass frowned back at her. She would never be the sort of woman who, on physical appearance alone, would attract a man of legend.

Hildegarde turned from the window. "We cannot forget what our host has done."

"His mother—Matthew's mother too—was rumored to be a beauty." Rowena edged from the pier glass with a wistful smile. "She was a lady's maid in a great house and caught the eye of a nobleman."

"Matthew told you this?" Hildegarde said in disapproval.

Rowena nodded. "She bore the nobleman's son nine months later, but by then the man was dead, killed in battle. Sir Matthew was the child of their union. She was put out into the streets in shame with her bastard."

"There is nothing of disgrace about Sir Matthew," Hildegarde said.

"Only because the nobleman's family came to the slums to claim Matthew when he was barely one. He was the only living link to their dead son, and they wanted to acknowledge him."

"But not the mother?" Hildegarde guessed.

"She was a disgraced woman," Rowena said softly. "Matthew's grandparents never allowed him to see her again. He did not know of her existence until his mother was dying."

"Matthew is a good man," Hildegarde insisted. "Clearly he trusts you to have revealed what he would not want the world to know. Still, he did not warn you his brother was a pirate."

"*If* he is a pirate," Rowena said. "Or was one in the past."

"How will you handle this matter, Highness?"

"I am not sure," Rowena said. "For now I shall simply play along with the man, accepting that he is what he appears to be."

"Matthew was never a pirate," Hildegarde said to herself.

Rowena nodded tiredly and returned to the bed, alarmed that when she closed her eyes, it was not Matthew's clean features that came to mind. The earl's dark face dominated her thoughts, his smile mocking . . . and seductive.

"Bolt the door, Highness," Hildegarde whispered from the outer corridor. "I suspect there is a secret passage leading from the fireplace, but it seems to have been sealed. I will not leave until I am sure you are safe for the night."

"Safe from what, you silly old thing?" Rowena grumbled as she trudged dutifully to the door.

She could have told Hildegarde not to waste her time in worries; if Rowena had her way, duty would soon lead her in a direction far more dangerous than anything either of them had ever imagined.

A light rain fell into the night. Their search of the outlying moor had been uneventful. Douglas motioned Aidan back onto the castle road. Then, on instinct, he stopped.

"One more ride around the glen."

Aidan shrugged. "Why not?"

The glen was undisturbed. The stone huts sat in darkness; a dog or two growled at their passage. Then, a half-mile or so beyond the village, Douglas noticed an isolated hut with peat smoke drifting up into the drizzle.

A woman's voice, softly pleading, broke the silence. Two horses were hobbled in the encroaching woods.

Douglas dismounted. "Search those trees, Aidan."

He walked to the hut. The door stood ajar. He made no sound as he entered, his eyes adjusting to the smoky glow of a dying peat fire.

A woman huddled against the wall, begging for mercy as a man in a frayed plaid buried his face in her breasts.

"You've had a busy day, lad," Douglas said.

The man whirled, his eyes wild in his bearded face. "Who the hell are ye?"

Douglas ignored the question. He heard a jar shatter in the adjoining room.

"I'm the Earl of Dunmoral," he said, prodding the tip of his sword into the man's belly. "And you, who has the manners of a jackal?"

"He's Liam of Glengalda," the woman burst out, taking cover behind Douglas's back. "He raped a f-friend of mine today, and beat wee Davie senseless. His brother is—"

The man drew an ax from his belt before she could finish. He died instantly, staring down at the sword that impaled him.

"The other," the woman whispered, tugging on Douglas's free arm. "He was stealing my food, and threatened to kill my bairns."

Douglas rushed behind the leather partition. A man in a hooded plaid had just climbed out the window, a sack of oats clutched to his chest.

Douglas hurried after him, throwing down his sword to climb through the narrow window. A light flared in the loft above. He assumed someone had lit a candle. A child whimpered. But he had no time to investigate.

He ran outside into the rain. At the edge of the woods he flung himself down on the man who'd fled the hut.

"Have mercy on me," the man said with a sob. "I didna want to join the outlaws. They'll kill me if I dinna steal food for them."

Douglas could not see the features obscured by the hood. "Where is Neacail of Glengalda?" he demanded.

"The coward hides and sends puir folks like me to do his bidding."

Douglas leaped to his feet. "Come with me," he said in a harsh voice.

"Aye," the man said docilely, and as he rose, the hood fell back, revealing a grinning face with battered features.

"My bairns," the woman cried from inside the hut. "He's set fire to the loft!"

"Jesus," Douglas heard Aidan shout. "Woman, get outside! The roof is falling. Help me, Douglas!"

The man took a step from Douglas.

"Ye canna put out the fire and hold me prisoner," he said shrewdly.

Douglas stared at the man's face. "Who are you?"

"Who do ye think?"

"Neacail," Douglas said, reaching for his belt. "You mad bastard."

Aidan stumbled from the hut with a child in his arms. The sight distracted Douglas, and Neacail used the advantage. He turned to flee into the woods.

Douglas broke into a run after him, wrenching his pistol from his belt. He squeezed the trigger. The pistol misfired; rain had dampened the powder.

"God," he roared, clenching his jaw in fury.

Neacail looked back to laugh. Douglas pulled

the other flintlock out to fire again. This time he hit the outlaw in the arm.

Neacail stiffened but did not stop. Douglas could only hope to find him later in the woods, dead or wounded.

"Douglas," Aidan shouted. "Help me for the love of Christ!"

There was no choice in the matter. Douglas could not give chase. He would not let those children burn to death.

Chapter 9

Scotland was a world away from the Spanish Main.

Douglas stood several hours later in the pre-dawn darkness on the pebble-strewn shore of Loch Dunmoral. Thunder resonated overhead in the heavens like an echo of divine laughter. Rain struck his rough-hewn face.

The pirates had played a joke on their captain.

Actually, it was meant to be a tribute.

They had taken the castle rowboat in the loch and lovingly converted it into a full-rigged miniature version of Douglas's last sloop, the *Delight*, which had been wrecked on the coast of Cuba during his final raid.

Phelps, the ship's carpenter, had even mounted a topsail and prow carved into the shape of a black fire-breathing dragon. The reflections of tiny brass cannons gleamed upon the darkened water.

Douglas enjoyed approximately fifteen seconds of nostalgia before panic set in. "And how the hell am I supposed to explain this to the princess?" he shouted. "What will the gentle folk of the glen think to see a pirate ship sailing the peaceful waters of their loch?"

The loch, in fact, was anything but peaceful, rain slashing the surface. A rising wind churned the water into powerful waves that pounded the shore. It took an hour for Douglas and Dainty to row to the small tidal island where they hoped to catch Neacail's men taking shelter from the storm.

They found only a few stones, a bird carcass, a merlin's nest.

"We will try again tomorrow," he said grimly as he brought the outrageous rowboat back to shore. "Perhaps they have gone out raiding. 'Tis almost light now. The last thing we need is for the princess to see her host sailing a pirate ship under her window."

The princess slept all day in her tower, guarded by her gargoyle of a governess. She slept through the thunder and lightning. She slept in innocence, oblivious to the black atmosphere that surrounded her.

Douglas paced, cursing the storm that prevented him from searching the outlying heath and hills. Rain gushed from the cannon spouts, muddying roads and overflowing rivers. He did not know this wild land he lorded over, but he would learn.

He went to bed that night without seeing Rowena once. Yet he felt an odd contentment, knowing she lay protected within the tower, safe from the elements that battered the stone castle.

Safe in the lair of a dragon and not the white knight with a broken leg she undoubtedly dreamed of and deserved.

Neacail of Glengalda stood by the fireplace of the tower bedchamber. He had remembered the hidden passage inside the castle he hoped to claim.

He watched the woman who slept in the bed only steps from where he stood.

A few hours earlier he had been watching the tall man, his enemy, brave the storm to pace the parapets. The man had stolen what belonged to Neacail, he'd tried to kill him, and he would pay. The pain of the pistol wound in Neacail's arm strengthened his hatred.

Neacail was the rightful heir to Dunmoral, or so his whoring mother had confessed to the priest on her deathbed last summer. She'd sworn that the former earl's nephew was Neacail's father, and any fool could see a family resemblance.

There were no papers to prove this. The former earl and his nephew were both dead. Yet Neacail had always known he had been born to privilege.

Six months ago Neacail had carried his blood claim to the Scottish Court of Session. The judge had laughed in his face.

"Perhaps the papers proving your nobility were burned at your birth," the judge had suggested with a sneer.

A week later Neacail had burned the judge's country house to the ground, not caring that the magistrate's bedridden sister was trapped within.

He'd watched her beat at the window like a caged bird. There was pleasure in that, and a lesson to those who laughed at him.

He wiped his nose on the sleeve of his torn saffron shirt. His deep-set eyes smoldered with thwarted ambition. His arm ached, but that weakness would not stop him.

He would sleep tonight in a cave like an animal. He would awaken amidst men who smelled like swine when he should be living in this castle like a lord.

Neacail had worked as a servant once in the castle scullery years ago. He had learned a few of the secret passages that others had forgotten, thinking such knowledge might prove useful.

He was not a fool though. He had not entered the castle to be caught. He had a grander plan.

The people of Dunmoral would pay first for branding him a fugitive.

Then the stranger who had stolen Neacail's birthright and those he hoped to protect would suffer.

He gazed across the room at the woman who slept so peacefully in her bed. The storm did not seem to disturb her. Neacail wondered whether she would waken if he touched her.

He touched the lace-edged chemise that lay across her bed instead. "Pretty," he said quietly. "And clean." He took one of the silken stockings that had fallen to the floor. He would use it to bandage the arm.

She stirred, flinging a hand across her face. Neacail had never seen such a woman in his life. Did she belong to his enemy? Where had she come from?

He backed away from the bed into the passage-way beside the fireplace. The next time he visited he would leave a gift.

She would be so surprised.

Chapter 10

THE NEXT MORNING, MRS. MACVITTIE BROUGHT Gemma a burgundy leather book with gilt-edged pages. "I found this last night and thought of your brother. It contains the memoirs of a Scottish viscount who lived at the court of Louis the Fourteenth."

Gemma glanced around the empty courtyard. "Thank you so much, Mrs. MacVittie. Douglas needs all the help he can get. Will this book explain how we should behave in the princess's presence?"

"It should help, although some of the confessions are rather risqué. I thought the descriptions of a royal feast might be enlightening."

"A feast?"

"Well, you must have a banquet to welcome the princess. 'Tis expected, even in the most remote regions such as ours. Royalty has been honored with feasts since ancient times."

Gemma bit her lip. "I see."

"You do have a cook in the castle, don't you?"

Gemma hesitated. The only cook to speak of was Frances, who'd owned a thriving brothel on a pirate stronghold. What Frances lacked in culinary skills she made up for in her determination to better herself.

"We have a cook," Gemma said firmly.

Mrs. MacVittie nodded. "Good. There's a menu in the book she might use as a reference. Now I don't mean to be unkind, my dear, but you and your brother's men ought to peruse these pages yourselves to pick up the wee hint or two on deportment. You'd not want to offend your royal visitor."

Gemma swallowed, hugging the book to her heart. She would do *anything* to please her brother. "Oh, no, ma'am. We wouldn't."

Hildegarde was standing outside Douglas's door when he opened it the next morning. He stifled a swear word at the sight of her.

"Good morning to you, madam," he said.

"I am on my way to the kitchen to deliver the royal breakfast requests to the cook."

"I shall do that, madam," he responded, thinking that Hildegarde and Frances might be too alike for their own good.

"If 'tis not too much trouble."

"'Tis no trouble at all," he said.

She nodded. "On Sundays, we will take toast and blackcurrant jelly. Coffee and chocolate should be served at every meal."

"I understand."

"On Mondays we will have calf's-foot jelly and toast. Tuesday is for toast and jelly à la Russe. On Wednesdays you have a choice of serving either ox-foot or orange jelly. We enjoy elderflower jelly on Thursdays."

Douglas sighed. "With toast?"

"With toast."

"Friday?" Douglas said.

"Friday is for quince jelly."

"Saturdays, madam?"

"On Saturdays we have an assortment of the above." She smiled at him. "Do you know what day it is?"

"'Tis Saturday," he said heavily.

"It might also be a good idea to display the princess's personal pennant in the great hall," Hildegarde concluded. "I hope this will not put you to any trouble."

"Anything to please the princess," he said grimly.

A few minutes later the princess's personal advisor cornered Douglas in the kitchen. The man was preparing to leave the castle, clearly eager to be gone so he could finish his military business and be back at Rowena's side.

Douglas listened to the man tell him in no uncertain terms that the princess must be protected. He made it clear he did not approve of leaving Rowena and Hildegarde alone.

"I will not let them take one step beyond the drawbridge unescorted," Douglas promised.

Frederic left without another word.

"'Twill not be easy to entertain that woman," Frances predicted.

Douglas sighed. "Do we have a good store of jellies?"

"Aye," Frances said in surprise. "Why?"

"A well-fed woman is easier to entertain," he said. "Or at least 'tis so in my experience."

Pale shafts of morning sunlight penetrated the high windows of the hall and illuminated the heraldic panels on the wall. A fire burned low in the huge hooded fireplace. Douglas felt a stab of anticipation as he watched the tall princess walk across the floor.

Daylight flattered her classical features, playing up the purity he had begun to believe he must have imagined. It also emphasized the intelligence in her eyes.

She looked straight at him. Astonished, he realized she was assessing him in the same forthright manner one would assess a horse at market. He wondered if he should show her his teeth and paw the floor with his right foot.

"You slept well, Your Highness?" he asked dryly

as he rose to escort her to the dais for a late breakfast.

"Yes, thank you." She sat at the elaborately laid table, studying the damask cloth and china. "And you, my lord?"

"Never better," he lied, looking over his shoulder.

He couldn't believe his luck. They were alone. Hildegarde the governess was probably sneaking a bottle of schnapps. The rest of the castle's inhabitants were obeying Douglas's strict orders to stay out of trouble.

He frowned. Pirates staying out of trouble was a contradiction in terms. What were the rascals up to?

Rowena was staring at the assortment of pots and platters on the table. She looked bemused. Douglas realized she was probably waiting for him to serve her. He thought she must be impressed that he had managed to find her favorite foods.

"Toast and jelly, Your Highness?" he asked. "We have blackcurrant, calf's and ox-foot, jelly à la Russe, elderflower, orange, and quince."

She was quiet for a moment. "Do you always eat this much toast and jelly, my lord?"

"Don't you?" he asked in surprise.

"No," she said. "I hate toast and jelly. Hildegarde likes them though."

"What about the coffee and hot chocolate?" he demanded.

Rowena grinned. "What about them?"

He grinned back, his large hand hovering over the two polished silver pots on the table. "Which would you prefer?"

"Chocolate, please." She studied the hammer-beamed ceiling with an expert's eye. "Fifteenth century?"

Douglas examined the silver pot in his hand. "I wouldn't think so. 'Tis in rare good condition if it is."

Rowena bit her lip. "I meant the castle keep, actually. The ceiling moldings."

He gave her an indulgent smile. "I knew that, Your Highness. Yes, 'tis fifteenth century." Or thirteenth or fourteenth. Damned, if he could remember Dunmoral's history. He put down the pot, suddenly realizing that danger lurked in the simplest question. He would have to take his own advice to be on guard against his invented background. A simple question about even the latrines could show him to be a liar. Or a lunatic.

"Do you live in a fifteenth-century castle in Hartzburg?" he asked cautiously.

Rowena looked suddenly distressed. Douglas wondered if he'd asked something appallingly stupid. Didn't they have castles in Hartzburg? Did they live on caves? Matthew, he was sure, would know such a thing.

"I have been exiled to the pink summer palace in the forest," she said quietly. "The castle proper is under siege by rebels."

"Besieged? By rebels?" Douglas, who didn't have a political bone in his body, was indignant at the thought. "In your homeland?"

Rowena smiled in gratitude at his genuine display of outrage. "That isn't the worst of it, my lord."

"There is more?"

"The rebels are holding Papa a virtual prisoner. He can keep them at bay for five months before he will be forced to surrender. They're threatening to behead him if their demands aren't met."

"That's—that's—"

"—treason."

"Yes, treason and intolerable." Douglas might rank with the world's greatest sinners, but even he possessed a certain sense of order. "Why hasn't someone gone in and thrashed the bast—the bad men?"

Rowena looked at him, her brow raised.

"I share your feelings exactly," she said. "I have tried to roust the rebels and failed. I refuse to sacrifice any more of my loyal young subjects. Some of the boys who want to fight are barely twelve years old. All our able-bodied men are dead or wounded." She paused. "Or they have betrayed me and thrown their allegiance to the other side."

"I'm sorry to hear that," Douglas said with a frown, surprised to find he meant it.

"Papa's enemies have an army of mercenaries and seasoned soldiers," Rowena said. "I simply didn't have the talent or leadership ability to muster up enough force on my own."

"The situation needs a warrior, not a woman," Douglas said forcefully.

"I've done what I can." Rowena sipped her chocolate. "You have heard of the Peace of Westphalia?"

"Hasn't everyone?" Douglas said.

"Then you will recall that while France gained sovereign power over certain territories, Hartzburg kept her independence."

Douglas was silent. Not only could he not recall it, he didn't know what the devil the woman was talking about.

"France and the Emperor were fighting over us," Rowena added.

"Well, so would I," Douglas stated.

She frowned. "We cherish our independence, my lord."

"As indeed you should." His frown deepened. "I seem to recall hearing that you have three older brothers. Perhaps 'tis not my place to ask, but why is a helpless woman defending a castle and trying to rescue her father?"

"I do not consider myself helpless, my lord."

Douglas studied her face, hiding a smile. "Defenseless then—but only in the physical sense."

"Your question is valid," she said ruefully. "My eldest brother Prince Erich has mysteriously vanished during a hunt. Rupert is in the Mediterranean on a merchant expedition. He was unexpectedly waylaid last spring."

Chasing women, Douglas said to himself.

Rowena continued, "The youngest, Anthony, is pursing a monastic life in the French Pyrenees."

Afraid of women, Douglas thought. He resisted the urge to shake his head. The men in her family were all but useless. He would like a week to set them straight on the role a woman should play in war—none. "Do your brothers know of the rebellion?"

"I've sent numerous messages—Matthew has helped me—but if they do not return home soon, or if they get themselves killed, I shall not only have to rescue Papa alone but also produce heirs to assume the dynastic succession."

"Heirs?" Douglas took a scalding sip of coffee to cover the fact his voice had just climbed an octave.

"I have to have babies in a hurry," Rowena said frankly. "The dynastic succession must be continued without interruption or the rebels who are holding my father will use that as a case to persuade our people to turn against us."

"This is an intriguing dilemma," Douglas said. Especially the part about having babies in a hurry.

Rowena sighed. "My sister Micheline has been banished to a convent for misbehavior, so naturally she cannot get pregnant."

"Naturally," Douglas said.

"Of course, with Micheline, such a thing is entirely possible."

The thought of producing heirs with the princess did dangerous things to Douglas's imagination. For a reckless moment he considered offering to whisk her upstairs and help her fulfill her political obligations. She was the first woman he'd met who made the prospect of having babies seem even remotely enticing. Lust and tenderness rocked him as he pictured them surrounded by a sea of little pirates and princesses.

She stared past him in noble innocence, lost in thoughts of plots and waylaid princes. Or was she all that innocent? he wondered cynically. A scowl settled over his sun-burnished features.

The woman was anything but stupid. Was she putting his character to the test? Did she mean to uncover his true intentions? Few were the men someone in her position could trust. She had been betrayed. She would be understandably cautious in her personal dealings.

She was confiding in Douglas because he was Sir Matthew's brother. A pirate would jump at the chance to bed her, let alone get his hands on her fortune.

A peer of the realm, however, would exercise a little more self-control. Hell, if she guessed that only a few months ago he'd been stalking Spaniards, sweating half-naked with a knife clamped in his teeth, she'd run gasping back to her pink summer palace in horror.

Douglas would have to earn her trust. He would have to impress her with his sense of dignity and self-restraint. Of course first he would have to *find* some dignity and self-restraint within himself. He wasn't sure he had ever possessed such sterling qualities.

He pursed his lips, forcing his attention back to what she was saying.

"—and as stated in the marriage contract, I will retain control of the truffle business."

He leaned forward to refill her cup. "You have trouble with business?"

"Were you listening to me?" Rowena asked.

Douglas bit back a grin. She was a spirited little princess, but he didn't mind that. "I certainly was, Your Highness. And do I have troubles of my own? Why, just last week—"

Rowena released a loud sigh. She looked at him as if he were a trifle dimwitted. "I was not talking about troubles. I was talking about truffles. T-R-U-F-F-L-E-S. Hartzburg is renowned for them. They're a great delicacy which we export all over Europe. Have you ever tasted them?"

"Certainly," Douglas lied. *We ate truffles every day aboard ship right along with our wormy biscuits and salted pork.* "There is nothing quite like a truffle to top off a meal, is there?"

Rowena's smile sparkled with mischief. "Apparently the rest of the world agrees. I can't stand them myself. What could be worse than a platter of black warty fungus to kill one's appetite? Papa serves them at every function."

Douglas leaned forward on his elbows, as if truffles were the most fascinating subject on earth. "Does he?"

"He used to make us hunt the horrid things in the beech woods with his trained pigs."

"How thrilling," Douglas said.

"He was good fun in those days, before my mother died," she said, her smile wistful. "He changed after he lost her. He became withdrawn and distrustful."

Douglas noticed the tension in her slender fingers as she gripped her cup. His gaze lifted to her face.

"I've spoken too much," she said. "You are a man who listens, my lord, and that can be a dangerous thing."

"Surely you know that your secrets will never leave this table?" he said quietly.

"I don't know you at all yet," she said, her smile returning. "But if Matthew insists I trust you, then you must be a trustworthy man."

A voice from the doorway doused the pleasant flames of intimacy that had begun to kindle between them.

Hildegarde clumped up to the table in her clogs, her scowl like a rainshower on a summer picnic. "'Tisn't a good idea to burden our host with our troubles," she said with a sharp look at Rowena.

"We were discussing truffles, not troubles," Rowena said, winking at Douglas.

Hildegarde sat down beside the princess. Lines of worry wrinkled her forehead. "I know why you have troubles in this castle, my lord," she said. "I stayed up all night and discovered the evil secret."

"Secret?" Douglas raised his head, his skin prickling with apprehension. Faith, had he been found out already? "What secret?" he demanded with all the bravado he could muster.

Gemma had called an emergency council in the pleasure garden to give lessons in royal protocol. Mrs. MacVittie's book passed from hand to hand, the elaborate sketches eliciting sniggers and outbursts of alarm.

Baldwin peered nearsightedly at the pictures. "And they call pirates nasty. All these French noblemen do is eat and have orgies. My old brain is shocked."

Mrs. MacVittie, standing over him, smiled. "A valid observation, Mr. McGee. The French Court is famous for its licentious behavior."

"'Tis lewd too," Willie exclaimed. "Gemma read that the king's own brother dresses up like a woman and dances with men."

Baldwin shook his head. "That doesna bother me as much as the part about the courtiers using the fireplaces as a privy."

"Wouldn't that put the fires out?" Willie wondered aloud.

"I do not care to discuss such things," Gemma said. "I called you here to practice protocol. Baldwin, as castle steward, do you know what your duties are regarding the princess?"

He looked uncertain. "Aye."

"'Tis your responsibility to see to her comfort," Mrs. MacVittie said. "This is a position of some importance."

"Ye mean I'm to bring her a hot brick if her feet feel cold, or a cup of peppermint tea if she gets a little windy after supper?"

Gemma sank down on the bench, staring forlornly at the dead leaves scattering across the flagstones. "'Tis hopeless."

Mrs. MacVittie patted her on the shoulder. "I do not think you need worry about the princess getting a little 'windy,' Mr. McGee," she said tactfully. "As to her cold feet, well, her companion can handle that personal matter. 'Tis *your* duty to show Her Royal Highness around the castle and make sure she always has a supply of candles to see in the dark."

"Don't curtsy to her again, or I'll gut you," Gemma added.

"There will be no need for that," Mrs. MacVittie said diplomatically. "Mr. McGee understands his part, don't you?"

"What part?" Baldwin said.

Mrs. MacVittie shook her head. Then she

turned to the frail-looking woman who stood alone by the hedge. "And you, Frances," she said, "how are your preparations coming for the feast?"

"There isn't going to be a feast if I can't find any decent food." Her delicate face sour, Frances folded her arms over her chest. Her blond curls were piled loosely on her head in a beribboned topknot. "All we have in the storeroom are oats and dried peas. Hardly royal fare. I gave a supper once for a duke in the bawdyhouse. He told me he ate queer things like fish eggs and peacocks and—and oysters on the half-shell," she said excitedly. "Surely we can manage some oysters."

"Common folk eat oysters," Gemma said with a frown.

Willie threw a stone into the air. "The nearest market town is four days ride each way. The oysters would stink to heaven before you cooked them. Douglas wouldn't want us to poison the poor princess."

"The cove is only a few miles away," Mrs. MacVittie said thoughtfully. "I have never eaten a Dunmoral oyster, if such a thing exists, but I do believe the viscount mentions mollusks on a menu for the king."

"'Tis worth a try." Gemma cast an anxious look at the keep. "They must be done with breakfast by now. I suppose we'll have to put in an appearance, or the princess will think we're ignorant peasants."

"We are," Baldwin said.

Gemma looked over at Frances. "You didn't meet her last night. Are you coming?"

Frances shook her head. Gemma suspected that while the woman was happy to work herself ragged to please Douglas, she privately believed he'd prefer her to stay out of sight on account of her past as a prostitute.

"Come and meet her, Frances," she said.

"Are you joking?" Frances straightened her apron. "I have a bloody feast to prepare. 'Tis going to take magic to turn oatmeal bannocks into a banquet."

Douglas leaned back in the ornately carved oak chair on the dais. His languid pose gave no hint he was on the verge of breaking into a cold sweat. "Secret?" He smiled as if sharing a private joke. "Don't tell me you've discovered tulip bulbs under your bed. I believe they were left there to germinate about a decade ago by the dotty old earl."

Rowena smiled. "What a peculiar way to speak of one's late father."

"Whose father?" Douglas grinned in response to her infectious smile. "And what was he late to?"

"Your father." Rowena gave him a questioning look. "The dotty old earl."

"The—ah, yes. Poor old Papa." Douglas's grin froze on his face. Naturally, not knowing his true origins, the princess would assume he'd inherited the earldom from the previous earl. Well, the odd old earl had just gained a son, and Douglas had gotten himself another father who was already closer to him than the lousy sire who'd abandoned him months before his birth.

" 'Tis a good thing to jest," Hildegarde said with an affectionate smile at Rowena. Her face hardened as she looked again at Douglas. She stabbed a beefy finger in his face. "But I tell you I know why you have troubles in your village. The loch that surrounds the castle is haunted."

"Haunted?" Douglas ignored the impulse to touch his earring for good luck. No pirate worth his salt sneered at superstition. Trust his luck to inherit a haunted castle.

Rowena sighed. "Hildegarde kept me up half the night with her imagination. She insists there was a water horse frolicking around in your loch."

Douglas stared back at her with a guileless expression. Ye Gods, was it possible? Had Hildegarde sighted *Delight* bobbing in the wind? "A water horse?" he said in polite disbelief.

"You Scots refer to them as kelpies." Hildegarde crossed herself, her plump hand resting on the amulet of elf bolts she wore for luck. "Evil creatures. They devour men and breathe brimstone. I was afraid to leave my lady alone until morning light."

Douglas affected an unconcerned chuckle.

" 'Twas pitch-black last night, ma'am. What you probably saw was an illusion of waves and water grasses."

"The creature had scales down its neck like a mane," Hildegarde said, her face dark with distress.

Douglas steepled his hands under his chin, his face betraying no sign of his anxiety. The water horse could only be that damned vixen *Delight*. She'd always gotten Douglas into trouble.

He wondered how quickly he could run down to the loch and hide her before anyone noticed his absence.

Who could he trust to keep Princess Rowena and her eagle-eyed governess occupied in the meantime? Dainty had not returned from patrolling the glen, a fact which, after the recent violence, caused him a moment of concern. Aidan had wandered off by himself. However, if any two men could take care of themselves, 'twas that unholy pair.

There was a rumble of voices as the doors opened to admit a small band of his retainers. Douglas narrowed his eyes, cringing inwardly as they approached the dais to pay their respects to the princess.

Or to shock the woman senseless.

Chances were that at least one of the troublemakers would make a fool of himself.

Gemma curtsied and shyly inquired if the princess had slept well. You'd never dream she'd been nursed on a pirate's knee since the tender age of three, that the first words out of her wee rosebud mouth were, "No prey, no pay, you stupid pig."

Mrs. MacVittie presented the princess with a pot of heather honey tied with a tartan ribbon.

Willie bowed awkwardly. Douglas noted with relief that the man had remembered to put in his false walrus-ivory teeth.

But Douglas's very heart stopped as Baldwin approached the table, staring at Rowena in awe.

Silence mounted.

Douglas cleared his throat.

Finally Baldwin bowed.

"Very well done," Douglas said in an undertone, waving the man away. "You may all go back to your posts now."

"Wait." Hildegarde's voice rang out with authority. She reached for a piece of toast. "Perhaps one of them has seen the kelpie."

"Kelpie?" Mrs. MacVittie looked intrigued. "In our loch?"

"What's a kelpie?" Gemma asked.

Douglas slid to the edge of his chain, his spine rigid, his black eyes flashing a warning.

"The castle is under a spell," Hildegarde said with such conviction that even Douglas for a moment entertained the bizarre possibility. "There is a water horse in the loch."

"No one has sighted a beastie in that loch for

nigh on a hundred years," Mrs. MacVittie said reflectively. "I wonder what brought it out."

"I'm afraid 'tis attracted to the princess's unblemished soul," Hildegarde said in a quavering voice. "Purity always draws the perverse."

Douglas stole a look at Rowena from beneath his heavy eyebrows. He was tempted to admit the truth just to quiet the old woman's fears. The princess, however, appeared unmoved.

"There are no such things as monsters," Rowena said. "To prove this I will row out on that loch myself this very morning."

Douglas suppressed a shout of horror. "You certainly will not. This is a matter for me to handle."

Hildegarde granted him a look of grudging approval. "That is all very well and good, my lord, but I think I must advise my lady to leave this castle immediately. There are other dangers here."

A shadow crossed Douglas's face. He felt a wave of panic welling up. "Leave? But you only just arrived."

"What dangers do you speak of?" Rowena asked sharply.

Hildegarde lowered her eyes. "The brigands who attacked his lordship's village. A young woman was raped and left for dead in the river. A boy was beaten viciously only an hour before our arrival last night. I heard the servants talking."

"That matter has been taken care of," Douglas said in a voice of ruthless arrogance that brought Rowena's head up in surprise. "The worthless turd responsible for the rape will never threaten another helpless woman with his blade again. By now his tongue is probably bulging from his head, and the crows pecking out his eyes."

"Douglas," Gemma whispered in warning, her hand flying to her mouth.

He could not stop himself. His pirate's wrath had been aroused and he was out of control. He leaned forward, looking fit to pound the table into the floor. "No one will harm your lady while I am here," he shouted. "As to the other outlaws—any man who looks at her askance will find his guts spilled at his feet before he knows what struck him. I will personally draw and quarter the swine myself—"

"*Douglas,*" Gemma said frantically.

"—and I will throw his bones to the dogs with his flesh still attached."

Douglas sat back in his chair, his spell of anger suddenly broken.

The hall was utterly silent. His outburst overhung it like a thundercloud.

Hildegarde was staring up at him as if he had just sprouted horns.

Rowena looked utterly stunned.

He'd done it now, he realized in self-contempt. He had spoken like a pirate. No gentleman would address gently bred ladies in such graphic terms. He had shocked the holy hell out of the princess.

The Earl of Dunmoral lived by tact not terror, he realized belatedly.

How much harm had he done with his wild dragon's fury? How much of the truth had he unwittingly revealed with his outburst?

Chapter 11

"I WAS SPEAKING FIGURATIVELY, OF COURSE," HE said with a penitent smile, hastening to repair the damage. "The reivers must be dealt with in a court of law, as the Crown has decreed. Far be it from me to take justice into my own inadequate hands. Forgive me for such offensive language. Violence will only beget more violence."

Rowena frowned. "Sometimes one must act and consider the consequences later."

He schooled his features into a self-righteous expression. "I am bound to obey the law, Your Highness."

"I understand that the British government has removed its troops from the Highlands," Hildegarde said in disapproval.

"That's true, madam," Douglas said.

"Then who will protect the princess?" she asked worriedly.

He bowed his dark head. He tried to look pious. 'Twas hard after you'd just spewed a tirade about worthless turds and spilling guts. "We shall trust in divine protection. And not let her wander anywhere unescorted."

This brought more silence. Now instead of the Dragon of Darien, he would be called the Chicken-Heart of Caledonia. Was this an improvement?

"And what about the kelpie?" Hildegarde would not let that ridiculous matter rest. "I have heard of water horses choosing human women to mate with."

"Heavens above," Douglas said.

"Yes." Rowena's voice was wry. "Apparently, the lustful creature came close enough to her window so she could see the fire-breathing snakes writhing in its mane."

"Hildegarde is convinced that it wants to make passionate love to me," Rowena added.

"I don't blame it." Douglas blinked. "I mean, I don't blame *her*—for being convinced, that is. A young woman in your position is considered booty by every eligible bachelor in Europe."

A puzzled but pleased smile brightened Rowena's face. "Booty?"

Douglas frowned. "Beauty. I said that your beauty has Europe on its ear."

"No, it doesn't," Rowena said.

"Of course it does."

Rowena scowled at him. "Now you sound like your brother Matthew."

"Thank you," Douglas said.

" 'Twas not a compliment," Rowena said crossly.

" 'Twasn't?"

"The matter of handling the water horse must be decided today or I will insist the princess leave," Hildegarde interrupted them. "Catching a kelpie requires a special bridle."

Baldwin, Willie, Shandy, Phelps and the other crew members of the *Delight* present were listening to every word in growing distress.

Like all pirates, his crew respected the powers of the supernatural. Take out your earring and lose an eye. Spit three times on your palm before firing a cannon. Never let a sea bird land to your left. They believed wholeheartedly in monsters.

Shandy, a short wiry Englishman with a black mustache, spoke for the others. "Something needs to be done about that creature, sir."

"There was a banshee in the village where I was born," Baldwin said with a shudder. "The awfulsome beast killed five people."

Douglas rose from the table. "I'm certain that you have neglected your duties in your desire to see the princess, but now 'tis time to return to

your posts. As to the matter of the loch monster—"
He paused meaningfully. "Perhaps he's a kind-
hearted beastie. Perhaps, if we got to know him
better, we would even discover that he's a real—
Delight."

Gemma's eyes lit up in instant understanding.

The message sunk into the men's heads one by
one. Except for Baldwin, whose skull, Douglas
lamented, seemed to be denser than the castle
walls.

"Kelpies are not known for their kindness,"
Hildegarde said. "They devour men on stormy
nights. I think we ought to exorcise it."

Baldwin's mouth dropped open. "Beggin' yer
pardon, ma'am, but that doesna sound like a good
idea. Best to leave the nasty thing be. Exercisin' it
will only give the teukin beastie more of an
appetite. It might take to eatin' women and bairns
then."

A grin flashed across Rowena's face. It faded as
Douglas clamped his hand down on Baldwin's
bony shoulder.

"I noticed that the torches in the corridor
outside the princess's chamber are low on oil. We
would not want Her Highness to stumble in the
dark, would we?"

Baldwin frowned, dimly aware he had done
something wrong and he'd better make it right
before Douglas killed him. Oh, hell, what was he
supposed to say? Gemma had made him stud

that silly French book all morning. Douglas had been hammering warnings in his head for a week. And now all this talk of that mean loch monster had scrambled his wits.

Then he remembered. He was the castle steward. He was to make sure that the princess was comfortable and that the lass didn't get lost.

He stood up straighter. He raised his voice to a wobbly shout. "The privy is the second door down the hall from yer room, princess—I dinna want ye to lose yer way in the dark so X marks the spot."

Gemma stomped up to him, murder in her eyes. *"Baldwin—"*

He gazed at the princess in adoration. "I marked it just minutes ago in case the urge took ye to use the head in the wee small hours."

Rowena's eyes widened.

Douglas closed his.

"He means use your head," Gemma said forcefully.

"I do?" Baldwin said.

Gemma smiled grimly. "Yes, you do. Why, didn't you tell me only an hour ago that you were concerned the princess would run out of candles if she wanted to read late at night?"

"No," Baldwin said, looking confused. "I said nothin' of the sort."

Rowena smiled in embarrassment. "I'd hoped

that we could overlook my rank and forget protocol during my stay."

"That shouldn't be hard," Gemma said under her breath, "seeing that we never knew protocol in the first place."

"X marks the spot! Worthless turds and booty!" Douglas grunted in exasperation as he propelled the rowboat toward a cluster of cattails. "Why didn't we just run up the old Jolly Roger or break open a cask of rum with our cutlasses? Why didn't we knock her over the head with Simon's wooden leg and announce, 'We are bloodthirsty pirates?'"

"Hell, Captain," Baldwin said, "ye've got nothin' to be ashamed of. I'm proud to have served under the Dragon."

Night was falling over the glen. Douglas plied the oars in silence, staring at the grinning dragon on the prow. His brooding gaze drifted to the sheltered tidal island in the middle of the loch.

"Where is Aidan?" he asked suddenly.

"Aidan is off by himself, sir, doing whatever 'tis he does when he is all alone," Dainty said. "Besides, you've warned everyone not to offend the princess. He's probably staying out of the way for fear he'll say something oafish in her company."

"Aidan is not the only one who must watch his behavior," Douglas said. "The princess is challenging me. All that talk about producing heirs. I begin to wonder if the woman means to bait me like an animal."

Dainty grinned, rowing in rhythm with Douglas's broad strokes.

They had met as galley slaves on the Barbary Coast about fifteen years ago. Due to his size, Dainty had soon become the captain's overseer. He had saved Douglas from a flogging or two, given him a few more, and by the time they'd staged a mutiny, they had already plotted a future of piracy together.

Douglas sighed. "She could possibly mean to divine my true nature. I wonder why Matthew has not informed her I'm a pirate and first-rate rapscallion."

"Ye are that, sir," Baldwin said. "The biggest bastard I've ever served."

"I told Matthew I'd reformed," Douglas said. "Could it be that he actually believes me?"

Dainty chuckled. "Where are we going to hide *Delight*, sir?"

"In those trees over—" Douglas stared in disbelief at the figures gathered along the shoreline. He swore. "So much for privacy."

The two other men in the boat swung their heads around to look. About thirteen or so villagers stood at the water's edge. The women wore worn loose-spun kirtles, the men age-faded plaids. Several of them doffed their bonnets in respect at Douglas.

Pirate lord or not, he belonged to them and they to him. Along with his charter for the earldom, he had assumed the burden of defending the dying clan MacAult, whose back had been broken by the tyranny of Oliver Cromwell.

A few of the braver souls waded out into the loch to help him bring the boat to shore.

Douglas expelled a deep sigh, not certain what to do with these people.

They weighed him in the silence, the pirate he'd been, the nobleman he now claimed to be simply because the Stuart king had put his signature to paper.

And in the end they obviously chose to believe the kinder illusion, castle laird and defender, a man with a dutiful heart.

Or no heart at all. It did not matter.

Douglas wasn't sure who he was himself, and he felt faintly ridiculous as they studied him with their wry Highland humor, and acceptance of life's absurdities, each pretending not to notice the replica of the pirate ship pulled up on their shore.

The Dragon of Darien, Scourge of the Seven Seas, now in a Scottish Loch.

"Good afternoon, my lord."

"Out fishin', were ye, yer lordship?"

Delight bobbed up between the weeds. Douglas sat in the boat, not having a clue how to explain her. Perhaps if he said nothing, the gentle people of Dunmoral would continue pretending not to notice.

They knew he'd been a pirate. Gemma, of the loose tongue that flapped like a topsail in a gale, had let the secret out their first night in the castle.

They asked little of him—only that he protect them from the predators who took advantage of their vulnerability.

Protect them—a pirate who had preyed on vulnerability.

Then one of the children, fearless and observant, darted forward. "'Tis a pirate ship!" she exclaimed. "Can we ride it?"

Her mother stumbled down the incline to pull the child away.

A bearded man in a blacksmith's leather jerkin approached the boat. He grinned in amusement as he looked Douglas in the eye.

"Caught yerself a right prize there, my lord. My name is Henry. That's my smithy at the end of the lane."

Douglas met the man's shrewd gaze. He couldn't think up a lie to explain *Delight* to save his life. He was forced resort to the truth.

"I need help," he said bluntly. "I want to hide this vessel. For sentimental reasons, my men cannot bring themselves to burn or dismantle the damned harlot."

Henry scratched the side of his jaw. "Hide her from the princess?"

"You know about her too?" Douglas said in disbelief.

"Oh, aye. Ye can hardly keep such a secret in these parts."

Douglas sighed. "Well, we have to keep this ship a secret."

Henry took a long draw on his briarwood pipe. "There's an empty barn in the village where we can keep an eye on her."

"I appreciate this." Douglas jumped from the rowboat to clap the man on the back. "I'm going to help you too. I'm sending men here to stand guard."

The sparkle faded from Henry's eyes. "Neacail's younger brother was found at the crossroads this morning with a single swordthrust through his chest. He was the raider who raped wee Aggie and the one who beat that boy Davie within an inch of his life."

Douglas's expression did not change. Aidan had left the body in open view as a signal to Neacail's men that Douglas would let no injustice go unavenged.

"Perhaps this will warn Neacail that the people of Dunmoral are not to be attacked with impunity," Douglas said.

Henry lowered his voice. "That family and their followers are a vicious lot, fugitives from the army, put to the horn by our clan. They willna let the loss of a brother go unavenged."

"I am prepared for that," Douglas said.

Henry shook his head in concern. "I've known Neacail since he was a wee bastard who took pleasure drownin' small animals in the loch. He'll take on the Devil himself to get what he wants."

Douglas's voice was soft with a steel core of confidence. "Then let him. The Devil is always ready for a challenge."

Chapter 12

A FEW MILES AWAY FROM LOCH DUNMORAL, A fishing boat bumped between the ridge of rocks that carved a jagged passageway into the shore where the river met the sea. Gemma leaned over the side and scanned the dark green waters for Dainty's bald head.

It was a chilly gray gloaming with mist in the air.

"He's been down there a long time," she said. "Perhaps Baldwin ought to go in after him."

"Me?" Baldwin said in horror.

"Don't look at me either," Frances said, burying her hands in her skirts. "I owe Douglas my life, but nobody is getting me in a Scottish sea in November."

Suddenly Dainty burst from between the rocks

like Poseidon, his lips blue and trembling, his eyes bright with triumph. "The princess will sup in style," he announced.

Gemma grinned. "You found them?"

"That I did." He clambered into the boat, a fishing net slung over his naked shoulders. "You'd never believe where—I near drowned in that diving bell hunting for the buggers, and there they were all the time plastered over the rocks of the shore for the taking."

The small group stared in anticipation at the black shiny mess he'd dumped into the bottom of the boat. Beaming with pride, Dainty shoved his knife into the waistband of his soaking trousers.

Frances glared at him. "These aren't oysters, you lackwit. They're big nasty mussels. *Ew.*"

"Mussels!" Baldwin stomped his feet in glee. "Ye're so stupid, Dainty! What kind of pirate canna tell a mussel from an oyster?"

Dainty flushed to the dormant roots of his bald head. "Well, you try finding the accursed creatures with the water cold enough to freeze your eyeballs in your head. That's the best I could do."

Disgruntled, he thumped down on the thwarts, nearly capsizing the small boat.

"Oysters live in beds," Frances said disgustedly.

Baldwin chuckled. "Aye, ye should have looked for their mattresses."

Dainty crossed his muscle-knotted arms over his chest. "Tell Her Highness they're Highland oysters, or dress them up in sauce. I'm not diving again."

Gemma pushed her toe against the gleaming mess of mussels. "Do you want to sicken the princess? Some mussels can be deadly."

"We have less than a week to give the feast," Frances said grimly. "I insist on serving oysters on the half-shell, and I have to have a peacock for the center of the table."

"A peacock?" Dainty cried.

"Yes," Gemma said. "A peacock. And after you've found me a decent one, you're to report to Mrs. MacVittie for lessons in deportment." She picked up the oar. "After all Douglas has done for us, we owe it to him to make him proud."

She did not say it but more than a debt of gratitude hung in the balance. If Douglas sought redemption, then so did they. If he found it, they would too. But if he failed and fell flat on his face in this bold venture called reform, they fell with him.

They would willingly follow him into hell, and it wouldn't be the first time.

Douglas waited on the dais for the princess to join him again the next day for breakfast. It was Sunday—blackcurrant-jelly day. He had bathed in cold water and scrubbed himself with birch-bud soap. He had changed from his hunting clothes into a clean shirt and plaid, his long black hair secured in a black ribbon. Yet his mind was not on social niceties.

'Twas on murder. Specifically, 'twas on finding Neacail of Glengalda and his men and bringing them to justice.

He was in a dark mood. He hated it when matters did not go his way.

Pirating had been play. Navigating the waters of polite behavior was a pain in the arse. Simply put, courting a princess was downright dangerous. He liked her, and he was just learning that 'twas not pleasant to deceive someone you liked. Nor was this masquerade easy to maintain.

Moreover, despite his efforts to remain detached, he liked the trusting Highlanders of Dunmoral too—*his* village, if you could believe it.

He would honor his vow to end Neacail's reign of violence and intimidation. Call him a harsh disciplinarian, a cutthroat, a mercenary, but no one hurt what was his.

Douglas reserved that right.

Several hours ago, acting on a hint that Henry MacAult had given him at the loch, he had ridden up into the wooded hills to hunt down Neacail but found no trace of him.

Fury and frustration gnawed at his vitals. He sensed that the outlaws were watching him in secret while he searched for them; a small army could have easily hidden in any of the caves or crag crevices of the outlying moor. Or perhaps

Neacail was licking his wounds; it seemed too much to hope for that he had not survived that single shot.

"I am going to stop them," he said, as if voicing the vow aloud gave it power.

Still, he could hardly keep cantering out for these rousing manhunts, then trot back as fresh as a rosebud for a respectable meal with Her Royal Highness.

Respectable.

He glanced up in slow-dawning horror at the dozen fat tallow candles protruding from the pine chandelier above the dais table. Candles that his men, in a moment of boredom, had carved into a circle of naked frolicking women.

"Oh, Lord," he said, vaulting up out of his enormous chair.

Gemma, engrossed in her book of French court life, looked up with a puzzled frown to see Douglas dancing around in the center of the table. "What in the world are you doing?"

"The princess! The naked candles. Help!"

'Twas too late. While Douglas had been quick enough to stuff the offensive candles in his pockets, he hadn't managed to climb off the table before Rowena and her governess approached the dais.

He stared down at Rowena with an embarrassed smile. She wore a gown of sky-blue silk with an embroidered silver girdle. Her golden-brown hair flowed loose over her shoulders. She looked so sweet and graceful that Douglas's mind froze in its tracks.

How could he hoodwink this woman?

The contours of her mouth curved with a naive sensuality that set his nerves on fire as she smiled back at him. He fought the surprising tender impulse to reach down to touch her face, to sift his hands through her hair, to breathe her womanly scent.

He also fought the more urgent need to take her to his bed and bolt the door while he taught her in graphic terms what it meant for a woman to belong to a man.

This, this grandiose scheme of seduction, took shape in his mind while he stood before her smiling like a clodpate on the very table she was expected to eat upon, wax figures of wanton women bulging in his pocket. "I imagine you're wondering why I'm standing here like this," he said.

Rowena's mouth twitched at the corners. "I'm sure there is a reasonable explanation."

"There is." He glanced at his sister. "Isn't there, Gemma?"

"'Twas a mouse," Gemma said quickly. "It ran across Douglas's foot. He's been terrified of them since . . . since he was locked up in a cellar overnight by accident when he was three."

"A mouse?"

Rowena looked startled. Not, Douglas assumed

disgustedly, because she was afraid of rodents herself but because one didn't expect a man of his stature to behave like such a faint-headed fop.

He jumped down to the floor. "Thank you, Gemma," he said in a clipped tone.

"You're welcome." The girl hardly spared him a glance, oblivious to his annoyance. She just gazed in awe at Rowena. "Shall I see about breakfast then?"

"What about this mouse?" Hildegarde asked, her gruff voice jolting Douglas out of his dangerous mood.

"I chased it away," Gemma said. "Douglas was too scared to do it."

Rowena arched her brow, her gaze lifting to the still swaying chandelier. She wished to be alone with Douglas, away from this castle and his retainers, in an atmosphere where she might probe deeper into his character. More and more she believed that his behavior was a pose, but whether he meant to please her or deceive her, she did not know.

She had been in his company only four days, 'twas true. Hardly long enough for him to prove himself the ruthless leader of legend. Perhaps he feared the Crown would punish him if he reverted to his past behavior. Still, she had to penetrate his guard quickly. Once Frederic returned, 'twould be impossible.

"I will eat later, thank you," she said. "Right now I'd love nothing more than a ride across the

moor. Is it possible, my lord? I have hardly moved
a muscle since I arrived. You could show me your
holdings."

Her simple request sent a chill of apprehension
down Douglas's spine. Rowena, riding alone on
the moor, a rare jewel to tempt the raiders who
had no regard for beauty or human life.

He shook his head. "I don't think so."

"Highness." Hildegarde sent Douglas a beseech-
ing look. "'Tis not wise to let her leave this castle.
She must be protected."

"You could accompany me, my lord," Rowena
said with a beguiling smile.

That tempted him. To ride alone with her in the
wind, to watch the furtive passage of deer
through the woods. And, if the moment came, to
woo her with a few well-chosen words, a kiss.
Strangely, winning her fortune was the farthest
thing from his mind. She was a treasure unto
herself.

But he could not court the woman and pay
heed to his surroundings. He hated to admit to
her that he'd allowed a handful of savage men
to intimidate an entire village. He did not wish
to appear even weaker than this absurd masquerade made him act. Instead of strolling in the
garden, he should be riding down an outlaw.

"There are raiders in the area," he said in an
apologetic voice.

"My brother has always preferred reading a

good book to any outdoor activity," Gemma said ruefully. "He had a delicate constitution as a child. Mama fretted herself into a state every time he had a cough."

Rowena stared up at Douglas in wonder. "Indeed."

"We almost lost him several times," Gemma went on, ignoring the killing gleam in her brother's eye. "A rheumy nose would lay him at death's door."

Douglas forced a smile. "Pray do not bore our guest with the details of my invalid youth, Gemma. You exaggerate."

"I'm not bored," Rowena said hastily. "I find your past a fascinating subject. Perhaps a canter across the moor would improve your . . . constitution."

Douglas looked down at her. Secrets and deception hung between them like a shimmering veil of mist that grew more dense with every second.

He could still put his hand through the mist, shatter the illusion. 'Twas not too late.

He could confess, come clean, admit he was an impostor, that he had committed acts bordering on barbaric. But then the mischief in her eyes would sharpen into mistrust. She would flee in panic.

He would lose her.

"I had planned another activity for the afternoon," he said evenly.

"Such as, my lord?"

Her gaze met his.

"I thought we might"—he took a deep breath—"read Shakespeare to each other in front of the fire." He struck a dramatic pose. "'O flesh, flesh, how art thou fishified!'"

"Fishified?" Rowena said, a frown wrinkling her forehead.

Hildegarde sighed in relief. "An excellent suggestion, my lord."

"I am beside myself with anticipation," Rowena said.

Douglas inclined his head. "I think only of your welfare."

"I'm sure you do," Rowena retorted. "However, if I may not ride, then I insist on taking a walk around the castle gardens. Gardening is a secret passion of mine, and I understand a green thumb runs in your family."

"The gardens." Douglas glanced to Gemma for help. He knew there had to be a garden somewhere in the castle. He'd never bothered to look. The former earl had cultivated a hothouse, but Douglas didn't have a clue what he'd grown.

"I suppose we could manage a brief stroll," Douglas said cautiously, his mind already on the search he and Aidan would make afterward.

"If it does not fatigue you," Rowena said wryly.

"The garden is in a terrible state," Gemma said.

Rowena squared her shoulders. "I will have my

walk, or go stark raving mad. And *that* is a royal command."

Douglas walked Gemma back against the table, his mask of docility slipping to reveal the devilish anger beneath. The princess sailed from the room with Hildegarde in tow to fetch her cloak.

"Why the hell did you have to tell her I'm afraid of mice?"

Gemma edged around a chair. "What was I supposed to tell her?"

"Couldn't you have said I was replacing the candles that had burned out in the chandelier?"

"Couldn't you?" Gemma retorted.

He wheeled to look away. His temper was not improved by the reminder that Rowena had rendered him incapable of straight thinking.

"The princess wants to walk in the garden," he said dourly.

Gemma grinned. "She has given you a royal command."

He waved her away. "Run ahead, lass. Make sure the men haven't filled the fountains with rum or littered the pathways with dead bodies and empty tankards. We must give her a nice garden."

Gemma sighed loudly. "I expect to be repaid for all this, Douglas. And by the way, you still have all those naked candles in your pocket. If the princess keeps addling your wits, you'll probably pull one out and pass it to her instead of a handkerchief."

Common sense told Rowena that one could not rouse a retired dragon without the risk of starting a fire. Intuition also warned her she was definitely courting danger.

Yet in what guise she could not decide. The Dragon of Darien was undoubtedly a dangerous man.

The Earl of Dunmoral, who appeared to be frightened of mice, preferring Shakespeare to physical exercise, was not.

Was the dragon of her dreams all smoke and no fire? Had the stories exaggerated his exploits?

"Delicate constitution," she said to herself. "If there is a delicate bone in that man's body, then I am the Dey of Algiers."

Hildegarde snorted. "Appearances lie. To look at *you*, one would not guess you are as headstrong as a donkey and persistent as a ferret."

Rowena smudged a dab of rouge across her lips. "He didn't notice I wore my hair loose. Or the embroidered silver girdle that even my boar-mannered brothers said looks well on me. There. Is that red enough?"

"Your mouth is a beacon in a storm, Highness."

Well, let's just hope his lordship decides to bring his ship to port, Rowena thought.

But she said, "The man expects me to believe he is afraid of mice. Why does he lie to me?"

"Would you admit you were an infamous barbarian if you had been offered a second chance at life, Highness?"

"I hardly know," Rowena said. "I have never been an infamous barbarian before. I think I might enjoy it, though."

"Perhaps 'twas a condition of his receiving the earldom, that he assume his new identity in both thought and deed," Hildegarde said speculatively.

"Then how do I bring out the beast in the man?" Rowena wondered aloud. "How can I trust him?"

"You cannot." Hildegarde arranged the sable-lined cloak around Rowena's shoulders as if it were a suit of armor. "Wait. We forgot to pin this on your bosom. You can trust no one, Highness. No one."

Rowena stared at the crudely twisted cross of sticks in the woman's hand. "You want me to wear a brooch of dead branches?"

"Rowan twigs," Hildegarde said. "A Scottish charm to protect you from danger."

Rowena vented a sigh. Resigned, she allowed the woman to fasten the strange symbol to the underside of her bodice. Arguing with Hildegarde never proved wise.

Yet it seemed pointless to wear a charm against danger when Rowena was working so hard to attract it.

"Shall I confront him outright?" she asked Hildegarde.

"Every man deserves a chance to reform," was

the response. "If you confess to knowing his past, which he obviously wants to keep secret, you will damage his pride. Worse, you will find yourself at the mercy of a man who has nothing left to lose. Perhaps 'tis only the illusion of decency that prevents him from hurting you."

"Then you advise me to continue playing along with this masquerade?" Rowena said.

"Until Frederic returns, yes. You must pretend he is the earl's genuine son."

"I have watched him with his sister and his men," Rowena said. "I have seen him show anger, affection, and authority. But 'tis like watching him through the castle's portcullis. I catch glimpses of the man, but I cannot sneak past his guard to see who he truly is."

"Which is probably a good thing," Hildegarde stated. "He who digs enough dirt will eventually come face-to-face with the Devil."

"I am drawn to the man behind the barrier," she admitted softly.

"Highness! Do not say such a thing. You have no experience with men."

"And I am never likely to gain it," Rowena said wryly.

Chapter 13

NOTHING MUCH GREW WITHIN THE SHELTERED walls of the castle garden at this time of year but for the evergreens, a few clusters of rosemary and thyme, some thistles, a forlorn Michaelmas daisy or two.

Rowena gazed at the neglected flora of the former earl's garden in open delight.

Douglas studied her with nonchalant amusement underlaid with a primal attraction that had begun to plague him like a physical ache.

Afraid of saying the wrong thing, he said little.

She did not seem to mind. She twirled around a wheelbarrow to disappear down an overgrown path. "I never knew you had a plesaunce, my lord," she shouted over her shoulder.

Neither did Douglas. In fact, he hadn't the

vaguest idea what a plesaunce was. It sounded like some sort of edible fowl.

"Shall we go in the maze or the rose arbor next?" Rowena bellowed happily.

"The rose arbor."

A safer choice. Douglas didn't trust himself alone with her in the shadowy tunnels of privet that the previous earl had cultivated. One inadvertent brush of her hand on his back, an accidental bump against each other, and he would lose the advantage, *take* advantage, proving himself to be unworthy of her.

Her mouth curved in a enchanting smile as she beckoned him. He felt himself moving toward her, drawn to the innocence he could destroy, uncertain suddenly of what he wanted from her. And she of him. An hour from now he hoped to be hunting down a deadly enemy. How could he plot vengeance in her presence?

"How very intriguing." Steps ahead of him, she stopped in front of a warped trellis with dying branches that produced a string of red flowers. "Don't tell me that's a *Rosa cinamomea simplex* at this time of year."

"All right," Douglas said. "I won't."

"What floribunda," Rowena said with enthusiasm. "What—"

"—in God's name is a rosy cinnamon complex?" Douglas asked himself, strolling up behind her for a look at this natural wonder.

His dark eyes narrowed in suspicion.

The flowers displayed on the trellis in such artful profusion were not to be found in any botanical encyclopedia. In fact, they looked suspiciously like the gaudy silk rosettes that had adorned the tiered petticoats Gemma had begged for in Nairn.

"Is it?" Rowena asked.

Douglas turned, surreptitiously scouring the garden for sign of his crack-brained little sister. "Is it what?"

"A *Rosa cinamomea simplex?*"

"No." Douglas scowled at the flamboyant bush. "'Tis a *petticoatalis Gemma idiotica.*"

"A—" Rowena stepped closer to the trellis. She let out an alarmingly loud whoop of laughter. "That is such a good joke," she said. "I was well-deceived."

Douglas drifted away from her, half paying attention. He'd just caught a glimpse of Gemma sneaking through the maze. She, who'd thought to trick the princess by pinning pieces of her petticoats to a trellis.

"I don't suppose you ever have to prune them," Rowena said, still chuckling.

"What?"

"Do you prune them?"

"Prunes don't do well in the Highlands," Douglas answered distractedly.

Rowena frowned. "What?"

He made a menacing motion at the maze. Rowena glanced around unexpectedly, catching him just as he shook his fist in Gemma's direction.

"What on earth are you doing, my lord?" Rowena asked.

He uncurled his fingers and swatted the air in front of his face. "Midges. You can snatch them by the handful. Pesky things. Did you say you liked prunes?"

"I think you are a dreadful tease," she said in a low voice.

"A tease? Who . . . me?"

"I am a sister myself," Rowena said. "I do have brothers of my own."

Douglas ran his hand through his hair. "I daresay you don't embarrass them by leaving bits of your personal undergarments around the garden."

"I daresay I've done worse." Rowena's smile was disarmingly wicked. "They claim I ruin their lives."

"You?" His gaze dropped to her mouth, lingering on the plum-red underlip. How could she ruin anyone's life? This woman was made for loving and causing laughter. His body tightened at the temptation. His heart ached with a desperate need he dared not acknowledge like a stone overturned to the sun.

"You're staring at me, my lord," she said.

He took a step toward her. "You're staring at me too."

"You were staring at my mouth," she said in an undertone.

Was this an invitation, or another test of character? The princess played with fire. She was a maiden-warrior throwing stones into the sleeping dragon's lair. If she persisted, she would find herself facing a fully-roused monster.

"I was staring at the rouge you are wearing on your lips," he said.

Her fingers flew to her mouth. "You noticed?"

"I am a man, Your Highness."

"You certainly are." Then, without warning, she added, "I have never been kissed."

Douglas drew his breath in through his teeth. God above, now she wasn't throwing stones into his cave. She was hurling boulders.

She looked up into his face. "Tell me the truth, my lord. Am I unattractive to men?"

Surprise darkened his eyes at the absurd question. But then it was gone, supplanted by a dark scowl of disapproval. How could her feminine powers even be in doubt? And who was it she wished to attract? Certainly no one in *his* castle, not if the man valued his life. "Why do you care whether you are attractive to men or not?" he demanded.

"I am to be wed within the year." Another sigh

escaped her. "Papa was interviewing suitors when the rebellion started. He led me to believe the list of decent men who desire me is limited."

"Decent men," Douglas murmured. "They are rarer than diamonds these days." The role of indecent men who desired her was no doubt endless, and his name would lead the list.

"I do not understand Papa much," she said. "He drinks and plots petty wars on his neighbors. He gallops out in the dead of night to arrest insurgents. Sometimes I wonder if he isn't hoping to be killed himself."

"There are men like that." Douglas said quietly, thinking of himself and Aidan, of their reckless exploits and disregard for death. Aidan had lost his wife. Douglas had lost his soul. They were a compatible pair of sinners. "Men whose secret burdens become more than they can bear."

Rowena's voice was subdued. "His last words to me were, 'This is the kind of world that kills helpless women and children, Rowena. Never trust it for a moment. Never trust anyone you have not tested.'"

"Your father is wise to warn you."

"But I need to trust someone," she said. "I need to listen to my own heart. Papa's heart is shriveled with grief and bitterness."

"What does your heart tell you?" he asked slowly.

She closed her eyes. His mouth grazed her hair, or did she imagine it? Did she imagine the delicious tension that spun them together like an invisible thread? "It tells me . . ." She turned toward the trellis. "It tells me that you did not answer my question."

He stepped into her. The hard contours of his chest felt like the castle wall, solid, intimidating, holding her captive. She ached suddenly to feel his arms around her. Then in a deep lyrical voice that sent shivers down her spine, he said, "Your loveliness eclipses the sun. Your eyes reflect the light of a thousand stars. Your—"

"—brain is as inflated as a pig's bladder if you imagine I want to hear that nonsense." She whirled around, her face hurt and angry. "I asked for honesty. If you are incapable of it, then please keep your horrid flattery to yourself."

A pig's bladder, she had said.

His first reaction was to give the royal hellion exactly what she was begging for.

A kiss that would shock her to the tips of her slippers, a kiss that tasted of such black desire it would brand her his forever. Princess or not, she was looking for trouble.

As fate would have it, she was standing before the very man who would like nothing better than to give it to her. Aye, he could this moment show her just how attractive she was. His racing pulse was a testament to her allure.

She claimed to value honesty.

Should he tell her that he honestly believed she

would not leave this castle with her purity intact? Should he drop his masquerade before the damage was done?

"I wish to be kissed," she announced without warning.

Douglas did not move a muscle. For the life of him he didn't know how a gentleman was supposed to react to such a statement. He knew how a rogue would react though. Unfortunately, bedding her in the potting shed was not an option.

She raised her voice. "I said—"

"I heard exactly what you said." He clenched his jaw and grabbed her arm. Drawing her against his chest, he whispered, "As probably did my sister. She is hiding in the maze."

Rowena peered around his shoulder. "Why did you not tell me this before?" she asked, looking irritated.

"I did not guess our conversation would take such an . . . interesting turn." He propelled her back onto the path.

"Would you have kissed me if we were alone?" she whispered.

Douglas's hand tightened on her arm for a dangerous moment. His face unreadable, he released her. "Do you see those little brown flowers over there?"

"Those are thistles, my lord."

He knelt at the untended triangle of foliage, his body fully aroused. "I think you're right," he said between his teeth.

"I suppose I could ask Aidan to kiss me," she said in a museful tone.

Douglas looked up from the ground. His face was as dark as death. "I would not advise that," he said in a very quiet voice. "You see, Aidan is my left arm, and I would cut off that arm before I'd allow it to touch you."

She swallowed, drawing back a step. "I wasn't serious," she said.

"Good," he said, his expression once again neutral. But deep inside his emotions burned red-black like the very heart of hell. To think of her begging kisses from Aidan was a torment he would not endure. "Do you wish Aidan to kiss you?" he demanded.

"Of course not. The man barely looks at me."

He grunted, relieved he would not have to murder one of his best friends. Then he plucked the bristly plant up by the roots. "Perhaps the damn thing is an herb."

Rowena frowned at him, grateful that his anger had passed. "'Tis a cow thistle, my lord. Obviously you do not take after your father. I understood he was a passionate horticulturist."

"Actually, he was a thieving whoreson," Douglas said without thinking.

She pressed her hand to her mouth. Without realizing it, she had been baiting him, hoping to trick him into the truth. The Dragon of Darien was not related to the Earl of Dunmoral by blood. Had she hoped to catch him in a lie?

"Your father was a what?" she said.

Appalled, Douglas shot to his feet. The woman had unbalanced him once again with her outrageous demands to be kissed. "The secret is out," he said soberly, clasping his hands behind his back. "Papa used to pinch seeds and pods from other people's gardens. I hope you will not hold this shocking piece of family history against me."

Rowena could only stare at him. He covered his blunder so well she could almost believe it had not been a blunder after all.

And Douglas, looking guileless, stared right back. The masquerade was about to recommence. The Earl of Dunmoral, that pompous impostor, had beaten down his darker counterpart.

He affected a sigh. "Papa did so love his plants. To the point of criminal behavior."

Rowena's gaze was unnervingly direct. She might be young. She might be sexually naive. She was definitely a wily little princess. But if he managed to deceive her, he suspected 'twould be only because she had allowed it.

"You need not apologize for your papa," she said. "My great-great-great grandfather was a peasant who overthrew the government and crowned himself prince."

"Very ambitious of him."

She smiled. "The men in my family take what they want."

So, as a rule, did Douglas.

He guided her over an ornamental footbridge. A small wooden sign warned them to proceed at their own folly. "And the women?"

"There are none to speak of. Well, as I told you before my younger sister Micheline has been banished to a convent in Brittany. My mother died long ago."

He felt a curious urge to draw her against his chest, to protect her from the hurts of the world. "Life is unpleasant, then, even for a princess."

"Sometimes. Papa never recovered from her death. I am all he has left. For years I've been the only one who could coax a smile out of him."

And you sacrifice your life for your sire. Does he appreciate you? You rescue him from his grief. Would he not worry if he knew you had ventured into the lair of a man like me?

"Those are slender shoulders to bear such burdens." He leaned back against a stone fountain with a lion's mouth that was clogged with dead leaves.

"And your shoulders appear quite strong," she said.

His heartbeat quickened. She said alarming things, dangerous things. She made him feel brave and strong when inside he knew himself to be a blackguard.

"You should be proud of your innocence," he stated.

Rowena frowned at him. "Why?"

"Men admire purity in a woman," Douglas said.

"Indeed," she said wryly. "That explains why they spend half their lives robbing every female they meet of that exalted state."

"Not all men are that way," Douglas said, although to save his life he couldn't think of one who wasn't.

"I don't want to be admired by men," Rowena confessed. "I think I would prefer to be lusted after like my sister."

A wave of black heat washed over Douglas. He glanced around. If the lady knew how her outrageous remarks affected him, she would not sling them about in such a unguarded manner. "That is another inflammatory thought, Your Highness. The wrong man would use such a statement to take advantage of you."

Rowena ignored the warning. "Of course I would have to find a man worthy of my trust as well as of my lust." She grinned. "Did I just make a rhyme?"

He clenched his jaw. "A very bad one."

"A man with the power to deflower?"

He gave her a little push forward. "I think our tour of the garden is complete."

She sighed in resignation. "Thank you. I needed the exercise. My body was tense all over from lack of use."

"I have experienced that feeling myself."

"In fact," Rowena said, "if there's only one thing I love more than a good garden, 'tis falconry. I noticed the castle mews when we first arrived.

Did Matthew ever mention to you that's how we met? Falconing in my father's forest?"

Douglas summoned a terse smile. "The rogue never told me."

"I was so impressed," she said offhandedly, moving past him with her pert nose in the air like a princess passing a lackey in the hall. "You are so unlike him, my lord. I don't suppose you share his interest in the sport? You probably prefer a tamer pursuit such as poetry."

He followed her slowly, a chill smile on his face.

While you were riding your pony on the palace grounds, I was sacking a castle in San Lorenzo. You bathed in scented oil and sipped Spanish chocolate in bed. I bathed in blood and sweat and got blinding drunk on Spanish wine in a bullet-riddled canoe.

While you were studying Roman history, I was supervising a gang of street ruffians. Your schoolmistresses hoped to instill Christian character in your heart. I lived to instill fear.

And before you had even begun to dream of that first kiss, I was killing my first man.

Tamer pursuits, she'd said.

If only she knew.

Wonderful, Rowena thought, stomping up the stairs to her room. Now he shall think she was not only a pickle-head, but a most peculiar and desperate female as well. She had all but thrown herself at his knees.

"I wish to be kissed." She groaned, hiding her face in her hands. "'A man with the power to deflower.' Did I *really* say that?"

She reached her room and banged the heavy door behind her. She wrenched off her pearl-seeded slippers and sent them hurtling at the window like lethal weapons. She kicked the bed-post, pretending it was his lordship's leg.

Chewing her lip, she pulled every article of clothing from the pinewood wardrobe into a heap on the bed.

A gray traveling gown that would not show the dirt. A dull blue dress that made her eyes appear lighter. Garments of murky green and brown because a princess must maintain a dignified appearance at all times.

And then, at the bottom of the unappealing pile, the watered raspberry silk with gold-threaded tissue underskirts and deep scalloped neckline that bared shoulders, breasts, and back. The scandalous garment of a courtesan had been created in Paris, a gift from one of her sister's admirers.

Her exiled sibling, Micheline of the daring heart, had forced the gown on Rowena as a gift before leaving for the convent in France.

"I can't wear that!" Rowena exclaimed. "It shows—"

"—that you are an alluring woman, a woman of

grace, not a drab and dutiful daughter who has never done a disobedient or exciting thing in her life." Micheline's cruel words had been thrown like a gauntlet. "I pass the torch to you, sister. Live your own life. Cause a stir. Break a heart or two."

"But—"

"Show off your bosoms, Rowena. They're bigger than mine."

Douglas felt a little better. After the walk with Rowena, he and Aidan had ridden across the moor to find two of Neacail's men hunting grouse.

Douglas had battled with the first outlaw, and the man now lay injured in the dungeon where he would probably die.

The second man had surrendered without a fight. He too awaited his fate in the dark vaults of Dunmoral.

Aye, Douglas had enjoyed his late-afternoon conquest. He would have felt better yet if 'twas Neacail he had brought down. Or if he could claim the princess on his own merit without this masquerade.

Chapter 14

GEMMA DROPPED HER MUDDIED SHOES ON THE castle steps. "Why didn't you kiss her in the garden yesterday, Douglas? I don't understand you. You like kissing women. Have you gone daft?"

"Probably." He released a morose sigh. "I don't suppose you can find me a falcon."

She plunked herself down on the steps and glared up at him. "Hell's bells. What kind of falcon?"

Douglas stared over her head at Rowena practicing archery before a courtyard of enrapt servants and retired pirates. She had the scoundrels eating out of her hand, tripping over themselves to carry her quiver, to bring her a glass of water from the well, to show her the newborn kittens in the stables.

"What was it about her that charms even the lowest element on earth?" he wondered aloud.

"She's just plain sweet and she treats everyone with respect," Gemma said thoughtfully, her small face scrunched in her hands. "She called Baldwin 'my good man' and we'll never hear the end of it. No one has ever called that moron a good man before. And she gave Dainty some ointment for his sore knee." Gemma sighed. "She even went searching the kitchens to praise Frances for those nasty oatcakes. Frances, who was bellowing at customers in a brothel last year."

"We're all frauds," Douglas said. "Impostors. I don't know why I thought this would work."

"You should have kissed her, Douglas. She all but ordered you to do it."

"She isn't a whore," he said stiffly. "She's a young lass just like you, and if I caught a man kissing you before you're betrothed, I'd crack his head open like a hazelnut."

Gemma giggled, then clapped her hands as Rowena hit the center of the target. "What kind of falcon am I supposed to find?"

"I don't care. Big. Little. Brown. Black—" He frowned at the sight of Shandy, Willie, and Baldwin trotting after Rowena like lap dogs. "I'm jesting, Gemma. I'm not a falconer. I'm not Matthew. I don't know who the hell I am anymore."

"Do you still want her fortune?" Gemma asked. He hesitated, his frown deepening as he

watched Rowena coax Aidan into taking a turn at
the target. "I don't know that either, lass."

"Oh. Douglas," Gemma's voice was mournful.
"Now you've really got me worried."

"'Tis dead!" Dainty's shout of disbelief resounded through the solar. "This is a stuffed bird,
Gemma! What the blue hell is Douglas supposed
to do with a dead bird?"

Willie and Baldwin, standing guard at the door,
grinned in enjoyment as Gemma sprang off the
window seat to calm the giant.

"Use your imagination, Dainty. We'll prop it up
on the tower. No one will ever know the difference."

"The damn bird is dead!"

She crossed her arms over her chest. "And if
you don't point out that fact with your bellowing
the princess probably won't even notice."

Dainty smirked. "What if she wants Douglas to
fly it?"

Fear deflated Gemma's confidence. Her arms
dropped to her sides. "I didn't think of that."

He picked up the bird from the table. "'Twas a
good try, girl."

"Better than yer nasty mussels," Baldwin said
with a gleeful crackle from the door.

Gemma blew out a sigh of exasperation. "I'm
not beaten yet. Come on, Dainty. This creature
has to be back in Dr. MacVittie's parlor before

bedtime, or else. Mary says he counts the birds in his collection every night."

The giant didn't move as she yanked the bird from his hand. "What evil are you planning?"

She strode to the door with the stuffed bird under her arm. "Something I saw at a country fair, and you're all helping me too."

Chapter 15

THAT SAME DAY, GEMMA TALKED DAINTY INTO fashioning a pulley-and-string device to fly the bird back and forth between the two tower windows. Gemma manned the east window. Dainty took the west. Willie hid on the walkway. Aidan refused to have anything to do with the affair. He wanted to watch from a safe distance when Douglas found out and the killing started.

Baldwin stood below in the bailey making signals to prevent Gemma from flying the falcon smack into the wall.

It was a staged production not unlike the Punch-and-Judy puppet shows so popular at fairs.

Gemma had a flair for drama. She thought her ruse might work. Seeing Douglas so despondent over a woman broke her heart. He deserved a

princess, although Gemma still thought he would
be wiser to stop trying to impress Rowena and
simply be himself. How could anyone not love her
brother?

Douglas felt a warning chill crawl down his
spine. His body felt suddenly cold below the
heavy plaid, his skin prickling with pinpoints of
anxiety just beneath the surface. Gemma had
summoned everyone into the bailey, promising
an hour of entertainment.

It had sounded harmless. Rowena had been
delighted at the prospect, complaining that she
was beginning to feel like a captive in the castle,
not allowed to leave for almost a week. But now
Douglas wondered what awful scheme Gemma
had concocted.

"Trust me, Douglas," she said with a confident
grin as she'd bolted up the stairs.

He moved up behind Baldwin. "What has my
sister planned?"

" 'Tis a secret, sir."

"You will tell me, Baldwin, or I shall hang you
by your ears from the portcullis."

"I promised I wouldna tell, sir." He glanced
back up at Douglas, cringing at the merciless
expression that met his gaze. "She's found ye a
falcon, sir."

"A falcon?" Douglas smiled reluctantly, pleased
despite himself. "She didn't? The clever girl."

"Aye." Baldwin's lips puckered as if he ached to add more.

"A genuine living falcon," Douglas mused softly. "And it has been trained?"

Baldwin sucked air in through his teeth, pretending to stare up at the tower.

Douglas's expression turned deadly. "Out with it, Baldwin. What manner of falcon has my meddlesome sister found?"

Dead. Dear God. Douglas could only shake his head and hope that the princess was nearsighted, or that Gemma's sad display of falconry would be received in the spirit it was given. The mist, drifting in thick across the tops of the castle towers, ought to help. Another deception, he thought with a sigh.

"The falcon seems to be hovering," Hildegarde murmured, leaning around Douglas to pull Rowena's mantle over her shoulders. "You must stay covered, Highness. The mist brings on illness."

Rowena shrugged the woman's hand away, her head tilted back to the tower. "I have never seen a falcon strike such a pose in midair."

"And you're never likely to again," Douglas said, glaring at the small face of his sister in the tower. "He always does that to get attention."

"She," Rowena corrected him.

"What?"

"*She* does that to get attention," Rowena said.

"The female is called a falcon. The male is a tiercel."

"That's what I meant," Douglas said irritably, pacing a circle around her, hoping to obstruct her view with his shoulders. "She's a dreadful show-off."

"I assume you took her as an eyess."

"Of course I did." Whatever that meant.

Rowena edged forward. "Could we climb to the battlement walk for a closer look?"

"I don't think so." Douglas nudged her back. "She's breeding, Your Highness. You know how sensitive falcons are when they breed."

Rowena gave Douglas a searching look. "'Tis a pleasant surprise to learn you share my passion. Falconry is a dying art."

He glanced up at the stuffed bird. "It certainly is."

All of a sudden Gemma appeared to lose control of the pulley. The falcon did a series of death-defying somersaults in the air. Douglas cringed.

"She's diving," Rowena said in surprise, shoving Douglas aside for a better look. "She's doing a flip—she's flying backward! Magnificent."

The skin across Douglas's broad cheekbones stretched white and taut. The damn bird wasn't diving; it was hurtling hirdie-girdie toward the princess's head. Dainty had allowed the string to unravel at an alarming rate.

Douglas broke away from the crowd in the

courtyard, trying the guess where the bird would land. He hopped this way and that. Then suddenly Dainty got the string straightened out, and the falcon lifted back above the walkways, a handful of feathers floating slowly down as it spun up into a graceful spiral.

"She's flying backward again," Hildegarde said in wonder. "I did not dream such a thing was possible."

"Neither did I," Rowena said in a skeptical voice.

Hildegarde gasped. "She's losing her feathers!"

"She's molting," Douglas said quickly.

Suspicion drew Rowena's face into a scowl. "I thought you said she was breeding."

He caught a feather in his fist. "Breeding and molting. 'Tis amazing how many things those birds can do at once." He forced Rowena farther back into the bailey. "I only wish I could train my retainers half as well."

"What will his lordship do with her eggs?" Hildegarde asked Baldwin, who stood beside her observing the spectacle in guarded silence.

"I dinna know, ma'am," he said honestly. "Poach 'em, I reckon."

"*Poach* them?" the woman said in horror.

Douglas glared at Baldwin. "He meant to say," 'Approach them,' ma'am. I will approach them carefully so as not to crack their precious wee shells."

Rowena looked up at him, her gaze unwavering, and Douglas knew he'd been found out. He gave a low whistle through his teeth, deliberately looking the other way.

"'Tis a rather early time of year to mate, isn't it, my lord?" she asked with an acidic smile.

"Not really," Baldwin said before Douglas could come up with a plausible answer. "We mate year-round here in the Highlands. Is it different in your country, princess?" he asked sympathetically. "Are ye only allowed to couple at certain times?"

Chapter 16

MARY MACVITTIE CAME TO THE CASTLE THE NEXT morning on a crusade.

A true believer in tradition, she was determined that Dunmoral should have its own princess. The presence of a princess would bring fame to this woefully forgotten hamlet.

She marched across the great hall to the dais with her infamous book of manners in hand. Her heart trembled in her breast at the task she was about to undertake.

Her pirate prince lounged in his chair with the wicked look of a man who could never truly be tamed. Why, he had his boots on the table! If Mary had brought her fan, she would have smacked him on the ear.

"You are late, madam," he said idly, his eyes half-closed.

She tried to catch her breath. He was a big man, intimidating. He was slapping a jeweled dirk across his massive thigh, and who knew what he might decide to do with it? "Your sister has been studying this," she said bravely, showing him the book. "'Tis a treatise on social intercourse."

"Social inter—" Douglas threw Gemma a furious look, swinging his long legs to the floor. "I ought to clap you in the tower, reading this rubbish."

Mrs. MacVittie felt rather faint, daring to contradict a man of his reputation. She wondered if he might make her walk the plank, or God forbid, if he might auction her naked to his men. The thought made her head reel. "Etiquette books are quite the fashion," she said. "Manners are essential, my lord, and if I may be frank, your retainers display a remarkable ignorance of the art of civility."

"What the hell did that woman just say?" Baldwin whispered.

Willie shook his head. "I think she said her name was Frank."

"For example, Gemma," she went on, turning to the girl, "did you know 'tis impolite for a young lady to hitch up her skirts in front of a fire when the opposite sex is present?"

"Is she supposed to take them off?" Baldwin wondered aloud.

"Of course she knows that," Douglas said indignantly.

"Well." Mrs. MacVittie gave him a searching look. "Did *you* know, sir, that it is considered the height of rudeness to fiddle with your fire irons at a party?"

"I make it a point never to fiddle in mixed company, madam."

"Only in his cabin," Dainty said, earning a poke in the ribs from Gemma.

"Fine dining is an art unto itself," Mrs. MacVittie said. "Proper social conduct requires that one learn to lay a table. Everything must be perfect for the princess. The King of France is served one hundred dishes at a sitting."

"One hundred?" Willie gave a long whistle. "We'll have to roll the poor princess from the table after that."

Mrs. MacVittie walked around the table, lips pursed in dismay. "Let us hold a mock banquet. You remain in your chair, my lord. For practical purposes, I shall play the part of the princess."

"Can I be the prince?" Baldwin asked.

"There is no prince, blockhead," Douglas said. "You're going to serve the wine."

"My lord." Mrs. MacVittie stopped to nudge Douglas's elbow into his lap. She felt braver now, realizing how desperately these poor souls needed saving. "All uncooked joints off the table. Now pretend we are passing around a platter."

"A platter of what?" Phelps asked.

"Haggis," Douglas said. "Frances has been practicing her receipt for it all week."

"So that's what I smelled," Baldwin said. "And here I was thinkin' some poor soul had died in the kitchen and hadna got buried yet."

Gemma wrinkled her nose. "I hate haggis. I'm not having any."

"You will if the princess takes some first," Mrs. MacVittie said sternly as she lowered herself into her seat. Then, "Mr. McGee, what in the world are you doing?"

"Pickin' the onions out of this haggis. They give me heartburn."

"Picking at one's food is not allowed," she said with a shudder of distaste. "Dainty, why are you making that horrible face?"

"I burned my tongue on them onions."

"I burned my tongue, Your Royal Highness. And do refrain from eating until I begin. Mr. McGee, uncork the wine."

Baldwin cast a puzzled look around the hall. "Where is it?"

"Use your imagination," Douglas said in exasperation. "Mrs. MacVittie, may I have a word?"

"Certainly, my lord. 'Tis your table."

Douglas glowered at his men. "No throwing food. No belching or farting out of your favorite songs. Willie, don't pick your false teeth with your knife." He nodded to Mary. "That is all."

"And very sound advice that was," she murmured. "Shall we continue?"

"Aren't we supposed to wash up in a bowl of scented water first?" Gemma asked.

"Indeed, we are," Mrs. MacVittie said. "Here is the bowl. Let us begin again."

"What happened to the haggis?" Dainty said.

"Do we wash our feet in the bowl?" Willie asked.

"You certainly do not," Mrs. MacVittie said. "In fact, in your lowly positions, 'tis highly improbable you will dine in the royal presence."

"The Dragon let us eat biscuits with Don Alfonso's daughter," Willie said.

"That was different," Dainty told him. "We were holding her for ransom. The princess is a guest."

Mrs. MacVittie frowned. "It might be a good idea to refrain from mentioning your past exploits in front of Her Royal Highness."

"What did she say?" Baldwin whispered.

Douglas glared down the table. "She means I'll knock you senseless if you tell the princess we were pirates."

Mrs. MacVittie swallowed a gasp. "Mr. Willie, pick up your knife."

"What knife?"

"The hypothetical knife."

"I never heared of such a thing," he said. "What is it?"

Dainty snorted. "A knife for eating your hypothets, stupid."

"I don't think I've ever eaten such a thing before," Willie said. "How do I know I'll like 'em?"

"I heard the captain call Henry Morgan a hypothet a few years back," Baldwin said thoughtfully.

Dainty flashed him a grin. "That was a hypocrite."

"Do they have their own knives too?" Baldwin asked curiously.

"No, Baldwin," Dainty said. "Hypocrites are eaten with spoons."

Baldwin stared across the table at Mrs. MacVittie. "Is your name really Frank?"

"Dear, dear," Mrs. MacVittie exclaimed. "The need for social correction in this castle is more urgent then I dreamed." She turned to Douglas. "Sir, I don't think I can help them."

"Neither do I." He looked around him in resignation.

"Would ye like a glass of wine, sir?" Baldwin asked, brandishing an imaginary bottle. "Ye look as if ye need it."

Douglas took Rowena on a ride through the village at gloaming that same day. Two hours earlier he had patrolled the moor and woods, hoping to catch the outlaws hunting again. Rowena was waiting for him when he returned. The princess had been pestering him for exercise, and he had secretly enlisted the help of his people to impress her.

Henry, the village smithy and clan spokesman, had promised the full cooperation of the village elders.

Douglas had never dreamed how far "cooperation" could go.

A fanfare of pipes, fiddlers, and offbeat drums greeted Rowena's arrival in the glen. Three young girls presented her with a basket of autumn nuts and apples. She graciously accepted this gift.

"I am deeply touched," she began. "His lordship has told me of your hardships—"

She never had a chance to launch into the uplifting speech she had prepared. The people of Dunmoral barely let her get in another word.

"Hardships?" a woman in a hooded plaid said. "Our hardships would have put us in the grave if not fer his lordship."

A young man raised his voice. "The good earl put out a fire in my auntie's cot last month. Wi' his bare hands, I might add."

Rowena looked up at Douglas. "Did he indeed?"

Douglas shrugged. "'Twas nothing."

A man with long gray hair came up to Rowena. "He yanked my rotten tooth right out of my head when the blacksmith couldna get it." He opened his mouth like a cave. "Reached in and got it wi' one tug. Ye can put yer finger in the hole if ye like."

Rowena pressed her lips together. "That is quite all right. I will take your word on it."

Douglas frowned at this nonsense.

A wee boy of five, prompted by a poke from his brother, stumbled forward. "His lordship saved our sister from drownin' when she went fishin' in the loch."

"He nursed my sick granny when she had the grippe."

"He nursed my sick wee goat."

Douglas stole a glance at Rowena, standing motionless beside him. Were those tears of admiration in her eyes? Was the woman moved by this fiddle-faddle?

"He drove my da to the market just to buy us a new churn."

"He birthed my baby brother."

"He carved a new headstone fer Uncle Angus."

Douglas looked at Rowena again. Her eyes were not just glazed. They were crossed. The princess looked as if she were in a trance.

He cleared his throat. "That will be enough—"

They ignored him, surging forward to sing his praises, their voices growing louder and louder as if they were competing for compliments.

"He fixed the well."

"He knitted a blanket fer our ailin' cow."

"He's a saint, that's what he is."

But the crowning moment came when Robbie, the ancient wheelwright, bent on arthritic knee with bonnet in hand to gaze up at Rowena as tears streamed into his beard.

"He's our guardian angel, and that's the truth. Why, the laird is so pure at heart, he's even taken a vow of chastity until he sees every last one of us safe and secure."

"I have?" Douglas said in a horrified voice.

Rowena did not utter a word to him the entire ride back to the castle. No doubt her poor head was pounding with tales of his legendary kindness. A kindness, judging by the look on her face, that indicated she might like to kill him.

Douglas did not blame her. Not only was he a pompous pretender, he had just become a virgin into the bargain.

"The man claims to have taken a vow of chastity!" Rowena shouted with a snort of laughter, falling backward onto her bed. "There goes my hope of begetting any heirs in a hurry!"

Hildegarde rushed forward to close the chamber door. "Calm yourself, Highness. Vows can be broken."

"How?" Rowena demanded.

"Well, there are potions—" Hildegarde's hands flew to her face. "God, what am I saying? If the man wishes to remain chaste, 'tis a sin for us to tempt him."

The evening of the feast had arrived. The castle hummed like a beehive with secret activity. Douglas dressed for the affair with the enthusiasm of a man going to his own execution. 'Twas clear he could not keep Rowena captive much longer. She had been at Dunmoral for over a week. 'Twas also clear that the woman was not overly impressed with his image as the "Virgin Earl." She gave an evil chuckle every time she saw him.

He turned to examine his lean profile in the pier glass. "Well, how do I look?"

"Put on that quilted waistcoat, sir," Willie said from the wardrobe.

Gemma shook her head. "It might make him look fat."

Douglas frowned. His crew had indeed grown slothful in their retirement. They'd put on weight. Even he had begun to feel a wee bit sluggish in the mid-section.

A month ago he'd started to swim faithfully every morning in the bone-numbing waters of the loch. One hundred exhausting laps as if preparing to woo a princess qualified as a marathon event.

He slapped his rock-hard stomach. "A pirate with a paunch, or the Laird of Lard? Not as long as there is breath in my body."

He strapped on his sword. His golden earring winked in the candlelight.

"Ye look lovely, sir," Baldwin said in approval. "I've never seen ye look nicer."

"You look like a pirate," Gemma said, frowning.

Willie came up behind him with a flagon of scented water. "What's wrong with that?"

Gemma gazed at Douglas's reflection. "He's

supposed to look like the laird. Why aren't you wearing the red high-heeled shoes we bought in Nairn?"

"Because I do not wish to wobble about like a woman." He stuck his fingers into the cravat that spilled from his strong brown throat. "Who lit that fire? I'm roasting in all this lace. Willie, touch that perfume stopper to my wrist and die. I'm not smelling like a French lily for anyone. I tire of playing the twiddlepoop."

"If you won't wear the heels, then you must wear the plaid," Gemma said. "Take off your clothes again, Douglas."

"In a pig's eye," he retorted.

"Red heels are the fashion at court, Douglas."

He put on his plumed hat. It overshadowed his sun-burnished face, carving hollows beneath the angular bones. "How does this look?"

"The hat is a dead giveaway," Gemma said in exasperation. "The laird is supposed to wear a bonnet with a feather in it."

"A bonnet?" Douglas laughed at that. Then he took a pair of scrolled pistols from the dressing table and stuck them in the sash over his shoulder. "Is that better?"

Gemma stared at him. "If you're going to challenge the princess to a duel."

"Should he wear the diamond cross he stole from Cartagena?" Willie asked.

Gemma shook her head. "Too crass. He has to wear the plaid."

"No," Douglas said.

Dainty pulled a shriveled gray object from his pocket. "Here's a shark's fin to tie on your bowsprit for good luck."

"I will not. God above."

"Those tight leather trousers make you look like a blackguard, Douglas," Gemma said.

He rubbed his jaw. "Dammit, this dressing up has taken so long I shall have to be shaved again."

"There isn't time." Gemma darted to the door, motioning everyone to follow. "Baldwin, Willie. You're getting dressed next, although talk about hopeless causes. Douglas, I still think you should wear that plaid and brooch."

Douglas sneaked back into his room five minutes later. He changed into a plaid of blue and grayish-green wool, dyed with heather and bramble. He refused to wear high heels. Then he slipped the shark's fin beneath his shirt. He figured he could use the luck.

Highland laird on the outside, pirate beneath.

The deception could not last much longer.

Douglas walked around the table, his hands locked behind his back. "What manner of dish hides on that platter?" he demanded.

Candlelight flickered across Baldwin's grinning face. "That's the peacock for the princess."

"Peacock." Douglas gazed at the covered centerpiece. "I was not aware we had peacocks in

Dunmoral. If this is another one of my sister's half-brained—"

He broke off in alarm as a trumpet blared from the gallery above. The music of bagpipes and fiddles swelled to a deafening pitch. The flames of the pinewood chandelier trembled and swayed.

He plugged his ears. "God's bones. Who is making that infernal noise?"

"The village musicians," Baldwin shouted. "The princess must be comin'. The lads were to start playin' the moment she left her room. 'Tis to honor her."

"Deafen her is more likely," Douglas said as he strode across the hall. "A few minutes of that racket, and we'll all be raving mad."

Rowena had just reached the bottom of the stairs when he found her. A gray silk dress graced her willowy frame. Her glorious hair waved over her shoulders like a goddess of fertility, a dangerous reminder to Douglas that the woman wished to have babies in a hurry. His heart gave a traitorous thump at the thought while his barbaric male body tightened in arousal.

He felt a jolt of guilt-tinged pleasure as their eyes met. She looked at him with a hope and vulnerability that would be utterly destroyed when he was done deceiving her.

She believed herself so strong, this maiden princess who wanted to lead an army to protect her papa. She thought she would succeed where hardened warriors had failed. She thought she could play with a dragon and not singe her delicate fingers.

But Douglas only played to win. She was a mere apprentice at the wicked games he had mastered, invented. Yet his plans for her had changed. He no longer wished for her money or influence. To his horror he wished to win her heart.

"And where is your shepherdess, little lamb?" he asked in an amused undertone.

Rowena gave him a grin. "Praying in the chapel for my protection. She's had a premonition that my very life is in danger."

A cold infusion of fear seemed to settle in Douglas's bones. Hildegarde, he remembered, considered herself something of a seer. "Premonitions should never be ignored."

Rowena shrugged to dismiss such a notion as he took her hand. "I would have been dead at the tender age of three if predictions like Hildegarde's are to be believed."

He closed his fingers over hers, surprised at the power of his protective instincts. "We must guard you more carefully, perhaps."

Rowena slanted him a look at the sober note in his voice. "Do you think I am in danger?"

Douglas hesitated. A boyish smile broke across his deeply burnished face. "'Tis hard to say. There are all manner of mysterious dishes arriving at our table. We may neither of us survive our supper."

Rowena peered around him. "Where is that unearthly noise coming from?"

"The minstrel's gallery." He let out a rueful sigh. "To honor you."

"Oh, dear. We'd best hurry to the table then before they bring down the walls."

He guided her down the corridor and into the hall where candlelight glinted on the silver dishes placed upon the damask-covered table. The music swelled to an ear-splitting crescendo at her entrance. The guests at the table rose, bowing and curtsying, along with his sister Gemma and Dr. MacVittie. Baldwin and Willie stood against the wall in white powdered periwigs and beribboned knee-breeches.

Rowena raised her voice to be heard above the music. "You've gone to far too much trouble, my lord. I shall have none of this 'above the salt' nonsense."

He cupped his ear. "Pardon me?"

"I will have to compliment the cook's efforts," she said in an even louder voice.

He looked blank. "What did you say?"

"The apple tarts look exquisite," she shouted in his face. "T-A-R-T-S."

Douglas drew away from her with a droll smile. The delighted compliments on her lips would probably turn into shrieks of outrage if he told her that this time last year the cook had been serving up an entirely different type of tart.

Rowena bit her lip. "Bring the cook to me, my lord. I'll tell her myself."

"I'm sorry." Douglas spread out his palms. "I can't hear you."

"I WANT TO SEE THE COOK!" Rowena roared across the room.

The music stopped abruptly. A targe dropped from the wall and thudded to the floor. Baldwin pulled off his periwig and wiped his forehead with his sleeve.

Rowena blushed.

Douglas motioned to the table. "Why don't you sample a tart if they tempt you?"

"She can't have a tart yet." Gemma hurried between them, dropping another curtsy. "The oysters are coming."

"Oysters?" Douglas said, frowning.

"The tarts weren't supposed to be served until after the main courses," Gemma explained. "Shandy got confused and brought the wrong dishes out. Frances nearly murdered him." She looked at Rowena. "I hope you'll forgive this outrageous oversight."

"It doesn't matter," Rowena said graciously. "I could eat apple tarts all day."

Douglas led her to the dais. Servants, who a year ago had been chasing a Spanish squadron to the West Indies, paraded in from behind the screens bearing the banquet dishes. Rowena sat down, looking pleased at their efforts.

A roasted lamb wearing a crown of pearls was placed before her. Then came marchpane, and a gilded salmon pie.

Dainty appeared at the dais with a wobbly blancmange shaped like a fairy-tale palace. The turrets collapsed before he reached the table, but that didn't stop him. By the time Hildegarde arrived at her seat, the drawbridge had collapsed in a quivering blob.

Baldwin came forward to pour the wine. Everyone at the table ceased breathing as the man filled Rowena's goblet with a delicate claret.

"I didna spill a drop," he announced when he finished, and the table released its collective breath.

"Very good, Baldwin," Douglas said in an undertone. "Now put your wig on the other way around."

Hildegarde and Dr. MacVittie began to discuss the treatment of bunions and the art of bloodletting. Mrs. MacVittie orchestrated the serving of dishes with covert hand signals.

"The oysters are coming," Dainty announced from the end of the hall. "Make way for the OYSTERS."

The highly touted oysters arrived at the table, artfully arranged on the half-shell. Douglas's jaw tightened as Willie moved from guest to guest to offer the platter of the most peculiar-looking mollusks he had ever seen.

Hildegarde held one of the white ridged shells

between her fingers. "I have never seen such a manner of oyster before."

"They're Highland oysters," Gemma said quickly, avoiding her brother's eyes.

"I have a pearl in my Highland oyster!" Hildegarde exclaimed.

Rowena arched her brow. "I have a pearl ring in mine."

Douglas stared down at his plate in distaste. "Gemma," he whispered between his teeth. "What is this?"

"They're mussels," she whispered back. "Dainty got them fresh from the cove this morning, and I painted them white."

He tried to smile. It came out as a grimace. "Mussels masquerading as oysters. Why did you not use oysters in the first place?"

"Well, Douglas, at first we couldn't find any oysters. Then Dainty found them, but by that time Frances remembered something about eating oysters in a month that has an 'R' in it." Gemma shook her head. "The trouble was, no one in Dunmoral could remember whether 'twas safe to eat oysters in such a month, or whether 'twas deadly."

Douglas sighed. "Dear Lord."

"Frances has been feeding mussels to the men all week to make sure they weren't the deadly sort. No one's died." She smiled. "Yet."

Douglas clamped his hand down on Rowena's wrist as she raised her fork to her mouth. "Don't."

She gave him a beguiling smile. "Oysters are an aphrodisiac, my lord. Haven't you heard?"

"An aphrodisiac? At the Virgin Earl's table?" He snapped his fingers over his shoulder. "Baldwin, take these offensive oysters away."

Rowena reached defiantly for her plate.

Douglas forced her hand down onto the table.

"What are you doing, my lord?" she asked haughtily. "*I* have not taken a vow of chastity."

Chastity. Aphrodisiacs. Douglas felt his blood begin to boil, remembering how long it had been since he'd touched a woman, and how badly he wanted to bed the woman at his side. He might as well have been a genuine virgin for the ridiculous length of time since his last sexual encounter. The scent of her befogged his brain, floral and female. Her easy smile bewitched him, and though he might hope to hold her captive, 'twas he who had been caught.

He glanced at his sister. He desperately needed a distraction. "Is it time to uncover the centerpiece?"

Gemma nodded, and Willie came forward to whisk the cover off the platter. Silence descended. Douglas swallowed a groan. Rowena grabbed her goblet to hide a sudden fit of giggles.

A scrawny moor grouse sat in the center of table, the dyed peacock feathers from Mrs. Mac-Vittie's best court fan protruding from its behind.

Hildegarde half-rose from her chair, her brows

gathered in a puzzled frown. "Goodness," she said. "What is that thing?"

"'Tis a Highland peacock," Baldwin said proudly. "Willie and me bagged the wee bugger all by ourselves. 'Tis so fresh you can still hear it breathin' if ye listen close enough." He clapped Rowena on the back. "Eat up hearty, princess, while 'tis good and hot."

Aidan appeared suddenly in the gallery, staring down at the festivities like an avenging angel. Douglas needed only the man's slight nod to know that something was seriously amiss.

He excused himself while Rowena was nibbling her third tart.

Dainty followed Douglas up the stairs. The three men proceeded down the long portrait-lined gallery in silence until they rounded a torchlit corner.

"What is it?" Douglas demanded.

Aidan lifted an odd-shaped bundle in his left hand.

"Dear Jesus," Dainty exclaimed. "Where did that come from?"

Aidan unwrapped a wolf's head from a blood-stained chemise. Rowena's chemise, Douglas thought, his throat closing in fear. No other woman in the castle wore a garment of such finely wrought lace.

He gazed at the animal's face, fangs frozen in a snarl.

"This was nailed to the inside of her door," Aidan said quietly.

Douglas felt a wave of panic engulf his entire body. "When?"

"During the banquet," Aidan said.

"Someone in the castle then." Dainty stared down the length of the mural passage. "They could be hiding anywhere. Why the hell are we standing about like a trio of trembling virgins?"

Aidan shook his head. "Gunther swears the guards did not see a soul enter or leave the castle. I searched her room. No one was there."

"I want whoever did this caught." Douglas swung around, then stopped, searching the shadows of Aidan's face. "How did *you* happen to be inside her room?"

Aidan looked surprised. "You were all occupied with the banquet. I took it on myself to patrol the halls. I noticed her door was ajar."

"A damn good thing you did," Dainty said gruffly. "The woman would have had the shock of her life seeing that on her door, or worse, coming upon the intruders."

"A damn good thing indeed." Douglas gazed at the wolf's head. "Get rid of that thing, and meet me at the stable. Dainty, stay here with Rowena."

"What will I tell her when she asks where you've run off to?" the giant asked.

Douglas and Aidan were already halfway down the passage. The flares in the wall rings died at their rushed exit, booted feet ringing against stone. Smoke lingered in their wake, and Douglas's troubled voice drifted from the depths of the stairwell.

"Tell her—tell her a rabid wolf was spotted near the castle. Tell her we have gone to hunt it down before it hurts anyone."

"I am not afraid of wolves," Rowena whispered hours later from the window. "But I am afraid I have come all this way for naught. I am afraid that I've fallen in love with an illusion."

The clatter of hooves over the drawbridge broke the silence of the night. Then came the grinding grooves of the portcullis chains. Minutes later she saw Douglas striding from the stables, his broad-shouldered figure dark and dominant, drawing the eye straight to him. Aidan followed at his heels. Dainty ran out of the keep to question them. His left and right arm, his closest friends, striking warriors in their own right.

Her breath caught at the raw energy that emanated from Douglas, unaware he was being watched. He moved with elemental power and ruthless grace. She suspected, by the impatient rhythm of his strides, that he had failed to accomplish whatever goal had dragged him from the banquet.

Hildegarde's urgent voice broke into her sleep. "Highness, we must leave here at once."

Rowena sat up with a start, her heart pounding

at the abrupt awakening. The thick ropes of her braided hair fell across her lap. She stared grumpily at the familiar figure who hovered over her bed. "What has happened?"

"I have an awful feeling in my heart about Frederic."

"Frederic? It has not yet been a fortnight," Rowena said. "Could this not wait until morning to be discussed?"

"I had a dream, a nightmare."

Rowena released a long-suffering sigh into the darkness.

"You were chained to a cross." Hildegarde's chin trembled. "'Twas so real I could see the raindrops on your face and the wind blowing your hair."

"Hildegarde," she said gently, hugging the woman's shoulders. "'Twas but a dream. Frederic is finding warriors and will soon return. I am safe in my bed."

"There was a man at your feet, Highness," the woman continued, her gaze focused inward in remembered horror. "He carried a knife between his teeth."

"A supper knife?" Rowena said, teasing to break the tension.

"'Twas the man called Aidan," Hildegarde said in a hoarse whisper. "The man with secrets in his eyes. The one who looks like my poor Stephan."

"Aidan is the earl's good friend," Rowena said

firmly. "He is unfailingly polite to me, and there is a nobility about him that I admire. Besides, he is not the only one in this castle to keep secrets. Now go back to your room, woman. I was in the midst of a pleasant dream myself."

Hildegarde obeyed with reluctance. "The door was not bolted—"

"Out, Hildegarde. His lordship's guards patrol the castle grounds on the hour."

"There are dark stains beneath your door—"

"Bloodstains again?" Rowena scoffed. "Go to bed, Hildegarde, before you bring everyone to my room with your hysterics. Every princess needs her sleep."

Neacail remained hidden behind the stones that formed the forgotten passageway into the bedchamber. He had heard the conversation between the two women. He had planned to look upon the younger woman while she slept again, but the older one had spoiled his pleasure.

A princess, he thought in disbelief. A princess sleeping in his castle.

He wondered whether she'd liked the gift he had left her, and what he should do with her when he took up his claim.

The muffled shout of a sentry sent him darting back down the dark steps of the passageway. He could not visit her again for a while. There were too many guards prowling about, and one of them might discover his horse waiting by the loch gate. It had been daring of him to nail that wolf's head on her door.

Besides, he had work to do. There were plans to be laid and fires waiting to be set. In fact, Neacail might light his next fire in honor of the princess.

She could watch the flames from her window.

Chapter 17

THE FOLLOWING AFTERNOON ROWENA WORE THE raspberry silk gown of a hundred scandals. By revealing herself she was hoping to shock the earl into revealing his true nature. Hildegarde was scandalized at this bold gesture and refused to speak to her. The woman stalked off in a huff, muttering a warning that Rowena would come to a bad end like her exiled sister.

Rowena drew a small breath for courage. She would have drawn a deeper one but decency did not allow greater movement. Never had she exposed this much décolletage before. The boned bodice forced her breasts above the shimmering fabric. It plunged down her back, lacing against the bare curve of her spine. She wore no chemise beneath, and felt half-naked.

Thunder rumbled outside the castle. The sound

was muted in the upper floor where she paced the length of the Turkey carpet. She had sent word to Douglas asking for a tour of the portrait gallery.

She had not seen him since late last night in the bailey. The impression of suppressed power and elemental masculinity had stayed in her mind.

She shivered from cold and apprehension. What would it take to make him drop his masquerade? How far was she willing to go?

She heard his light tread on the stairs, and her heart quickened. Too late now to run back to her room for her mantle. Too late for modesty. Covertly she tried to pull her hair loose from the pearl-headed bodkins that held it in place. The act only served to make her look more like a wanton. A woman with bare bosoms and disarrayed hair.

Douglas slowed on the top step and stared at her for an interminable moment. Lightning speared the sky behind the window. He wore an embroidered black waistcoat and white Holland shirt with snug nankeen breeches. He looked dignified. She did not.

There was no doubt he noticed the change in her appearance. His gaze moved over her like naked flame before it lifted to her face. She shivered again at the untamed emotion in his eyes. Desire, possession, and then, disapproval.

Nervousness attacked her composure as he came toward her. "Did you hear the thunder? We're going to have—to cover you up," he said sternly. "You will take a chill."

Before Rowena could protest, he had reached for the yellowed lace runner on the alcove table behind them. Deftly he yanked it out from beneath a pewter candlestick.

Her lips thinned as he settled the dusty lace across the cleft of her breasts, his touch hasty and impersonal. "You are too considerate, my lord."

"Think nothing of it," he said. "You wished to view the portrait gallery?"

She wished to kick him in the shin, but she merely nodded, her face hot with humiliation as he motioned her to follow. *He wasn't a pirate,* she fumed inwardly. *He was a paragon of piety and pretension. He was a prude and a—a—*

"—pain in the neck," she muttered.

Douglas halted in midstep. "Your neck pains you?" he asked, clucking his tongue. "Well, I am not surprised, underdressed as you are."

Rowena very deliberately pulled the lace off her cleavage and dropped it at his feet. "I am in excellent health."

His gaze flickered downward for the briefest instant to the cleavage she displayed. His chiseled mouth tightened at the corners. "So I've noticed. However—" He retrieved the runner and settled it back over the swell of her breasts, his long fingers lingering for a dangerous moment. "—I should have to pinch myself purple if you came down with a lung infection."

Rowena's lips flattened. "How kind you are."

"Not at all," he said airily. "Now come, Your

Highness. The dauntless Earls of Dunmoral are awaiting your inspection."

"I was in the black class at the convent," Rowena said unexpectedly as they plunged down an unlit passageway. "I—"

The muffled echo of thunder interrupted her. The air grew damp and pulsed with unrest. Glints of gray-gold light broke through the leaded lozenge-shaped windowpanes. Douglas frowned into the gloom. He was lost again, and he'd never wanted to seduce a woman more than at that moment, to take her against the wall with thunder rumbling around them, to couple with her in a darkened corner. He ached with the primal need to mate. He ached to give her exactly what she was asking for. Yet it would not be enough. The bonds he yearned to forge were not only of the flesh. He had discovered that there was trust and tenderness in his heart that needed to be expressed.

"The black class?" he said "That sounds perfectly ominous."

"I supervised theatrical performances," Rowena said.

"Did you?" *I supervised pirate raids.*

He led her toward a heavy door. He could hear her breathing lightly to meet his pace. The sound aroused him. He could too easily imagine her breathless in the darkness of his bed, her hair tangled over their naked bodies, his shaft impaling her.

He found the sight of her creamy breasts and back unbearably arousing. He knew serious trouble when he saw it.

'Twas dangerous for a friendly ship to sail up to a frigate with her gun ports exposed. One good giggle in that gown, and she would expose herself too. His masquerade would shatter. Could she ever love a man like him? Could she forgive his past, his attempts to mislead her?

"We talked about forbidden things in the convent," she said.

He reached for the door's iron ring. "You naughty girl."

"The Dragon of Darien was a favorite subject," she said dangerously.

Douglas stared at the unopened door, his heart stopping before it began to pound in irregular strokes.

So she knew. Or definitely suspected. If she knew for certain, they wouldn't be standing alone together in a tunnel of black temptation, sexual attraction and an impending storm charging the air.

Would they?

An unpleasant possibility occurred to him. Women were fascinated by danger. They were often fascinated by the wrong man. Could the princess be attracted to the infamy he wanted to forget? Could he have been ensnared in a trap of his own making?

He could not tolerate the thought, even though he had lived for such risky liaisons in the past. He needed her to believe in him for who he was. He needed her to believe the lie he had created. It made him all the more determined to prove he'd chosen the high road of moral reform . . . a pirate resisting the charms of a princess. He sighed heavily, wondering if he were strong enough to withstand such temptation.

"Do you know of the Dragon?" Rowena asked.

"I have heard of him," Douglas said in a cautious voice.

"I memorized the tales of his exploits."

His shoulder muscles tensed. "Some people would consider that a deplorable waste of time."

"I thought he was wildly exciting."

"Wildly exciting." He turned around to face her, staring squarely into her eyes. "Do you have any idea what sort of temperament it takes to enable a man to live like that?"

"I know he has done things he probably regrets. I know he abducted the daughter of a Spanish don and held her for ransom on his pirate ship," Rowena said.

Did you know he blew up a shipload of innocent people?

"The rogue deserves to be horsewhipped," he said gravely.

"Some have said he should be hanged," she said.

Douglas mentally crossed himself. "Well, I wouldn't go that far. After all, he did have a letter of marque from His Majesty."

"No, he didn't," Rowena said.

"Yes, he did."

"No," she said slowly. "I've read everything ever written on the Dragon, and the scoundrel sailed under his own whim."

Douglas felt like putting his hands around her white shoulders and giving her a good shake. "I believe you are wrong."

She placed her hands on her hips. "I am an expert on the man, sir."

"And I am—"

He gazed down into her composed face. Calm on the surface, dangerous currents beneath. He wondered who was guilty of the greater deception, after all. He wondered, when all was said and done, who would emerge as conqueror. Purity had a power all its own. Even a sinner such as himself was not immune. "I am undoubtedly mistaken." His eyes glittered with cold irony. "Let us view the portrait gallery. I'll warrant there's not a pirate in the pack."

Rowena examined the painting of a florid-faced man in an ermine tunic. "Who is that?"

"That—that appears to be my great-uncle,"

Douglas said, deliberately standing away from the lady.

She rubbed the tarnished plate beneath the frame, chuckling to herself. "He's related to you?"

"Indeed, he is."

"The plate says Henry the Eighth. I did not realize you claimed royal ancestry."

"We try to keep it a secret," Douglas said, steering her to a portrait of a plain-looking woman in a ruffled collar and farthingale. "All those hangers-on, you know. Ah—now here is the queen."

"Queen Mary or Elizabeth?" Rowena said.

Douglas looked at the portrait. He didn't have a clue.

"Mary-Elizabeth," he said.

"Mary-Elizabeth?" Rowena said with a puzzled frown.

"She's a little known figure in Scottish history. In fact, she was beheaded days after this portrait was painted. 'Tis a most tragic story."

"Is she related to you too?" Rowena asked.

"I don't think so," Douglas said. "But then again no one really knows what she did during the Lost Years."

She brushed around him, the corners of her lips twitching in a smile. She held her body with an unguarded sensuality that almost brought Douglas to his knees. She lifted her face to another portrait, but he was more interested in staring at the curve of her back and buttocks. That dress of hers was indecent. He loved it.

"He does not look at all like you," she stated.

"Who doesn't?"

"Your father." Or the man they both knew bore no relation to him at all.

"How do you—" He lifted his gaze from her backside to the portrait of the seventh Earl of Dunmoral. Short. Fat. Caterpillar eyebrows drawn into a scowl. "Good God," he said, leaning back against the wall. "I should hope not. I take after my mother's side."

"Which would explain why you do not look much like Matthew either," Rowena said, turning to study him. "Except around the eyes. I do see a resemblance there."

His gaze was merciless. "And have you spent many hours staring into my brother's eyes?" he asked coldly.

Color crept into her cheeks. "Actually, I haven't."

"I suppose that was the purpose of the tryst, to stare into each other's eyes."

"The tryst?" Rowena looked offended. "The word has a romantic connotation."

Douglas searched her face. "You did not come here to seek a clandestine romance?" he said in disbelief.

Her fingers tangled in the lace at her throat. "Not with Matthew," she said irritably.

"You are not in love with my brother?" he demanded.

Rowena giggled. "You have such a silly look on your face, my lord."

She turned back to the portrait. And Douglas did not move, he could not move, wondering what the confounded woman was trying to tell him.

I outrank Matthew, he realized suddenly. *Me, the bastard, rogue, and raider, and now I am going to steal his woman because he's stuck in Sweden with a broken leg.* He grinned to himself. All in all, it was not looking like such a bad situation.

He frowned as he returned in thought to his previous realization. Rowena was not attracted to who he was but to what she thought he had been. The false romance of piracy had turned many a fair head.

The Dragon was dead. Douglas didn't think he could resurrect the wretched beast if he tried. He had become more like the man he masqueraded than his legend. Quite possibly he had become too high-principled for a princess whose mind was set on raising royal hell.

He was spared from further displaying his ignorance of Dunmoral's family history by Gemma's timely arrival. The girl hurried toward them, red splotches of color on her face. She forgot to curtsy, intent on delivering her message.

"There you are, Douglas, Your Highness.

There's been a little trouble in the village. You might want to ride down there right away."

"What manner of trouble?" Rowena asked in concern. "The wolves again?"

Gemma glanced up at Douglas. "The wind has brought a few of the old cots down. There . . . there was a fire. We should have been better prepared for the winter."

"Are the men ready to ride?" Douglas said grimly, knowing full well that "a little trouble" meant the reivers had struck again.

"Aidan has already gone with Shandy and Phelps," Gemma said quietly.

"Perhaps I could be of help," Rowena said. "I know how to—"

"No." The vehemence in Douglas's voice clearly startled her, but he didn't care. "You will stay here with my sister," he said sternly. "The storm is breaking, and I will not have the worry of you both on my mind."

Rowena scowled. "As you wish."

He strode away without another word. A blue streak of lightning behind the window threw his harsh countenance into shadow before he disappeared.

He took the wooden stairs to the hall at a run, hearing Dainty's gruff voice growling out orders. The former galley slave had gathered the men together, fully armed and eagerly anticipating a fierce battle.

He strapped on his bandoleer over the padded velvet waistcoat, cursing the fashionable breeches and ruffled shirt that would hamper him in the rain. Someone shoved a pair of pistols at him across the table. Gemma threw his brogues down from the gallery. Baldwin brought him his good-luck Spanish broadsword. He gripped the dragon-embossed hilt and felt blood surging through his veins, empowering him.

"I thought I ordered Martin and Roy to guard the village," Douglas said. "They are capable men."

Dainty hadn't taken the time to shave. He wore a black leather jerkin over his bare chest. With his bald head and giant's build, he looked every inch as menacing as the first time he had bullwhipped Douglas senseless in the galley hold.

"They were on guard, sir. But the raiders set fire to a hut where a grandmother watched over five youngsters. The men had a choice of saving lives or taking them."

Douglas cursed. "How long ago did they attack?"

"They hit only an hour ago, in broad daylight," Dainty said. "The bastards have no fear of anything."

Douglas pulled on a pair of black leather gloves. "Then let us teach them what the fear of hell feels like."

Chapter 18

THE RAIDERS HAD RIDDEN ROUGHSHOD OVER THE humble preparations for the harvest festival. Shattered crockery and broken trenches lay strewn over the turf. A long trestle table had been cleaved in two by a battle ax. Geese scavenged the torn bags of precious oats and barley. A goat butted its head to be free of its byre, frightened by the confusion.

The heather-thatched roof of one stone hut had been set afire but hastily extinguished. Stinging rain fell on the smoke. No one had been hurt, but quiet terror bruised the faces of the Highlanders huddled at the base of the hill, waiting for their laird.

He walked through the wreckage in grim silence, startled when a child ran up to grasp his large hand for comfort.

His hand.

A half-crippled elderly man, sifting through the debris for his cane, straightened painfully to give him a nod. "Thank God, ye're here."

And like a chorus the words carried across the ravished glen. "He's here. The laird is here. Did I not tell ye he would come?" And he could feel their relief, their hope, their anxiety abating just because he stood in their midst.

A freebooter who had never done an admirable thing in his life. A stormy man who had left carnage in his wake without a backward glance.

And they were his reward, these people and their troubles, granted on the whim of the king known as the Merry Monarch.

He hefted the girl into his powerful arms. "Are you frightened, lassie?"

"Aye, I was." She buried her face in his long black hair. Her chin rested on the strong column of his throat. "But not now."

Henry broke from the huddle to walk with him. "They were full of wickedness, my lord. I canna believe no one is dead."

Douglas gently set the child to the ground. The acrid tang of dying smoke stung his eyes as he glanced around. "What stopped them?"

"Old Bruce the Blind Seer stumbled up to the top of the hill in his nightshirt and pointed his scrawny finger straight at Neacail. The old man looked like a banshee with the wind blowing his gray hair. Gave Neacail the Evil Eye."

Douglas stared through the wisps of smoke and rain, imagining the scene. "I will send more men to stand guard. If there is any sign of trouble, have Gunther move the entire village into the castle."

"They'll be back." Henry scrubbed his hand over his soot-blackened cheek. "They promised they'll be back."

Dainty plucked a wreath of dried broom and gorse from the wreckage. The villagers watched him in awe, a monster of a man in an armless jerkin who did not seem to feel the icy rain. They did not fear him, the laird trusted him, and that was enough.

"We'll need better horses to ride them down, sir," Dainty said as he settled the wreath on the little girl's head. "Swift retaliation is the only way to stop this sort of intimidation."

Aidan stepped out from behind an overturned cart, a sack of shriveled apples in his arm. "The three of us will go alone," he said.

Douglas looked around at the devastation. "No. Aidan, you stay here to patrol the glen. Dainty, go back to the castle and watch the women. I'll find Neacail."

They didn't argue. They'd watched Douglas pull off too many impossible raids and rescues to doubt either his instinct or ability.

He wanted to bring down his nemesis by himself. If he found satisfaction or even death in this, then so be it.

Douglas would do as he pleased anyway, and they would not interfere with what another man needed to do.

Douglas's ride across the storm-swept moor aroused an unexpected reaction. In a strange way it felt like he was back on the Main, chasing some coveted treasure with a single-minded resolve that bordered on obsession.

Except that instead of muggy swamp, he struggled through bracken underbrush and peat bog that slowed his mount's progress. At least an alligator or Spanish soldier in a steel helmet wouldn't appear out of the shadows to attack him. A Scottish outlaw with a deadly grudge and claymore would. The huge fang-toothed rocks that protruded from the hills could shelter a deadly enemy.

The rain fell now in a gossamer film that clung to his lashes and chilled his skin. Sunlight could blind a man. Mist could deceive him.

Neacail might hold the advantage of knowing the land, but Douglas learned fast, memorizing every boulder and fox den that he passed. He would study the moods of the moors and mist as he had the wind and sea.

A tawny owl hooted from the womb of a pine wood that bordered the moor.

Douglas stiffened and slid from his horse. He

lowered his hand to his sword. Unmoving, he listened. Pewter shadows of gloaming gave way to evening.

The woods were alive with the stirring of nocturnal predators. A wildcat stalking a blue hare. A vole shuffled through a tangle of conifers and fallen needles. Water rushed over the smooth brown stones of a burn. He studied the rhythm.

A footfall. So stealthy, so controlled he might have imagined it. A human predator lying in wait. He exhaled in measured breaths.

He unsheathed his sword. The beveled blade shone like silver against the mist. He melted through the trees, his spine rigid with anticipation. Then he was backing toward the burn, his brogues brushing wet clumps of bog myrtle.

"I've been watching you," the man before him said.

Dying wisps of light outlined the male figure in a filthy tartan who stood alone on the footbridge. Neacail of Glengalda, his shaggy ashen hair framing a face that some women would find intriguing. Broken nose. Cruel mouth. Nordic features. He was a head shorter than Douglas but bulkier with the mean strength that comes from surviving on the land. His right arm was bandaged with what looked like a woman's stocking.

Douglas felt a surge of gratitude for the bone-numbing mornings of swimming in the loch and the hair-raising races he and Dainty had taken across the moor on horseback. He hadn't lost his killing edge.

His blood quickened with battle instincts.

He glanced around, assessing the field. "No huts afire, Neacail?"

Neacail hurled a stream of spittle at his feet. "The village is mine. No Sassenach king has a right to deny a blood claim."

Douglas stepped into the warped footbridge. The ropes sagged beneath his weight. "Why would a man destroy what he fights to gain?"

"I'll kill them one by one if I like," Neacail said with a sneer. "I'll saw off their heads and serve them to my hounds on a silver platter if it pleases me."

"It doesn't please me," Douglas said. "Do you know who I am?"

"The jackadandy lord who stole my birthright." The man wiped his mouth on his forearm. "Do you think yer titles will help ye now?"

"The jackadandy lord." Douglas raised his sword, his smile chilling. "To the death then."

Neacail sprang into motion like a statue awakening from a spell. He swung a battle ax over his head, and a sword in his left hand. Sweat carved runnels in the creases of his face. His brown eyes narrowed into slits, taunting, like a maddened boar.

Douglas raised his sword arm; strange thoughts ran through his mind. Was his own face a merciless mask of inhumanity? Had he looked like that to his enemies? A man without a soul. Steal, plunder, roar in victory. If he killed him, did he kill that kindred hatred in himself or resurrect it? Dear God, did he *enjoy* hurting others?

Why should Rowena feel safe with such a man?

His body met Neacail's challenge, detached from the moral conflicts of his mind. Reflex took over. Conscience fled. He slashed upward with his broadsword and sent the other man's battle ax flying over the footbridge.

Before Neacail could react, Douglas smashed the flat of his blade against the other man's arm. Neacail groaned. Aidan had taught Douglas how to fence with finesse. Dainty had taught him how to break a Barbary horse. Growing up in poverty had taught him how to fight dirty.

They fell together, unbalanced, off the foot-bridge into the burn. The laced brogues Douglas wore enabled him to gain his footing on the grassy stones. They clashed. Separated.

Neacail charged him like a centaur. Douglas kicked him in the groin. Then a dirk flashed in the man's hand, and Douglas wasn't fighting for ideals or salvation, or even to avenge an attack on his people. He fought for his life.

He danced back, slick black hair dripping down his back; he reached for the short knife in his belt. And froze as a familiar figure bolted across the bridge above.

"Jesus, no," he said in a breath as Rowena reached the bank of the burn, her face coming into focus. She carried a basket of food and wore a black silk mantle. She flaunted perfumed gloves and pearls as if she were sneaking out on a midnight picnic instead of witnessing a lethal fight. Fear for her near immobilized him.

"Go," he said between his teeth. "Go—_go!_ Get the hell out of here!"

She gathered up her skirts, confused by his tone of voice. Then her face registered shock, as if she'd only just realized what she had interrupted.

"Douglas—" She gestured behind him, her eyes wide with horror. "Douglas—_watch out!_"

He pivoted a split second before Neacail could stab him in the throat. The dirk sliced down his shoulder. The man had intended to sever his jugular vein. Instead, he tore a jagged trail into the thick biceps of Douglas's right arm.

Douglas ignored the shock of burning pain. He was staring in disbelief at the pistol that had suddenly appeared in Rowena's hands.

"Give it to me, Rowena. _Now._"

She wavered, starting to obey. Then, panicked, she aimed the pistol at Neacail as he scrambled up the bank toward her.

She stood in his path, a sentinel of defiance. Douglas saw Neacail stare at her for a second in hesitation before shoving her aside. A princess in pearls was probably the last thing a Highland outlaw expected to encounter. She fell back into the tangled cattails, the pistol sliding into the water.

Douglas let out an unholy roar that was borne more of frustration than pain. His left hand clamped to his shoulder, he bolted up the bank and ran after Neacail before the loss of blood made him too lightheaded to continue.

Rowena's horse had already climbed halfway up the hill. Neacail paused to make an obscene gesture before he vaulted onto the saddle and galloped away.

"He's gone, my lord." Rowena slid down the brae into the burn, dipping her mantle into the water. "You need help."

He wheeled, his mouth a flat line of fury and pain. "Woman," he shouted at her. "Are you daft? You could have been kidnapped or killed!"

"I wasn't," she said in a crisp undertone, bracing him as he swayed.

Delirium swam in his head. The edges of his vision blurred. "What goddamned mule-headed notion brought you here against my orders?"

She stared at him, twisting the damp mantle in her hands. Irritably he wondered if his abrupt transformation from bumbling courtier to swearing warrior had unbalanced her more then watching him bleed to death.

Apparently he was wrong.

Rowena calmly began to wrap the mantle around his arm, tying the silk fringe beneath the ridge of bloodied muscles. White-lipped, she countered, "You told me you were rebuilding the huts. How was I to know you lied?"

"How in the name of God did you get past Dainty's guard?" he roared.

Rowena anchored her arms around his waist. "I will not answer while you address me in that hideous manner."

He laughed between his teeth. "Forgive me, Highness—or is it hoyden? I'm going to kill Dainty for this."

"You're in no condition to kill anyone," she retorted.

"Thank you for the reminder. Let go of me, woman. I can walk myself, even if I'm not capable of fighting like a man."

"Kindly do not fight *me,* my lord. I am trying to take you to safety."

Another laugh, this one weaker. His breath grew labored. "What do you think it means when a pirate must be rescued by a princess?"

"A fairy tale in reverse, I suppose." She looked around her, studying the woods. "Honesty would have made this completely unnecessary."

"Do you want honesty? I'll give you honesty. I lust for you, Rowena. I lust for you even now that my life's blood is draining from my body. You are beautiful."

She drew away only to throw both arms around his waist as he began to buckle at the knees. "Stop this talking. Conserve your strength."

"You asked for honesty. Dear God, my arm hurts. You are beautiful and I want you. Does that please you, lady?"

He stumbled. She swallowed a cry. His blood dripped down into her braid. He was heavy, and desperately wounded. Fear darkened her face.

"A fine time to extol my beauty," she said with a grimace as she shifted their combined weight to her other foot.

"I would have killed him this time if you hadn't popped up on the bridge like a blasted jack-in-the-box." His voice was faint. Then, almost conversationally, he added. "He had no idea who I really am. Not that it mattered. I fought like a blessed fairy princess myself."

"Not from what I saw," Rowena murmured.

He scowled. "I might have drawn a daisy from my sheath and attacked him with it. I have become my own creation."

"Please, my lord."

He sagged against her, and she folded under his weight, forcing him upright again. "I am the Daisy of Darien." He closed his eyes, chuckling darkly. "Have you heard of me?"

She swallowed a cry as an owl swooped down from an overhanging branch. The truth at last. "Everyone has heard of you . . . Dragon."

"I am not afraid of mice, Rowena. I would disabuse you of that humiliating notion before I die."

She faltered. Her fine quilted petticoats dragged about her ankles, stained with red loam, sodden and laced with pine needles. "You are not going to die."

"But you are beautiful," he said before he collapsed against her. "Beautiful and covered in blood."

He was delirious with pain, she realized, and therefore she would have to overlook his shouting and ranting. Yet even in his weakness, it took every ounce of strength she possessed to subdue him.

His blood soaked through her makeshift bandage into her bodice as she half dragged him into the woods. She felt its warm stickiness against her breasts.

"Woman," he groaned into her hair, trying to reject her support but unable to walk without it. "I could throttle you for this willfulness. How did you get past the castle guards on one of my own damn horses?"

Rowena said nothing. She concentrated on getting them to shelter in case the man who'd injured him returned to finish the job. This was not the time to inform him that, as her father could attest, the castle had not been built that could imprison her.

She led him to a stand of hazel trees, sweeping out a clearing for him to rest upon. She drew a hasty screen of branches and old bracken around his shivering frame. He struggled like a spoiled child, first pushing her onto her rump, then dragging her down by her braid onto his chest.

She fell heavily, tears of frustration filling her eyes. A thousand pinpricks of awareness tingled where their bodies touched. Wounded and stripped of pretense, he was nonetheless the most dangerous man she'd ever met.

Worse, she realized that although he had misled her and she could not be certain of his true feelings, she was attracted to him on a helplessly visceral level. The battered warrior who tugged her braid like a boy was both vulnerable . . . and alarmingly virile.

She still hadn't recovered from the shock of coming upon him fighting like a warlord in the woods. She shuddered as she remembered the sight of his powerful body in battle. She had felt the raw energy exploding from him like a lightning bolt.

"I would kiss you," he muttered. Or was it kill you? He was talking to himself. The broken phrases, spoken in Spanish with a soft Scottish burr, became unintelligible. He was sinking deeper, and she felt so helpless—

Alarm jolted through her—she had seen her brothers with deeper wounds from their mock battles, and they had not behaved like this. Only once, when Erich had tried to spear a boar, stabbing himself in the process with the tip that had been—

"Poisoned." She whispered the word in horror, and heard a sudden deadly silence.

Yet when she looked down, his black eyes bored into hers with chilling alertness. He knows, she thought.

"Could his knife have been poisoned, my lord?"

"Yes." He sounded calm, almost relieved, as if he too had wondered what weirdness had taken hold of him.

"I shall need help," she said. "You must be bled."

"No. *No!*" His voice rose to a raw shout, and Rowena, panicking that his adversaries would find them, laid her hand over his mouth.

"Don't go." He brought his hand up to wrench hers away, his grip still amazingly strong. "Wait. Dainty will come."

"There isn't time to wait." She rocked back on her heels and reached for the black velvet bag around her waist. A phial fell into the dirt, followed by a handful of peculiar-shaped stones.

Douglas watched her, his eyes narrowed into glassy slits. His breath came in shallow gasps. "What . . . what are those?"

She uncorked the phial, her fingers cold and clumsy. "Powdered unicorn's horn and bezoar stones. Hildegarde insisted I carry them as an antidote to poison."

"Unicorn's horn." A smile crossed his face, distorted by a spasm of pain. "Only a princess would carry such a magic treasure."

He lost consciousness a few moments after she had brought the ancient antidote to his lips; she had never had cause to test it before. "Dragon or Daisy," she said, "you are mine, and I will fight to keep you."

The muffled clamor of hoofbeats rose from the hills. Heart in her throat, she clasped his dirk in her hands and settled into a crouch, waiting, prepared to defend her wounded warrior to the death.

Aidan's first impression was of blood. In the woman's hair, on her gown. She crouched like a forest animal over Douglas with his knife clenched in a death grip.

His gaze flickered grimly to Douglas, noting the rise and fall of his chest. He held out his hand to Rowena. "Come with me. 'Tis all right now. I will take care of this."

Chapter 19

WAS HE IN A CAVE?

Chills ran over his body. The air smelled thick and musty, unpleasant to breathe. He could not escape from the strange images that flitted through the dim mist of his mind. He realized he was dreaming.

He could see Aidan on horseback, his arm locked around Rowena's waist, her head resting on his shoulder. They made a striking match, the austere rider in black and the princess with the flowing chestnut hair.

Not Aidan, his mind shouted. Don't ride away with Aidan, Rowena.

His hands tightened into fists, yet he could not lift his arms. By the saints, he had been bound, and he had to rescue Rowena from . . .

The dream changed unexpectedly. He saw a

strange man riding to the castle, a red-haired man in gold-embroidered clothes. The man took Rowena in his arms and kissed her on the steps of the keep.

By God, Douglas would not stand for this. He would kill both Aidan and this stranger who kissed his woman on his very castle steps. He reached for his sword.

"He is fighting in his sleep," a voice said from far away.

"He will reopen his wound," another said.

He groaned, straining to be free.

Rowena came to him in the dream. The female scent of her teased his senses, aroused him like a stag in rut. He kissed her until neither of them could breathe. He suckled her soft breasts until she whimpered for something more, begging him to take her, needing him as he needed her. His body pulsated with a desire so powerful he shook from limb to limb.

He dragged his mouth down her belly, lured to her woman's musk, the cleft between her thighs. He would die if he could not taste her.

His large hands gripped her hips. He burned to be inside her, ached to thrust, to spill his seed, to bond with her. Body and soul. He would dominate her once and for all. He would ride her until they could not move.

Yet fulfillment eluded him as the erotic vision dissolved like a reflection in a loch, and suddenly a claw bit into his shoulder. The pain was unbearable, a dagger thrust to the bone.

His bellow of fury resounded across the room. It brought Dr. MacVittie running out of the adjoining closet with a fresh poultice in his hands. It brought Gemma bolt upright from the trundle where she lay dozing, a book on her lap.

Douglas dropped back onto the bed, sweating, disoriented, swallowing a groan. He was beginning to remember what had befallen him.

He pushed the coverlet to the floor with a growl of impatience. "What happened to the princess? How did I get here? Summon Dainty—we have work to finish in the glen."

The doctor banged his copper bowl down on the nightstand. "Hold yourself still, my lord. I'll not be sewing you up again after you nearly broke my jaw. The princess is resting. Neacail got away."

Douglas barely glanced at his bandaged shoulder. It hurt; he'd known worse. He scowled ferociously at the older man. "You speak to me with disrespect. Need I remind you that I am your laird?"

The doctor looked him in the eye. "You had enough poison in your system to kill a horse. I've not slept in four days, watching over you. If I've forgotten my manners, I would hope to be excused."

Douglas grunted, then sat up straight again,

releasing a string of curses. "Four days? *Four days?*"

"Please lie back, my lord. I have made you a fresh poultice."

Douglas stared at the nightstand in suspicion. "Brewed in a chamberpot?" he said insultingly.

"'Tis a powerful remedy I have used on His Majesty: pulverized snails, garlic, onions, and roasted earthworms wrapped in a raw chicken skin." The doctor motioned to Gemma. "Help me hold him down. He must be poulticed daily until the moon enters Scorpio, or the humors will settle in his liver."

Douglas tolerated about two seconds of this before he knocked them away with his good arm. At the doctor's urging, Gemma ran from the room to fetch Dainty to help. Surly as a bear, Douglas lurched off the bed. Smelly lumps of poultice dripped down the contours of his massive brown chest as he pulled on a shirt, then a pair of black leather breeches and boots.

A reflection in the mirror caught his eye as he began to lace the thongs on his shirt. He turned to see Rowena enter the room.

They examined each other in silence. Heat flushed over Douglas as he remembered the sensual dream, the taste of her, the delight of exploring her soft body.

Yet there was a wariness around her eyes that he had not noticed before. Appalled, he wondered if in his delirium, he had tried to make his dream come true. Had he forced himself on her in the woods? Overpowered her? He did not remember much except that she had spoiled his chance of bringing down Neacail of Glengalda.

She came toward him. "I am relieved to see that you are on your feet."

A frown settled on his face. She did not seem to be a woman degraded. Yet his own self-disgust was unbearable—to have her come upon him fighting his adversary and then, indignity of all male indignities, to lose the fight because the sight of her had shattered his concentration.

The doctor coughed into his hand. "The poultice, my lord—"

"Damn the poultice," Douglas said.

"But—" The physician sighed in resignation, then packed up his bag and left the room.

Neither Douglas nor the princess seemed to notice.

Belatedly Rowena crossed her bare arms over her chest. "I rushed from my room when I heard you throwing your tantrum. I hadn't even finished dressing or brushing my hair."

"I do not throw tantrums. I threw a poultice."

Rowena glanced down distractedly at the mess on the floor. "I wondered where that hideous smell was coming from. I thought 'twas you."

Douglas might have taken offense at this, but he suddenly realized she was indeed half-dressed. He studied her with healthy male interest. A man would have to be half-dead not to appreciate the delicious swell of her breasts above her square linen smock. And those pretty feminine petticoats, sheer silk that billowed out from her rounded hips. His body reacted with a total disregard for its battered state. She was, he realized, only a few steps from his bed.

"I forgot my bodice and overskirt," she said in embarrassment.

His face unreadable, Douglas reached behind him and handed her another of his shirts of white Holland. She put it on, chewing her lower lip. The shirt came to her knees.

"Thank you," she said as she fumbled with the buttons. "Now we must get you back into bed—"

"You look well in my shirt, Rowena."

She looked quickly up at his face. "Perhaps we should not engage in conversation. The doctor said you would not be yourself for some time."

"I have not been myself ever since you came here," he said, surprising himself with this admission.

Rowena gave him a level look. "I am well aware of that." She threw up her hands. "It took a mortal injury for the man to come clean. Well, better late than never."

Douglas stared at her. Almighty God. So the truth *had* come out that night, or during his delirium. It did not really matter when. The deception had reached a disastrous end.

"You know about—everything?" he asked, scowling from beneath his brows.

Her voice was cool. "Do you mean that you were—what is the pirate term—flying false colors? That you are indeed the Dragon of Darien?"

"You know," he said sadly.

"You lied to me, my lord."

"I did," he said in a heavy voice.

"Why?"

"I did not think you would entrust yourself to a pirate," he said.

"Better a pirate than a man who talks to flowers." She sighed, making a small gesture of resignation with her hands. "Get back into bed, my lord. You have lost a great deal of blood. Talking will only tire you."

He frowned. This was intolerable. Now she thought him not only a liar, but a prick-me-dainty as well, too weak to hold a conversation.

"I am going out to finish what you interrupted," he said resolvedly.

"But you can't."

"I am not a daisy," he said as he stalked past her, wondering where on earth the preposterous thought had come from.

Rowena planted herself in his path. "You will have to trample me down before I let you pass."

He sniggered. Then he walked her backward into the wall, using the sheer brute strength of his body. "Is that so?"

"The doctor says I saved your life, you pig-headed pirate," she said.

"Saved my life?" Douglas allowed himself to

lean against her for several seconds. He would die before admitting he felt dizzy. Their bodies fit together so well that he shuddered. "If it hadn't been for you, I never would have let that man cut me."

Rowena was indignant. "Are you blaming me now because I saved your life?" She began to pull off his shirt, buttons flying in his face.

He grinned uneasily. He wondered if she were going to seduce him. She was choosing a hell of a time if she was. "What are you doing?"

"Making it easier on you. How many strokes will it be?"

He stared at her, horrified and hopeful. The room was beginning to spin. If he could make it to the bed, he might not faint. "What manner of strokes are you talking about?"

"The public whipping," she said.

Douglas put his hand to his head. One of them was definitely going daft. "What whipping?"

"The whipping you think I deserve for saving your life, or letting Neacail get away." Rowena tore the shirt open. "The Dragon never misses an act of discipline."

"I never said I was going to whip you," Douglas shouted. "The very thought sickens me." Taking off the rest of her clothes, however, did not seem like a bad idea. "What kind of man would whip a woman?"

Gemma appeared in the doorway, her face white with alarm. "Why are you shouting at the princess about whipping? Everyone in the castle can hear you. Douglas, get back to bed. You're delirious again. You've never whipped a woman."

Rowena looked at him in concern. "He doesn't look well, does he? I suppose I should take into account that the poison might have affected his mind."

"There is not a blessed thing wrong with my mind," Douglas yelled.

Suddenly Dainty appeared in the doorway, disgust on his bullish face. "There'll be no whipping of women as long as I'm alive. I've sinned aplenty with you over the years, sir, but I draw the line at that."

Gemma shook her head. "Matthew would never threaten to whip a woman."

That was it for Douglas. His deception had failed. He smelled like a chamberpot. Rowena believed him capable of hurting her.

He gave a low-throated growl and barreled through the doorway. He had naught left to lose.

Rowena ran past him, barefooted, his shirt trailing over her petticoats, all the way down the stairwell. She followed him as he strode into the hall and shouted for his men. Douglas ignored her. He was staring in astonished fury at the stranger ensconced on the dais.

A pale red-haired nobleman in gold-embroidered velvet stared back at him. The bold usurper slumped in the gigantic carved chair of the castle laird.

This stranger regarded Douglas with curiosity over the goblet of burgundy he'd just raised to his long pinched nose. He took two disdainful sniffs, then lowered the goblet. He looked scandalized at the sight of Rowena rushing into the hall.

"Rowena, are you wearing a man's shirt?" the young intruder demanded.

Douglas wondered if he should pick the scrawny twit up by the ears and hurl him out of the hall. After all, he spoke with a displeasing familiarity to her, and he was sitting in Douglas's chair.

Douglas glanced over his shoulder at Rowena, who was struggling to put on Gemma's cloak. "Who is this twit?" he asked tightly.

"He is my cousin Jerome," Rowena said. "Jerome, this is the Earl of Dunmoral, your host."

"You jest, Rowena," Jerome said with a delicate shudder. "I thought he was the village huntsman."

The twit rose from the chair, examining Douglas in fearful amusement. Douglas suddenly realized how he must look. His long black hair was crudely tied in a leather thong. His face was unshaven, the cheekbones prominent from four days of fasting.

The sword and pistols protruding from the belt of the breeches he had pulled on did not give him a friendly appearance. He probably resembled one of the castle's original inhabitants, a medieval warrior who would slaughter his guests if the fancy struck him.

"Your cousin?" Douglas felt a moment's uncertainty about killing the clodpate. 'Twas probably not a good idea to kill a future in-law.

Jerome gave Douglas a nervous smile. "We have hoped for your recovery, my lord. Rowena has refused to come home until she was assured you would survive. With matters taking such a drastic turn in Hartzburg, I have been quite frantic to pry her away from your . . . hospitality."

Now Douglas had a genuine reason to kill him: the twit not only sat in his chair and sniffed Douglas's wine, but he meant to take Rowena back to that dangerous land. He turned stiffly to look at her.

"Are you leaving me?" he demanded.

"Not yet."

"Not ever," he said emphatically.

He realized then how exhausted she too appeared, with purple shadows beneath her downcast eyes. He wondered if she had lost sleep by worrying over him, and the thought was strangely pleasing.

"Jerome's father has just been taken hostage." Her shoulders sagged with the burden that Douglas would gladly bear. "The rebels have almost broken past Papa's guard."

"Prince Randolph cannot hold out much longer," Jerome said. "That is why Rowena must hurry home to reconsider their demands."

Douglas poured himself a goblet of wine. "You would negotiate with kidnappers?" he said in disbelief.

Contempt flickered across Jerome's colorless face. "You do not understand the politics of a principality, my lord."

"I may not understand the principles of a principality," Douglas said without thinking. "But I do understand a kidnapping."

Jerome looked up at him in alarm. "From personal experience?"

"Highland history is rife with episodes of treachery and abduction," Douglas answered evasively. He narrowed his eyes as Jerome nervously took a gulp of wine. "Surely you've heard of the unwelcome guest who sat at a Scotsman's table only to have his own head served on the supper platter that same night?"

Jerome's breath rushed out in a startled cough. Douglas gave him a forceful thump on the back, leaning down to whisper in his ear, "I would not drink too much if I were you, either. I suspect someone is trying to poison me."

Jerome set the goblet down on the table. "If Rowena does not return with me, Hartzburg will fall to the—" He wrinkled his nose. "What *is* that disturbing odor?"

"His lordship's poultice," Rowena said.

Jerome pulled out a perfumed handkerchief. "Good God."

In his entire life Douglas had not had to struggle harder to subdue his emotions. He realized that Rowena was seriously considering returning to her homeland because of what her cousin had told her. He ached to grab the runt by the neck and use his head as a battering ram against the door. If the princess had not been present, he would have thrashed the twit for daring to entice Rowena into danger.

But Rowena was watching and God only knew what she thought of him since that debacle in the woods. Matthew would handle this situation with calm diplomacy and not the primitive rage that had characterized Douglas's reactions in the past. He would have to tread carefully around this matter of her father else he would risk losing her forever.

"Her Highness has a personal advisor," Douglas said, ignoring the anxious hammering of his heart. "What does he say of this?"

Rowena frowned. "I have not seen Frederic since the night I arrived at this castle. It does begin to worry me he has not even sent me a message. A full fortnight has come and gone."

Jerome's gaze darted to Douglas. "Frederic would not want Her Highness to stay here. He never really wanted to leave Hartzburg in the first place."

"You are a misguided fool," Douglas said smugly. "You hope to have her appeal to the kidnappers' higher instincts. I tell you that such men have none."

"My father's life is at stake." Jerome looked suddenly like a frightened young boy. "The rebels want Rowena to meet them in person. What else can we do?"

"Frederic wanted Matthew to take a small army of mercenaries in through the mountains," Rowena said quietly. "'Tis the only way."

Douglas stared down at her, striving to conceal his alarm. His lady did not belong in a battlefield. She belonged at his hearth, brushing out her hair, reading to their children. *He* would fight for her. She would not have to defend herself.

"Matthew is not the only authority on military tactics," he stated.

"True." She appeared to have missed the point. "But there are very few warriors who are experienced, willing, and available to help me."

"Mayhap you have not looked in the right place."

"I have looked everywhere," Rowena said in exasperation.

"I can help you," Douglas said bluntly, a trifle offended that he was forced to state the obvious.

Rowena studied him in rueful silence. "How?" she said at last. "The physician said you will need at least two months to heal. And your hands are full hunting down the outlaws who threaten your village. Uncle Walter is being held by at least twenty ruffians in a rocky dungeon."

Douglas was too insulted to respond.

What did he know of manly things like rescues and revenge? she might well have asked. What use was an injured warrior who let outlaws harass him when her homeland tottered on the brink of anarchy?

In all the days of playacting the gentleman, he had never dreamed he would be so convincing that his very manhood would be questioned.

"The Dragon of Darien could help you," Douglas said with steel in his voice.

Before Rowena could react, the doors opened and Aidan, spurs striking sparks against stone, strode into the hall. "The horses are saddled, sir. We have food."

"Where are you going?" Rowena asked Douglas in alarm. "No. Don't tell me. I know—'tis a dreadful idea. Aidan, tell him to wait another week. He isn't ready to go out again after those men."

Aidan didn't say a word. He merely squared his shoulders and stared at a shield on the wall. Rowena might as well have been bargaining with a stone effigy for all the emotion he showed.

She turned in desperation to the short bewhiskered man who sat in the corner cleaning a pile of swords. "Baldwin, tell His Lordship he isn't strong enough to fight Neacail. He'll tear his stitches. The wound will get infected."

Baldwin laid down his sword and cloth. He looked at Rowena. He looked appraisingly at Douglas. Then he went back to his work, shaking his grizzled head as if solving this problem were beyond him.

Rowena exhaled forcefully. "Douglas of Dunmoral, I *forbid* you to leave this castle."

Douglas regarded her in irritation. "Stopping Neacail is not a matter to discuss like a dinner dish," he said. "The man will strike again and again until someone catches him." He lowered his voice. "Privately, I appreciate the fact that you care enough to order me about. In public, however, I cannot tolerate this unseemly henpecking."

She ran her fingertips up his bronzed wrist. "Would you not rather spend time alone with me than chase after an outlaw?"

"You forget your place," Douglas said in a voice loud enough for every man in the hall to hear. And at the same time he suppressed a shiver of pure longing at her touch.

"We should talk about this in private, Douglas."

"We do not have time," he said. "We will talk later."

"We won't talk later if you're killed," Rowena said.

"We are talking now," he said impatiently, "and 'tis wasting my time."

"What is the point in talking about this later if what we wanted to talk about is already done?" she asked.

"What are you talking about?" he said.

Rowena shook her head. "I love you, Douglas, but you are of no use to me dead."

His heavy-lidded gaze swept over her with possessive hunger as he realized what she had said. She loved him. He was stunned that he could experience such a strange brew of gentle and barbaric feelings in one breath.

She had come after him that night in the woods because she worried about him. She had seen him at his worst, a humiliated warrior. He had sworn at her and said incredibly embarrassing things in her presence. Yet unbelievably the bond between them had been strengthened, not weakened by his failings.

He had never guessed that this sort of caring was possible between two people. He had not dreamed he could impress such a woman without resorting to deception. How he wished now he had been honest with her from the start.

He desired this woman and her depth of caring with a gut-wrenching pain that made the wound in his shoulder feel like a wasp sting.

He pulled her against his chest and kissed her in full view of everyone in the hall. His powerful hands gripped her shoulders. Her head fell back. A gasp caught in her throat. Then she locked her arms around his neck and kissed him back with a passion one would not exactly expect from a princess. Her soft mouth sought his. She all but backed him into the table. Blood roared in his head like a waterfall.

"Princess," he whispered against her mouth, grinning as he broke the kiss. "You are precious and most unpredictable. But this time you *will* stay here."

He set her away from him, casting a hard stare at the gigantic figure in the doorway. "Dainty, if you let anything happen to her, I will throw the flowers at your funeral."

"Be careful, Douglas," Rowena said, her face a study in anxiety. "Come back to me."

"I intend to, Rowena."

"You're a stubborn man," she added.

He scowled at her to show his displeasure. She scowled back to hide her fear.

Baldwin brought him his sword. Then Douglas pivoted, Aidan falling into step like a shadow.

Jerome, still in shock from watching Douglas kiss his royal cousin, had slipped back against the table to let them pass. His elbow hit the goblet. The goblet rolled off the table between Douglas's booted feet. With a fleeting frown of annoyance, Douglas reached down to retrieve it.

"You kissed the royal princess in public," Jerome said. "Aren't you even going to apologize?"

"No," Douglas said, swinging around again. "I am not."

* * *

Hildegarde closed the heavy bedchamber door in Dainty's face as the princess hurried past her. "What is it?" she whispered.

"The man is driving me mad," Rowena said. "I am a prisoner now. A true prisoner. The giant is my bodyguard."

Hildegarde looked around the room; she had spent days trying to uncover the secret passage she sensed had escaped her search. She was still afraid that Prince Randolph's adversaries had followed them into these Scottish wilds to kidnap Rowena.

"There is still no word from Frederic?" Hildegarde asked.

"No." Rowena bent to wrench off her kidskin slippers, hiding her worried expression from the woman's scrutiny. "He's probably on the way here with his army."

"That man has never broken a promise in his life," Hildegarde said softly. "Something must have happened. Someone has stopped him."

Rowena looked up, her blood suddenly cold. "Jerome, do you think? Could he have brought rebel soldiers with him and perhaps done harm to Frederic on his way back here?"

Hildegarde shook her head. "Jerome was always a gentle boy. He doesn't have a head for plots. I cannot believe he would hurt anyone or betray you, Highness."

"Nor can I," Rowena said. "I—"

She bolted to the window at the sound of horses

whickering in the courtyard below. Douglas was riding from the stable on a spirited black stallion that he controlled with the pressure of his powerful thighs. Someone had taught the pirate how to ride.

"God protect him," she said in a whisper. "Bring him back whole."

His dark head lifted as if he had felt her blessing. Their gazes connected, and Rowena shivered as a frisson of fear and physical longing danced over her skin.

"Where does he go?" Hildegarde asked over her shoulder.

"To meet Neacail of Glengalda."

"But he is not yet recovered," Hildegarde exclaimed. "How does he plan to fight in such a weakened state?"

Rowena gripped the windowsill, her mouth pinched white. "I suppose that depends on whether he is the Earl of Dunmoral, or the Dragon of Darien at the time."

Chapter 20

SHE WAS A PRINCESS WHO HAD LIVED IN A TUR-reted palace and who rode beribboned ponies in a pasture, but her life had not been a fairy tale. Her mother had died of blood poisoning when Rowena was three, and the royal family had never recovered from losing the high-spirited woman who had been its heart and guiding hand.

Bereft of a mother's wisdom, Rowena's sister Micheline had become a rebel. Rowena, a lonely child, had taken solace in nature, in archery and forbidden walks through the forest. She had spent most of her life trying to make her grieving father smile.

Prince Randolph barely knew his children existed. He fought petty wars as a distraction. His heart had never healed from losing his wife.

Rowena loved him anyway, but wished that for

once he would take responsibility for his own welfare. She saw nothing otherwise but a sad life of obligation before her, of battling little wars that would drain her land and spirit dry.

Here at Dunmoral she had finally found a world where she was allowed to live. To test her feminine powers. To follow her inner longings. To suffer heartache because the man she loved had misled her and she loved him anyway.

Queen Mary or Elizabeth?

Mary-Elizabeth.

This isn't the solar at all. It appears to be the chapel.

Of course 'tis the chapel. Silly me . . .

The rasp of stone scraping against stone startled her. She swung around and saw Jerome emerge from a frayed tapestry that concealed a side panel behind the molded fireplace—the secret passage Hildegarde had missed. Her breath quickened, but she remained in control. A scream, she knew would bring Dainty charging into the room.

Her arrogant young cousin was dressed in a brown hunting tunic and wolfskin cape. Her gaze went to the silver-scrolled pistols in his belt. He looked like a child playing soldiers.

"Rowena." He did not sound like the young boy she remembered who set rabbits free from huntsmen's traps. "I eavesdropped in the kitchens. One of the servants found this at the abbey crossroads. It belonged to Frederic, did it not?"

Rowena stared down at the shorn length of cloth he showed her. It was the sash and gold medallion Frederic had carried with such pride against his heart. Flakes of dried blood darkened the metal. She swallowed, feeling a wave of lightheadedness wash over her.

"I'm going to look for him," Jerome said. "He might have fallen into a ravine, unable to send for aid. He is not a young man. Will you help me?"

Silence fell. Dainty stood guard outside her door. Hildegarde had ventured down to the kitchens to oversee supper preparations, afraid they would be poisoned if she did not supervise the making of the soup.

Hildegarde and Rowena had liked Jerome as a child. But time and ambition stood between the two cousins. Was it possible the rebels hoped to put Jerome on the throne as their puppet? Had he really traveled here to engage her help, or to make certain she did not return home? Her father's warnings about trust echoed in her mind.

"You were always good at finding people in the forest," he said earnestly. "Animals and people."

It was true. Rowena possessed a gypsy's sixth sense when it came to following trails. She knew intuitively when a path had been disturbed. She was patient and perceptive and in touch with her instincts. Yet the Highland hills were not the familiar woods of home. The very mist here vibrated with mystical secrets.

She made the choice to trust her cousin, as she had decided to trust Douglas.

"Give me a moment to change."

He sighed in relief. "Hurry."

Douglas cantered across the inhospitable heath, clumps of turf flying in his wake. Cold air stung his face as he rode against the wind that came shrieking down from the mountains. It was still early afternoon, but eerie burgundy-gold clouds darkened the sky. A storm would break before twilight.

'Twas the kind of day that made even a pirate pray.

Aidan remained behind him, standing look-out on a lonely crag. They had searched every stream, cave, and copse in a widening circle for a place where a band of outlaws could take refuge.

Once the storm struck, they would have to find shelter themselves.

Douglas slowed his horse. A buzzard circled a distant cairn. He motioned over his shoulder to Aidan. He saw him draw a pistol from his belt.

"Don't come with me," Douglas said as the man reined in beside him. "This is a good place for an ambush."

Aidan's gaze lifted to the cairn in cool agreement. "Aye."

Douglas eased off his horse. He unstrapped his sword and secured it between two smooth oblong stones. Behind him Aidan readied his pistol and crossbow and laid both across his lap.

The wind had quieted. Douglas walked through the cairn, dying stalks of brown heather brushing his legs. He carried his pistol in his right hand, a dirk in the other. His shoulder ached, but sheer determination enabled him to ignore this weakness.

He sensed Aidan raise his bow.

He started to climb the hill to the cairn. The buzzard melted away into the blackening sky. A predator would not hover above a party of armed men.

A dead man was another matter.

His stomach tightened as he turned the body over. The man's velvet tunic had been slashed from throat to midriff. Blood from countless stab wounds had seeped through the cloth.

"Frederic," he said with a sigh. He'd barely recognized the princess's advisor, but the blue Hartzburg cross embroidered on the man's empty scabbard gave away his identity.

The attack had been brutal and clumsy. Wolves lying in wait, except that those animals did not maul for sport.

He pressed his thumb to the man's throat without thinking. The faintest pulsebeat throbbed, a thread of life, so tenuous he could have missed it. Frederic's breathing was so shallow he could not hear it. Yet there was hope.

A shadow fell across the cairn. Douglas looked

up to see Aidan standing over him with an enormous flat stone.

Aidan gave Frederic a sympathetic look, lowering the stone. "I will bury him if you ride ahead."

"No. He still lives." Douglas's voice sounded as hoarse as the cries of the ravens coming from the abandoned abbey beyond the hills. He was thinking of how he would explain this to Rowena.

He would be responsible if Frederic died. The elderly man would have been safe if Douglas had thwarted Neacail's violence in the first place.

"I will take Frederic back to the castle before the storm breaks. Perhaps his injuries are not as grave as they seem. Bring me the extra plaid from your horse, Aidan, and with luck we will not concern ourselves with the grim business of digging a grave."

Dainty was furious and afraid. He'd failed Douglas now twice in a row. How was he going to explain that a mere woman had tricked him? Why had he trusted her when she'd asked not to be disturbed in her room? The castle was a blasted honeycomb of secret passages.

"That idiot Baldwin was right," he said to himself. "What does a pirate want with a damn princess anyway?"

Hildegarde's hysterical ranting echoed in his ears as he thundered across the drawbridge. He had raided the guardroom and armed himself with every weapon he could lay his huge hands on. Dainty was determined to take on the Devil himself to save her.

"My lady will be dead by the time you find her!" Hildegarde shrieked as she pitched a shovel at him from the gatehouse. "This land is full of wolves and wickedness. What if Jerome has carried her off while you dozed at her door? What if villains have slit her throat while I made soup?"

Dainty drew a draught of damp air into his lungs. He doubted 'twas Jerome, or wild animals that he and Rowena would have to worry about. 'Twas the Dragon's wrath when he discovered that his right arm had let him down again.

Douglas leaned across the table, his face as gray as granite. "Woman, if you do not cease that bawling, I will not be responsible for my actions. When did your lady leave?"

Hildegarde moaned into her hands. "I don't know. Jerome took her. She left me a note—they were looking for poor Frederic. What if the men who attacked him find her? Why did I let her come here? Why?"

Douglas backed away from the table, regretting the time he had already lost returning to the castle. He could not afford to ready more fresh horses and provisions for a long hunt.

The storm had broken, and raw fear raked his mind at the thought of Rowena wandering beyond his protection.

Chapter 21

ROWENA'S LIPS WERE NUMB WITH COLD AND PRAY-
ing. "This isn't right, Jerome. Frederic was worried sick about leaving me alone. He would have
at least sent me word of his whereabouts."

"I told you." Jerome's gaze darted nervously
around them. "I told you that you should have
taken asylum in France instead of Scotland. The
people here are half-pagan."

Her laughter floated into the still air. "And we
at Hartzburg, with our worship of mountain
trolls and sorceresses, are not."

They rode bareback on the mare Jerome had
stolen from one of the guards patrolling the loch.
Rowena had diverted him by skimming stones
from a tree on the water's surface. It was a ploy
she and her cousin had used as children.

A couple of hoodie crows cawed from a stand of skeletal alders.

"Birds of death," Jerome murmured.

"You sound like Hildegarde." Rowena spurred the mare forward. She wore a pair of green woolen hose beneath the rucked-up skirts of her riding habit. "The poor woman is probably convinced by now that you've abducted me."

She felt him stiffen against her. "As if I'd hurt you."

She forced a smile. "You suggested only seven months ago that Papa imprison me in the dungeon if I refused to marry the Duke of Vandever. You said I needed peace to think."

"For the good of Hartzburg," he said indignantly.

"More evil has been excused by those same words, Jerome. I won't marry that man."

His knee bumped against hers. The sky had turned sullen, shedding only pinpoints of light that stabbed the forest like spears. "Because of Matthew the perfect and pompous?"

"Why does everyone think I am in love with Matthew?" she asked in annoyance.

"If you won't marry Matthew, then why refuse the duke? They are both handsome men."

"I don't know," she said. "Perhaps they are not my destiny."

He scoffed at her. "Destiny, Rowena. I warned your father he shouldn't shelter gypsies in the castle."

"There is love as a consideration," she said dryly, "or rather the lack of it."

"A woman of your position cannot squander her life on ideals."

"Why not?" she said quietly.

"'Tis the earl, isn't it?" he mused aloud. "The dark warrior always wins. You let him kiss you. I would not have believed it if I hadn't witnessed the shocking act myself. He would have been hanged for daring as much at home."

She grinned crookedly and said nothing, remembering the powerful thrill she had felt down to her toes when Douglas kissed her. The memory of it warmed her even now. There could be no doubt her Dragon had come to care for her, that she had won his warrior's heart.

Or that he faced deadly danger, perhaps at this same moment. Her grin faded as fear for him gripped her. How easy 'twould be for the raiders to ambush him, and no one would know of it for days.

"Let's go back," Jerome said without warning. "'Tis going to storm. I shouldn't have brought you. We will return and ask the earl to help when he returns from his quest."

They had ridden into the pinewood shadows of a ridge that overlooked the winding road to the castle. Rowena urged the horse down toward the fringe of forest on the other side, an area thickly clothed in bracken and bramble fern.

"I saw something. A man's cloak."

Jerome wriggled around. "I don't like this."

"Neither do I," she said. "Look, fern doesn't grow like that."

She halted at the edge of an ash coppice that was interspersed with overgrown hazel and holly. A woolen plaid hung between two trees.

"'Tis a hiding place," she whispered. "You can watch the road from here and not be seen."

"I see naught but tangled thorn and dying foliage," Jerome exclaimed.

"The woman is right, laddie."

The crude voice came from the surrounding trees. Before Jerome could raise his musket, trapped between Rowena's cloak and her backside, he was hauled backward off his horse by a small group of Highlanders in filthy plaids who burst from the underbrush.

Rowena sat motionless on the mare. Part of her upbringing, ironically enough, had consisted of the appropriate behavior during a political abduction.

She tucked her shaking hands into the sable muff suspended from her waist on a gold-linked chain. She did not want to show her fear, to give them any more power over her than the physical.

A short man with blackened stumps of teeth, his hair in greasy braids, tore off his bonnet and swept her a mocking bow. "Welcome to hell, Yer Highness. We have just recently learnt of yer esteemed identity. Did ye enjoy the present my brother left in yer room?"

"Dear God." She leaned down to examine him. "You need a dentist! You look like an All Hallows' Eve turnip head with hollowed-out teeth."

He frowned in confusion. "What does that mean?"

"She said ye're as ugly as a rotten turnip," one of his men laughed.

Rowena's heart hammered against her breastbone. A Damascus-steel sword dangled at the spokesman's waist, inscribed with a blessing from her godfather, the Archbishop of Hartzburg. Her composure crumbled. She knew the sword had belonged to Frederic, that they had found him. She prayed his death had been swift. She prayed she would remain strong.

No one seemed to know what to do with her.

Then one of the outlaws holding Jerome motioned to the man who wore Frederic's sword. None of the outlaws were Neacail of Glengalda. Rowena had gotten a fairly good look at Neacail's course-featured face that night he'd fought Douglas on the bridge.

This man was apparently another of Neacail's lawless relatives.

"What do we do wi' her, Eachuinn?"

He walked up to Rowena, eyeing her with suspicion. She stared at the dried blood on his breacan, wishing for Douglas, trying not to think of what Frederic had suffered. Of what might befall her.

"Pig," she said in her low smoky voice. "Swine.

Offal of a maggot. May you be carried to hell in a burning chariot."

He turned pale under his pockmarked skin. His men laughed again, albeit uneasily this time.

"She's curst ye, Eachuinn."

"A burnin' chariot. 'Twill be the first time ye'll ride like gentry."

"Awful maggot. That's ye, man. A squirmy wee grub."

"She's a witch, mayhap," someone murmured.

A muscle twitched under the man's hollow cheek. "Then let's take her up to the Witching Stone and let her summon her master."

"Neacail will want a ransom fer her," said a man positioned in the trees. "Should we not wait until he returns?"

Echoes of thunder resonated across the moor as the men debated the matter. Rowena glanced once at Jerome's face and saw that he looked ashen with terror in the diffused light. Jerome had dreamed of fighting battles, of proving himself a hero. Reality was not the epic battle with a rainbow at the end he had expected.

Her sable muff, and the pistol within, were suddenly torn from her grasp. Three men pulled her to the ground, feigning concern when she fell to her knees. Rough hands gripped her shoulders, her hands. She heard Jerome cry out a warning, and she closed her eyes.

Rowena managed to control her fear, relying on faith.

The outlaws didn't know it yet, but her instincts told her they weren't going to live long enough to collect any ransom.

Douglas and Dainty reached the hill where Neacail's men had taken Rowena within a minute of each other. Dainty's first thought when he saw Douglas cantering toward him, his face black with fury, was "I'm a dead man. I ought to just lie down on my goddamned sword."

But Douglas didn't waste his energy; he was staring up at Rowena lashed to a standing stone on the crest of the hill, the wind tearing her hair into ribbons around her oval-shaped face. Her riding habit had been shredded into rags. Her white throat glistened in the rain. Her eyes were closed, her neck twisted at a peculiar angle, and for a moment he could not breathe or move, wondering if she were even still alive.

She turned her head. Relief replaced the fear that paralyzed him; blood rushed back into his limbs and brain in a burst of rage he could barely restrain. To see his lady thus abused enraged him beyond human endurance.

She looked pagan and beautiful and rigid with resigned terror, a medieval sorceress in silken rags who was stirring up an unearthly storm. He swallowed over the knot in his throat.

He glanced at the giant beside him. "Where is her whelp of a cousin?"

"In the cave with the outlaws," Dainty said.

Dainty had never seen Douglas like this. His eyes burned with an unholy light. His being pulsated with a charge that seemed to harness the raging elements around them. Pirating had always been a game. This was not.

"Is the lad dead or alive?" Douglas asked.

"Alive the last I saw," Dainty said.

Douglas was silent, coiled energy gathering as rain washed down on his rugged face. Uncertainty darkened his gaze as he realized that Aidan was already halfway to the hill. The man crawled from stone to stone like an adder in the concealing blackness of the storm. Douglas knew he could trust him.

"Sir," Dainty said, shifting with impatience.

For the first time that day, Douglas really looked at his friend. "My God," he said with humorless smile. "A monster in mail-armor. You're a one-man arsenal, aren't you?"

Dainty grinned, ready to pay any penance. "I raided the guardroom before I left the castle."

A coat of chain mail covered his brawny chest. A steel fist-shield hung beside the sword at his waist along with a pole-ax. He was holding a medieval morning star, the spiked metal ball on a chain and handle that could smash a man's head open with one blow.

"I hope to God you don't rust in the rain," Douglas said softly.

Dainty swallowed, needing forgiveness. "Sir—"

Douglas turned away, his eyes narrowing in speculation. "Aidan has almost reached Rowena's stone. Do you remember our first raid on Cartagena?"

"You want me to wait here?" Dainty said in disappointment.

"Only until I enter the cave and flush them out." His teeth showed in an arrogant grin. "Then you may put your incredible arsenal to the test."

The icy terror had begun to melt the moment Rowena recognized Douglas galloping across the moor like a mythical warlord conjured from the mists of time. His shoulder must pain him, she thought. But watching him on the stallion, his controlled strength, one would never guess he had battled death only days ago. His dark figure dominated the barren landscape.

His black hair fell on his broad shoulders. He was looking at her. Even though it was too far to see the details of his face, Rowena sensed his anger and determination, and she drew upon his power to fuel her own dwindling courage.

A week ago, playing along with his masquerade, she might have expected this man to pray for the souls of her captors. Remembering how he had fought Neacail of Glengalda, however, she knew him more than capable of a brutal counterdefense.

She shivered, from cold and nervous anticipation. Rain struck her face and trickled down her throat. Thankfully she had not been violated. Eachuinn, thinking of the ransom, had refused to let the others touch her. He had struck her once, though, in a temper when he removed her rings and she had unwisely scratched his face. A bruise throbbed on her cheekbone. He had shredded her shirts and petticoats with his dirk, mocking her disheveled state.

Numbness had penetrated to her bones, her rope-bound ankles and wrists. The rain seemed to be easing, but the wind was worse, chafing her skin. *Hurry, my lord.*

Douglas had disappeared behind the outcrop of bare rocks that sprouted at the base of the hill. So had Dainty. Their horses were hidden beneath the shadows of a rocky overhang. Relief shuddered through her body as she looked down and saw Aidan crawling on his belly through the stones, a dagger in his teeth.

"Do not move, lady," he said in a precise voice below her. "Pretend to stare straight ahead."

Her stomach knotted as one of the outlaws swaggered to the mouth of the cave. He glanced up in appraisal at Rowena. Then he studied the sullen landscape as if searching for a sign that their bait had been taken.

A princess tied to a stone like a sacrifice. She swallowed over the lump of fear and indignation in her throat.

The outlaw looked at her again, taking a long swig of aqua vitae from a bottle. They had sent a message to the castle and clearly expected a response.

"There now," **Aidan** said very quietly. "He's gone back inside to enjoy the warmth of his fire before the Dragon dispatches him to an even hotter place. I am going to cut your ropes with great care. Pray do not move."

She exhaled in painful breaths. If she moved, she feared she would shatter like fine Chinese porcelain.

"Stay exactly as you are until I tell you otherwise," he continued in that even tone. "Then you must take cover behind the stones."

She ground her teeth together. She didn't even blink in acknowledgment, although tears of relief gathered in her eyes. Aidan slipped away, and before she could flex her fingers, Douglas sprang up from the concealing rocks and burst inside the cave.

Hoarse shouts of surprise from the outlaws blended into the quiet roar of the wind. Every so often she heard the clash of steel against steel, a frightened oath.

It became hard to obey Aidan's order, especially when the fighting moved outside. Darkness had fallen. Glimmers from the rising moon gave the battle an otherworldly quality. She spotted Jerome chasing a man into a tussock of broom with Frederic's sword. She ached to snatch up a bow to help.

Douglas emerged next from the cave. He

slashed at a pair of raiders with sword and dagger like a man possessed by demons. Rowena could almost see the fear and bewilderment on their faces, in their clumsy uncertain counterattack.

Who would expect a dragon to burst into a smoky cave to confront four armed men? They must wonder if he were inhuman, a devil, and if she were indeed a witch who served him.

The former Earl of Dunmoral had never raised a twig in his own defense. Surely they asked themselves who this broad-shouldered foe was who'd sprang forth from the rocks like Bran, Celtic God of the Underworld.

Not a legend.

Not an ordinary Highland laird.

Whoever he was, Rowena knew he hid a very great heart behind his masquerade, and neither she nor his people could afford to lose him. The true legend of this man would not be based on his piracy. 'Twould come from his compassion and courage.

Douglas would have paid a princess's ransom to have an artist on hand to record this battle. He wanted a sketch of the raiders' faces when Dainty came thundering toward them on his horse, swinging the morning star over his bald head like a crazed conqueror.

The first victim fell at Douglas's feet, whimpering, "Lord save us. We only did as we were told."

His companion struggled to swing his claymore at Dainty's huge legs. Douglas turned away as the morning star caught the man in the chest, crushing lung and ribcage.

He found three more men hiding behind the rocks before one ran away. He took care of the other two by himself, but the stitches in his shoulder had reopened. Furthermore, he had not caught Neacail. Pain and anger rendered his mood foul and unforgiving.

And there was Rowena to be dealt with. He scowled up at the Witching Stone, signaling to Aidan that it was safe to bring her down.

Safe in one sense of the word. She was safe from the outlaws, but not from *him*. Douglas felt like paddling her royal posterior with his bare hand.

She looked amazingly dignified as she paused to straighten her shredded skirts before climbing down the hill, and this too angered him. His insides felt raw. The woman could not know the agony he'd suffered as he searched the moor. She had no idea he'd half expected to find her body, like Frederic's, in a pile of rocks.

She had no idea that if he had found her dead, he would not have wanted to live himself.

"Good work, Aidan," Douglas said quietly as the man walked toward him. "Why has the princess not come down yet?"

"I think she needed a moment to herself, sir."

Douglas nodded, then looked back up at the standing stone, horror deepening his voice. "Oh, my God," he said. "Rowena."

Eachuinn, Neacail's older brother, had not run away like the other cowards. Instead, he had taken advantage of the fighting to climb stealthily to the standing stone from the other side of the hill.

He rose unnoticed in the dark. He drew his dirk from his hose and held the blade across Rowena's throat, shouting out into the eerie aftermath of the storm. "Drop yer weapons, or I'll kill her. And bring me that horse."

Aidan looked up, his face unreadable, and let several long moments pass before his sword slid from his hand.

Dainty dismounted, shedding weapons. He walked his horse to the bottom of the hill, his gait measured and deliberate.

"Hurry the hell up!" Eachuinn cried, his cheek pressed into Rowena's hair. "The other man, too. All three of ye. I counted three."

Jerome looked at Aidan and then threw down his sword, his young face white with dread.

A droplet of blood ran down Rowena's neck. She did not breathe. Nor did Eachuinn for very long after that. A scrolled dagger flashed, and the man sagged against her for a second before he collapsed, his sightless eyes staring up at Douglas's unsmiling face.

Aidan flicked her a curiously approving glance as he climbed toward her. "For a woman, you understand the power of silence."

"I understand nothing," Rowena whispered, leaning back against the stone to let the cold wind wash over her shivering body. "I was too afraid to say anything."

Then Douglas was towering over her, his face raw and implacable. "I do not appreciate this," he said, flinging a plaid over her narrow shoulders.

Rowena was indignant. "As if I got myself captured on purpose."

He wasn't about to humiliate himself by admitting how helpless he had felt. He wouldn't let her know he'd almost lost his self-control when Eachuinn had held the knife to her throat. The scene was imprinted on his mind like a scar. His knees had nearly buckled under his weight.

He would not further weaken his image by admitting that the smear of blood on her throat made him sick to his stomach. He did not even ease her anguish when she said in despair that Frederic was dead. Caring about her had rendered him soft inside. Yet that was the way of it. Self-disgust shook him to the core.

He walked away while she wept. He would resist the unmanly temptation to gather her into his arms and offer comfort. Especially with Aidan and Dainty watching to witness this weakness. Still, her quiet sobs struck at his heart.

"Sir," Aidan said in question, glancing at Rowena alone on the hill.

"Tell her that her advisor still lives if you like," he said wearily. "I am too angry to give solace."

He rode hard into the black rain that had started to fall again, Rowena a stiff bundle in his arms. When it became impossible to continue, he stopped to take shelter in the abandoned abbey. Dainty, Aidan, and Jerome fanned out on the mud-swollen grounds to stand guard. The horses were hobbled in the drainage ditch.

Douglas took Rowena into the ruins of the abbey refectory. Using Aidan's ax, he broke up a pinewood stool. With every chop, Rowena flinched. This made him chop all the harder. Then he started a fire in the hollowed stove pit of what was once a hearth. A ball of dead furze served as kindling.

Rowena neatly laid her sodden shoes and cloak by the fire to dry. Her face composed, she twisted some bracken into a makeshift broom and began to sweep rubble and shards of stained glass into the corner. Rain dripped down from various holes in the collapsed roof.

Douglas frowned disapprovingly at this domestic activity. "Are we expecting the royal family, Rowena?"

She stopped her sweeping. "I did not want you

to tread on broken glass with your big feet, my lord."

He stretched out before the fire. "A pity you did not consider my well-being when you caused me to lose the fight to Neacail," he said in an admonishing voice. "Or when you disobeyed me."

Rowena marched over to him, the broom in hand. "Do you always blame others for your woes? 'Tis not my fault you failed to catch this villain."

It was the wrong thing to say. Douglas sat up with an angry grunt as his plaid came unfastened at the shoulder. "I would have caught him if I hadn't been playing the buffoon to impress you."

She stared in concern at the dark blood seeping through his shirt. "Why would you want to impress me?"

Douglas saw no point in lying. It had brought him naught but trouble. "At first, I had my eye on your fortune."

Rowena leaned forward to unravel his plaid, chewing her lip as she worked the wool free from his wound. "What were you planning to do with it? Fund a raid on Maracaibo with Henry Morgan?"

"God's bones." Douglas stared down fiercely at her face as she began unbuttoning his shirt. " 'Tis unfitting that you know more about my life than I do."

"The Dragon of Darien is discussed in every salon in Europe," she said softly.

He caught her slender wrists in his hand. "*Was* discussed. No one believes in dragons anymore."

"They do not appear to have much respect for princesses either." She glanced down ruefully at her ruined skirts, her smoky voice subdued. "I would have given you the money."

Douglas swallowed, releasing her wrists. Damn, but he could feel his anger dissolving, and he was not yet prepared to forgive her. "I doubt Prince Randolph would have approved. A princess aiding a pirate."

"My mother left me a great inheritance in jewels. 'Tis my fortune to do with as I please."

He shuddered as her fingertips danced up his arm, circling the iron-hard muscles of his biceps. "I do not desire your money, Rowena."

"What do you desire, my lord?"

His strongest desire, in truth, was to bed her, on the dirt floor of this ruined abbey. He desired both her submission and her spirit. He ached to touch her all over, to taste her, to admit that she had captured him. He ached to worship at her feet and conquer her at once. His breathing quickened at the thought of it.

"I made plans to deceive you," he said starkly. "Your money was meant to help my village. Yet I did not plan well enough, it would seem.

"I did not plan to lose my heart to you the very evening we met," he went on. "But there it is, lady. The truth, perhaps for the first time in my damnable life. I love you."

She grinned. "Then all is well between us. I love you, too."

"Not quite," he said with a black scowl. "You disobeyed me. I will not tolerate this. You were told not to leave the castle."

"I was worried about Frederic."

"You should have worried more about me," he said arrogantly. "You should have worried about how I would choose to discipline you. No one may stay with me who disobeys."

Rowena's eyebrows arched. "Shall I leave now?"

He shifted forward, his big frame blocking the fire's light. Darkness engulfed her. She could see his pulse beating in the base of his brown throat. His scowl of displeasure made her shiver. So did the dangerous heat that radiated from his body.

It was at this point that Rowena realized it was time to make her own apology. She should express shame that she'd suspected Douglas was the Dragon all along, and that she had gone along with his masquerade.

But she just couldn't bring herself to apologize. For one thing she was determined to make the most of his contrite attitude about deceiving her.

For another she was afraid of arousing his dragon's fury. Not that she'd thought he'd hurt her. He wouldn't. But he might hurt himself if he worked himself up into another wrathful state.

So she held her tongue. She would tell him about the minister's rumor at a later date. Mayhap after the birth of their third child. Or on the eve of their tenth wedding anniversary. When he was too tired to get worked up.

"You will stay with me," he said.

"Make up your mind, my lord. You just told me I cannot stay unless I obey you."

He smirked as if the matter were settled. "You will stay *and* obey."

"I think this bears further discussion," she said diplomatically.

"You cannot leave me." This time it was not an order, but the plea of a proud man who was not accustomed to begging.

He leaned away from her.

Rowena lowered her eyes, peeping up through her lashes as he kicked off his trews and unlaced his brogues. His blood-stained shirt fell at her knees. Then his plaid. The smell of man, of horse and sweat and musk, rose to her nostrils.

She released a deep sigh into the silence. She laced her hands together.

"What are you thinking now?" he demanded.

"That another lie has just been laid bare." She shuddered. "There is not a delicate bone in your body."

He gave her a beguiling smile. "You are shivering. Remove your clothes."

"What?"

"Come under my plaid with me. We will share the heat of our bodies."

"Naked?"

"This is no time for maidenly modesty, Rowena. You have suffered a grave shock today."

"I do not know that cuddling naked with you is going to calm my nerves, Douglas."

"But 'twill warm you," he said with another arrogant grin.

"I have no doubt of that—" She fell back on the palms of her hands as he began to loosen her bodice with alarming expertise. His smile faded as he untied the tapes of her skirts and petticoats and saw the damage done to her. Ugly purple bruises stood out against her skin.

"Sweet Jesus," he said, breathing hard. "When I think of what they did to you, I want to kill them."

She touched his hand, emotion closing her throat as he caught her fingers in his. "You *did* kill them, my lord. And your men are right now protecting the village."

He rubbed his thumbs over the rope marks on her wrists. "I wish to kill them again. I wish to make them suffer a hundredfold for daring to harm you."

Afraid of the anger in his voice, she tried to lighten his mood. "You have a definite tendency toward violence, my lord."

"But not where you are concerned." He lifted his black gaze to hers. "I would not hurt you for the world." His voice broke. "For the worst moment of my life, I thought I had lost you."

"Douglas—"

"Do you still want that kiss?" he asked in the seductive voice that few women had been able to resist.

She closed her eyes with a sigh as he laid his hands on her shoulders. Her clothing fell away like a broken shell, leaving her vulnerable and exposed. She had no defenses to fight a man like the Dragon. Nor did she wish him to raise his guard against her again.

She rose onto her knees. He took her face in his hands and kissed her so deeply that she began to shake. His tongue plundered her mouth as if it were one of the treasures he was famous for stealing. Sweet darkness swam in her head before he was finished.

"Are my kisses what you dreamed of?" he demanded in amusement.

She couldn't answer. She just anchored her arms around his waist and hoped he would understand how he had overwhelmed her. She hoped too that he would continue his loving.

Which he did. He cupped the globes of her breasts, sculpting the shape in his palms. He circled her dusky nipples with his fingertips, plucking gently, and her head fell back as indescribable sensation streaked to every secret place in her body. The things he did . . . his knowing touch, flooded her with dangerous joy. She ached all over with the needs he had aroused.

Her response practically robbed Douglas of his

reason. He groaned in sweet agony as her soft breasts brushed his bare arm. He couldn't pretend that kissing her had not affected him. He had been a damned saint for too long. His manhood was in the mood to misbehave.

He gave a growl of male aggression. Rowena felt him pull the plaid from his body, and she couldn't stop herself from taking a look.

"I knew I wouldn't be able to stop if I kissed you."

His voice was so rough she almost didn't recognize it. She cracked open one eye. It was him, all right, her dragon, his battle-tested body a beautiful thing to behold. Physical mastery had been proven in every muscle. Raw strength rested within the broad contours of his chest, his flanks. He exuded a virility that made her mouth dry. She felt a compelling need to touch him.

Slowly her gaze fell to the scars that stood out against the musculature of his shoulders. His eyes met hers. He opened his mouth to explain, but she spoke first.

"Don't say a word. Those are the scars you got when you rescued a kitten from a tree during a thunderstorm."

"I was taken as a slave in Algiers," he said in a somber tone. "Dainty and I escaped together."

"I know that," she said softly.

He brushed her hair back from her face. "Frederic isn't dead. At least he was still alive when I found him."

"I know that too," she whispered. "Aidan told me."

"I wish to know as much about you, Rowena. We will start with the secrets of your delightful body."

He studied her with unashamed appreciation in the firelight. Belatedly she crossed her arms under her breasts. Yet there was not one inch of her flesh that escaped his scrutiny. "I have never desired a woman more than I do you," he said, his nostrils flaring.

She moistened her lips with the tip of her tongue. She was certain he could hear her heart pounding. She said the first thing that popped into her head.

"You are not anything like Sir Matthew."

His eyes narrowed on her face. "Brother or not, I'll kill the blessed dolt too."

Rowena tried not to laugh. She placed her hands on his chest, then shyly pulled them away. "Perhaps you ought to take up falconry in earnest, my lord. It might give you something to do besides killing people."

Douglas stared down at her in silence. No woman had ever touched him with such tender curiosity before. It undid him, that mingling of sweetness and sexuality. It reawakened a gentle side of him he would have sworn was gone forever. If it had ever existed. His loins pulsed with heaviness and arousal. Yet his heart felt pleasingly unfettered and light with hope.

"Touch me again, Rowena," he commanded her in an undertone. "Touch me as you just did."

She did, her fingertips tracing across the granite-hard muscles of his chest. He reached for her. His hand looked huge and ominous as it skimmed the curve of her hipbone.

"Be mine," he said, his gaze hooded.

The tip of his shaft rose against her belly. She buried her face in the hollow of his neck, whispering, "Yes."

He went still. A shudder tore through his powerful frame. His callused thumbs cradled her jaw. "Do you know the sort of things I've done? Do you know in truth who I have been?"

"I know." She kissed his warm brown throat. "But I believe in you, Dragon, and I believe there's goodness in you."

"And if there isn't?"

Her sigh rose into the silence. "I would be your woman anyway."

Mary MacVittie marched her band of reluctant followers deep into the woods. She would have preferred to lead them to the Witching Stone, this being an ancient Celtic ceremony. But the people of the small glen were too frightened by the violence that happened there earlier in the evening.

Revenge was certain when Neacail found out what had happened to his older brother Eachuinn. Gunther, acting on Douglas's earlier order, had instructed everyone to assemble in the castle before morning. The earl would protect them there.

"Needfire." Dr. MacVittie scowled at the bottle of aqua vitae that was being passed around the circle. "As if anyone believes in this nonsense."

A frosty moon shone down on the gathering. The promise of winter chilled the air and misted breath.

For good measure Mary had dressed in a pure white silk robe. Actually, 'twas a nightdress, but nobody in Dunmoral knew the difference. She had also enlisted the help of Old Bruce the Blind Seer, and Ailag, the village herbwoman who was said to have made a black wart grow on Oliver Cromwell's left kneecap.

Mary raised the virgin rowan branch.

Old Bruce blessed the flames that leaped from his bog-fire torch.

"Light," Mary said in a whisper. "Hold the virgin wood to the torch, and may the old gods look down on us with favor."

Chapter 22

DOUGLAS GRINNED, THE GRIN OF A PREDATOR ON the verge of a conquest. "You will start obeying me now, Rowena."

"I am a princess, Douglas. I do not take orders."

"You are a woman first."

He buried his head between her legs. Rowena wanted to hit him for his boldness, but her body apparently had a will of its own. It wanted to submit to the man. It wanted to be mastered. She wriggled to sit up, but by then Douglas was holding her bottom firmly in both hands. She was helpless.

"You're not—"

"I am," he said, his wicked voice a whisper.

His tongue taught her the meaning of pleasure. His breath burned and aroused her. He nibbled at her with his even white teeth. The sensations that burst in the pit of her belly could only be called indecent—he was making love to her with his mouth. She strained upward from the floor as he suckled her sensitive nubbin of flesh, then separated the dewy folds beneath.

"You were made for loving, Rowena," he murmured as his tongue drove even deeper inside her. "I have never tasted anything sweeter."

Rowena wondered if she would faint. He unleashed sexual feelings that stole her breath. She gasped. She might have sworn. He did not halt his invasion. Then when release came like a sunburst over her dazzled senses, she knew she wouldn't faint. Oh, no. She was going to die. Her body convulsed. Her heart actually stopped cold in her chest. Douglas didn't look anything like a mournful man, however. He was grinning up at her most luridly from ear to ear.

He drew back from the plaid. Rowena gazed up at his thickly muscled body in wonder and apprehension as her own throbbed and pulsed with dying impulses. She raised her hand to touch his thigh. He shuddered as if in mortal pain.

"I want to make you mine," he said, his voice raw with need.

His black gaze branded her naked body as his possession.

"Does this mean that you have given up the vow of chastity you took before the village?" she whispered innocently.

Douglas laughed, the dark notes of his voice

echoing through the ruined hall. Before the sound died away, he had pinned her down on his plaid.

Chills ran over her as he nudged her thighs apart with his powerful knee, spreading her wide for his entry. Then his mouth covered hers in an intimate kiss, taking everything she offered. His hard shaft pressed against her. The groan she gave blended into his growl of male dominance.

She tensed as he thrust through the barrier of her delicate tissue. His mouth absorbed her cry of discomfort. Slowly the burning inside her eased. He began to rock against her in a ritual she couldn't resist. Her back arched, and he slid his big hands under her buttocks to drive inside her, thick muscle stretching her, slowly making his mastery complete.

Fire shot through Douglas as he penetrated her to the hilt. She felt so fragile, and he worried he would hurt her. Yet he couldn't stop himself. Her sweet flesh sheathed him so tightly he could barely keep from thrusting like an animal. Primitive desires clawed at his control. His face was drawn into a mask of self-restraint. He'd wanted her for too long, and when she began to move against him, it sent blood rushing to his head, and male instinct took over.

They moved together in a mating dance even after the fire began to flicker low and darkness closed around them. He slid deeply inside and withdrew, repeating this arousing rhythm until

they were breathless, reduced to raw sensation.
She was his woman now, and he was deeply
satisfied as he spilled his seed in the sweet depths
of her body. She would have to stay with him
forever.

The virgin branch caught fire. Its flames
burned blue-gold and pure, shedding radiant
light into the sky. The pinewoods glowed with
soft gilded shadows.

Mary MacVittie sighed with satisfaction. Then
she handed the burning branch to the young
strapping man behind her. "Run now and light
every fire in the village from this branch. The
castle too. The flames must be kept alive in at
least one hearth for a year, or the ritual will not
work."

Chapter 23

DOUGLAS DREW THE PLAID AROUND ROWENA'S damp shivering body. Morning had just broken over the abbey. He had needed the rest for the battle that he knew he must face. He would not stop again until Neacail was brought to justice. "I wish I could let you sleep another hour," he said in a deep voice. "Drink some brandy, Rowena. I will add more kindling to the fire. Thankfully it has burned all night."

She began to draw her knees inward, but he stopped her, frowning. "There is blood on your thighs. Give me my shirt."

"I can do it, Douglas."

But he wouldn't let her, insisting on tenderly wiping away the dark stains with the rainwater that had been caught in one of the abbey urns. His touch was so gentle, she barely felt it. In silence he took her slender feet in his hands and rubbed until warmth spread through her.

"We will be wed as soon as I can make arrangements," he said thoughtfully. "As soon as Neacail is caught. I am grateful that I can go out again with peace between you and me."

Rowena sighed, weakened by the magic of wonderful hands. "I will have to make a petition for the wedding contract. A princess is supposed to remain pure for the bridal bed."

"This is Scotland, Rowena. Marriage is a simple matter. We need only give our mutual consent."

"Yes, my lord. The wedding contract is but a formality. However, its stipulations must be observed even by you."

He raised his brow. "What is the purpose of this contract? I do not want your money."

Rowena took a sip of brandy. "'Tis not a question of money. The contract must be approved by the Council to ensure dynastic succession. *You* must be approved. With my homeland in chaos, such matters are necessary. I believe I mentioned the importance of heirs to you before."

"I believe you did," he said lazily, tracing his forefinger down her arm, smiling at the tiny shiver she gave.

Rowena paused. "'Tis crucial to Hartzburg that you are able to perform your manly functions."

"Call it foolish pride, but 'tis rather crucial to me too, Rowena."

"Your virility will be questioned," she said.

His mouth stretched into a devilish smile. "I shall rise to the occasion."

" 'Tis a serious issue, my lord. Hartzburg cannot continue unless its men are virile."

"I feel virile enough to father a Chinese dynasty."

"But will you feel virile enough a year from now while the Council takes its time to give us its approval?" Rowena asked. "A year is required for a royal courtship. During that time we are not supposed to meet without at least two guards present."

"A year from now?" he said in alarm. "Do you mean I have to wait another year to bed you?" His voice rose. "Hell, I won't be virile. I'll be a volcanic eruption."

There was a snort of laughter from the sunken courtyard outside the hall where Dainty walked patrol. Rowena subjected Douglas to a reproving stare.

" 'Tis bad enough that I have let myself be compromised within the ruins of a religious building," she said in an admonishing whisper. "I do not wish to have the world know of it."

Douglas grinned at her. "If I'd known that you were a royal hellion at heart, I'd have compromised you in the comfort of my castle. And as to waiting another—"

He looked up in irritation as a succession of

dull thuds shook the heavy oaken door. "Stop playing with that morning star, Dainty," he shouted.

The thudding continued. Then Dainty burst into an obscenity. Rowena covered her ears.

"God above," Douglas muttered, coming to his feet as he finished securing his plaid. "My men have become children. Get dressed, Rowena. I would not have anyone else take the pleasure of seeing you like that. I am a possessive man."

Rowena struggled into her smock. Then she called out after him, "Watch out for splinters, my lord! There is much debris in the dirt, and your big feet are bare."

He grunted at such a silly thought, the woman worrying over a splinter when only yesterday he had survived a deadly battle.

"Take your sword!" she added.

"I have it, Rowena."

"What about your stockings? The air is chill."

"Ye Gods," he said.

"I wish you would put on your shoes."

He stopped, shaking his head. By all that was holy, only one night together and they already sounded as if they'd been wedded for years.

With an annoyed glance to make sure Rowena was decent, he flung open the partially unhinged door. He was ready to give Aidan and Dainty a severe tongue-lashing, or better yet knock their inconsiderate heads together.

Scowling, he stepped out into the mist-shrouded remains of the abbey courtyard.

Aidan sat astride his horse on the muddied slope above what remained of the vaulted crypts.

Dainty stood against a holy-water stoop plucking arrows from his coat of chain-mail. Jerome was hiding in the collapsed rubble of the thirteenth-century arcade.

"What is the meaning of this?" Douglas demanded. "Have you not had enough fighting that you must play at it?"

Dainty disgustedly threw a handful of arrows to the ground. "Who said we were playing?"

Aidan dismounted and slid down the slick incline, mud splashing to his thighs. " 'Twas another of Neacail's men, a single archer, a damn good shot."

"A single archer?" Douglas narrowed his eyes. "One man made of you a hedgehog, Dainty? What in God's name were you doing?"

Aidan stared up at the sky.

Dainty gave a delicate shrug. "Placing bets, sir," he said in a mumble.

"On?"

"On," Dainty said. "On—"

"—whether you would come outside with a smile on your face, sir," Aidan answered.

"And this wager on my personal satisfaction was worth all our lives?" Douglas said in a disbelieving voice.

Dainty winced as Aidan worked another arrow

free from his breastplate. "The bastard is dead. He was alone."

"And he did not shoot at you, Aidan?" Douglas said quietly.

"Aidan went after him, though," Dainty said. "But the bastard had already blown out his brains behind that wall. We covered him with stones so the princess wouldn't see his bloodied corpse when we left."

"Considerate of you," Douglas said. His gaze drifted to the arrow-riddled door of the refectory. "But if Dainty hadn't been trussed up like a turtle, it might be the princess we'd be burying beneath that tree." He glanced at Aidan. "Or even you."

"Do we give chase again?" Aidan said.

Douglas stared at the arrows littering the ground. "After I see Rowena safely locked inside the castle."

Thick tendrils of mist covered the moor.

The wind had died down but another winter storm raged behind the mountains. Douglas led his party home in watchful silence. Rowena rode with him on his stallion with Dainty and Aidan flanking her on their mounts. Jerome lagged behind, jumping at every crow and grouse that protested their passing.

Douglas drew his first free breath as they reached the drawbridge. Rowena was safe. He would do now what he needed to do with a clear mind.

"A fresh horse and food," he said as a stable boy came running out to meet them in the barbican.

Rowena dismounted stiffly beside him. "Your arm needs tending."

"I'll tend it myself." He did not want her touching him again. He didn't want to soften, anger fueling him for the fight ahead. The perfume of her that lingered on him was distraction enough.

"My lord—" She laid her hand on his forearm, but he bristled, refusing her concern.

He couldn't even pretend to be polite. His torn stitches burned like Satan's breath. In his mind's eye he saw her naked body burnished by firelight. He forced the image away, summoning the memory of her bound and helpless on the hill.

She drew away without another word. With a day's growth of beard, his garment stiff with blood, pistols and sword at his waist, Douglas embodied the dragon she had dreamed of—and suddenly might lose.

Hildegarde hurried up beside her, her face anxious. "May the saints be praised for bringing you back. But the man is not going off again without a night's rest?"

Rowena nodded, her throat too tight to answer as Douglas strode off to the stables.

He wiped his dirk on a clean rag in the darkness of the stables, shifting impatiently as Dainty examined and rebound his shoulder.

"Aidan could stay to watch her," Dainty said in a casual voice.

"Let Dainty stay," Aidan said, leaning against the doorjamb.

"If you're going to argue about it all the damn day," Douglas said, "I might as well just send the princess out into battle and solve the problem of guarding her here and now."

"She'd probably do a better job of it than we've been doing," Dainty said earnestly.

"She could outshoot me with a bow," Aidan said.

Douglas snorted. "That isn't saying much."

The three men burst into laughter, only to sober as Rowena squeezed into the doorway behind Aidan.

"I have brought you a warm plaid and a special medallion blessed by my father's priest, my lord," she said.

"That is considerate of you," Douglas said, his face still flushed with amusement. "Isn't it, Dainty?"

Dainty wiped the edge of his eye. "It's brought tears to my eyes, sir."

"You are priceless, princess," Aidan said with a solemn bow.

"She could teach us a thing or two," Douglas said, which set all three men off laughing again.

Rowena glared at them. "I am so happy to be the object of your private joke. Need I remind you, however, that this man is going off to confront a cold-hearted killer?"

They stopped laughing.

Rowena nodded in satisfaction. "Please leave me alone with his lordship."

"I want you inside the keep," Douglas said the moment the two men left. "I want to see your face behind that barred window before I go."

"Take them with you," she whispered.

"No. The pleasure of killing Neacail will be mine alone. Kiss me before I leave."

She raised her face in chaste offering.

The kiss he took was not chaste. It tasted of sin and promised dark passion. It made Rowena's heart race against her ribcage. He gripped her shoulders as she arched into him, hurting her with his hands.

"At least wait another day, Douglas," she said when he released her to lean back against the stall door.

"I can't." There was no place for compromise on that roughly chiseled face. He was, in fact, impatient to be gone from her. "I'm not waiting another year to bed you again either," he added with an attempt at a smile.

She turned to face the stall, refusing to be patronized.

Sighing, he kissed the back of her neck. She smelled like rain and soap and sex, and when he remembered how it felt to be inside her, his head swam with a haze of desire that the callous warrior in him coldly ignored. He had shown enough weakness.

He studied the purple rope burns on her neck. Raw fury swept away every last speck of refined feeling. There would be time for tenderness later. He would not return to her until he had done what needed to be done. And if he failed, well, he would not return at all.

"Do what Dainty asks of you," he said in a deliberately detached voice.

She turned, her fingers pressed to her mouth. "You're unwise to go alone. Take Aidan—"

He spun on his heel before she could finish. His obsession for revenge ravaged his fierce unshaven face. She stepped back at the bloodlust smoldering in his eyes. A stable-boy slipped into the stables, too intimidated by the sight of the warrior's resolve to utter a single word.

Black panic welled inside Rowena. She knew nothing she did or said would stop him. He had the look of her brothers and father when they went off to battle, to a world where women did not exist. He moved with a power that belied his wounded body. Strength flowed from a hidden source that overrode human limitations.

The Dragon would fight to the death this time.

Baldwin's voice rose into the silence of the stable loft. "The princess is worried about him. Why do women fret so much?"

"I'd have gone with him if he'd asked," Willie said, rolling on his back. "I could use a good battle to get my blood stirring."

"She said he was hurt." Concern darkened Baldwin's face. "He isna the type to complain or ask fer help."

Frances hoisted herself up on her elbows. "Some men catch a cold, and they're dying. Others, like Douglas, don't think 'tis manly to show any pain at all. They just cork up their complaining like wine in a bottle and when it gets full, they go out and kill someone to feel better. At least that's what the men I've known did."

"And ye've known quite a few, Frances," Baldwin said by way of a compliment.

She stretched back into the straw. "Of course, the men I knew were swine. Douglas is a gentleman now so I can't pretend to know his kind."

Baldwin chewed a piece of straw. "I wonder what it feels like to be a gentleman."

"Once a pirate, always a pirate." Willie passed him the bottle of rum. It was empty. "Have a drink."

"Once a pirate . . ." Baldwin shook his grizzled head in admiration. "That's the most profound thing I've ever heard in my life."

"I'm always profound when I'm drunk." Willie hiccoughed. "Isn't that true, Frances?"

"No, you're always stupid." She peered down into the gloomy stalls below. "But I'll tell you what *is* true. A pirate needs a crew. He doesn't need three fools in a loft."

"He doesna need an empty bottle of rum either," Baldwin said, peering down the hollow glass neck. "Willie, ye're a selfish dog, and that's the truth."

Chapter 24

Rowena could not stand it another second. The waiting was killing her. She opened her mouth to complain.

Her two bodyguards didn't so much as blink. They had stuffed lamb's wool in their ears after her first ungodly tirade three hours ago. They were afraid her caterwauling would weaken them.

She picked up a tapestried pillow and hurled it from the window seat. Dainty didn't look up. He just raised his leather targe, the Scottish shield, and kept playing his game. She pitched a goblet of wine next. Aidan simply ducked as a wave of burgundy flew over the table.

They were playing chess in the solar by candle-light in the afternoon gloom while the princess paced circles on the Turkey carpet.

"You should be with Douglas," she said. "Shame on both of you! Playing games while your lord risks his life."

They ignored her. They couldn't hear a word she said.

She marched over to the table. She leaned down, pulled the plug from Dainty's ear, and bellowed: "How can you just sit there moving those stupid things around when he's fighting Neacail alone?"

Dainty jumped, dropping his pawn.

Aidan removed his lamb's wool and gave her a blank look. "Did you say something, Your Highness?"

Her eyes blazed. "Go after him. He needs you. The village needs you. I don't."

"Can't," Dainty said.

Aidan shrugged apologetically. "We promised."

"I swear I won't leave here," Rowena said. "Chain me to the dungeon wall if you do not believe me. Just help him. His right and left arms—that's what he calls you. You are wasting your talents watching me."

Dainty and Aidan stared at each other for a moment, not denying there was truth in what she said. Rowena held her breath, hopeful, praying. She felt ill. She'd taken only a glass of mulled ale all day.

"No," Dainty said, shaking his bald head. "Can't leave you here alone. Douglas wouldn't like it."

"We could chain you in the dungeon, though," Aidan said politely.

She nudged the chess board with her hip, tempted to push it off the table. "Ride into the village, and summon Shandy and Phelps to assist him."

"That's not a bad idea." Dainty's face was thoughtful. "We'd have to wait for Douglas to give his approval."

"I'll do it," she said decisively.

They returned to their game.

Rowena slipped from the room.

Rowena wasn't rash enough to ride out after Douglas again with darkness approaching. She would only be in the way. She could help, though, by enlisting a few of his friends to follow him. He had ordered most of his men to guard the castle, or the village as the people of Dunmoral prepared to move into the outer ward. Rowena decided to order them to guard Douglas instead.

Within twenty minutes, she had discovered the escape tunnels that ran beneath the dungeon. Dust and sticky cobwebs decorated her hair as she scrambled up the steps and triumphantly shoved at the rust-hinged trapdoor to freedom.

She smelled mud and mildewed damp in the air, and suspected she had reached a postern-gate passage into the woods that encircled the loch. With any luck a boat would be waiting.

A boat was waiting in the fading light. So were Dainty and Aidan.

Dainty reached down, and calmly hauled her out of the dark hole.

"I was looking for the privy," she said.

He brushed a cobweb from her cheek. "We'll be happy to take you there."

"X marks the spot," Aidan added.

"I am worried sick about him," she said in a broken whisper.

"Would you like another cup of mulled ale to ease your worries?" Aidan asked.

She pulled a pistol from the heavy folds of her dusty velvet skirts. "Get out of the way."

Dainty backed up immediately. Aidan crossed his arms over his leather jerkin. "Which one of us are you going to shoot?"

"Shoot me," Dainty said.

"You can't shoot us both," Aidan said.

"I'd rather be dead than let Douglas down again," Dainty said.

Rowena ground her teeth. "I want to shoot you both! He's in no condition for another battle."

"Douglas is the Dragon of Darien," Aidan said. "He can't be hurt."

Rowena shook her head in frustration. "No one believes in dragons anymore."

Aidan gently took the pistol from her hand. "Well, I do," he said in a quiet voice, "because a dragon was the only one who believed in me. You see, my family thought I murdered my own wife because I was racing our carriage when I lost control of the horses. Never once has Douglas questioned my innocence."

"Come, princess." Dainty extended her arm. "I'll escort you to that privy."

Chapter 25

NEACAIL HAD TRICKED HIM. DOUGLAS HAD GAL-
loped across bare moonlit moorland and over hill
like an avenging chieftain. He'd searched musty
caves and secret crevices, his body tense with
anticipation, ready for battle.

All to stalk a shadow.

Neacail had laid a false trail, leading Douglas
farther and farther away from where he belonged. He did not doubt that the tracks were set
to lure him from Dunmoral.

A wolf howled from the distant woods. The
eerie sound echoed across the encroaching night
and raised the hair on Douglas's nape. There was
a warning in the animal's call. Another wolf
released a deep-throated reply from the hills.

His spine rigid, he wheeled the stallion's head
and climbed a stormy incline. At first, he did not

realize what had disturbed the wolves, creatures who lived on the fringe, as he had. Creatures who were either admired for their thieving habits or despised, but never understood for what they were.

He could not see the castle at all. Metal-gray clouds like thunderheads obscured the square towers, the irregular outline that strangely had become a home to him. The castle where his princess waited with his young sister.

Then the clouds began to part, illuminated from behind by a sky of black and gold. Smoke and fire. His heart stopped. For a moment he did not realize that it was the village, not the castle, that had ignited like a torch. Surely by now the Highlanders had taken refuge in the outer ward.

There would be no more innocent blood on his hands. He pressed his spurs to his mount, giving the animal its head. The horse needed little urging. It was trained to obey. The old earl might have been a flower-growing fool, but he'd recognized good horseflesh. A Scottish gypsy had raised the stallion for racing.

The fire would spread. The raiders, heady with success, would move to the castle unless Douglas stopped them.

Douglas and Jerome fought back to back as darkness fell. Aidan had apparently let the young whelp escape the castle to placate Rowena. The smoke was so overpowering that at times they knew each other only by the bump of a shoulder or disembodied shout. Douglas would not have thought the lad had the courage or stamina for such an undignified battle. But perhaps Jerome felt he needed to atone for leading Rowena out of the castle to begin with.

Douglas appreciated the help. Neacail's men fought mean, and Douglas was admittedly not at his best.

"Look out!" Jerome shouted as a burly Scots outlaw with a beard hanging to his belly came hurtling from the dark at Douglas like a boar.

And no sooner did Douglas stop the man with his sword than another jumped Jerome from behind, almost cleaving the lad in half with an ax before Douglas pulled his dagger from his waist and threw it with a deadly accuracy perfected from doldrum days at sea.

The smoke began to thin. The village lay in blackened ruins. Shandy and Phelps, the two men ordered to guard the deserted village, had climbed the hill to hunt for other raiders.

Douglas retrieved his dagger, and stretched, letting the cold air flow over his sweating body. The astringent stench of blood and charred wood clogged his nostrils. Moonlight fell across the grim scene. He could not afford to lower his guard. Neacail had not yet been caught.

Jerome leaped like an acrobat into the water

trough to wrestle a raider hiding there. The man died without a sound.

Douglas grunted in amusement. He admired the boy's energy. His own was dangerously lagging. "A useful skill. You were a traveling mountebank in your infancy?"

The lad somersaulted down at Douglas's feet. "I've counted three left still looting homes on the hill. What do we—"

Douglas's sudden shift in posture stopped Jerome midsentence. Simultaneously, they looked up across the moonlit clearing. A light-haired man with a muscular build had just bolted into the single hut that remained standing in a circle of destruction.

"That would be Neacail?" Jerome said, glancing at Douglas.

"Aye." Douglas wiped his sword across his breeches. "That's the hut of Old Bruce the Blind Seer. I thought Neacail was too superstitious to burn it down."

"Thank God you had the villagers moved before this happened."

Douglas strode past him. "Aye," he said absently. "Thank God."

Douglas had broken into a run before his companion realized his intentions. He threw his unhurt shoulder against the door of the hut with a war shout that sent a fresh surge of blood through his system.

He burst into a nest of cowering outlaws. Neacail crouched on the floor.

He sent three armed men flying before the other three wrestled him to the dirt floor. Somewhere behind him a cat mewed plaintively in a hidden corner of the loft. He struggled against the combined assault of the others, kicking one man in the teeth, breaking his jaw. A stool crashed against his legs. He gripped someone by the throat, and sent another headfirst into the hearth when the wild ululations rose from the night.

Pagan cries.

"What in the name of Christ is that?" Neacail said, reaching in panic for a pistol that had fallen to the floor.

Douglas grinned, his white teeth flashing like a wolf's as he slipped his hand into his belt. "Pirates," he said conversationally. "Not your garden-variety privateer who politely wipes his boots on the deck before helping himself to your hope chest, but the scum-of-the-earth, skull-and-crossbones, booty and bottle of rum pirate who's taken an oath in blood to the Brethren of the Coast."

The doors crashed open. Baldwin fired a pair of flintlock pistols into the air.

Willie had forgotten his false teeth.

"Demons," Neacail whispered. " 'Tis true what I heard . . ."

Douglas kicked the pistol from the man's trembling hand. He drew his sword. "Nothing short of the Second Coming will stop me this time."

Neacail bared his teeth and came at Douglas with a rusty dirk.

Douglas said a silent prayer and took his revenge, his death blow swift and clean.

Chapter 26

"I WILL NOT BE CARRIED TO MY WOMAN ON A stretcher," Douglas said, flat on his back, his face a hideous mass of cuts and bruises.

"Then we'll be rollin' ye in the rest of the way because ye canna walk," Baldwin said as he bumped into the roped bridge rail that hung over the black waters of the loch.

Douglas swore at the top of his lungs. "Are you trying to kill me when my enemies failed?"

"If we'd wanted ye dead, we wouldna have joined the battle," Baldwin retorted, backing up to the other rail, which sent a white-hot wave of agony crashing over Douglas's battered body.

He groaned, trying to ease his frame into a bearable position. "I suppose I should be grateful," he said, staring up at the midnight sky. "No doubt you dunderheads meant to be helpful."

"'Twas our pleasure," Baldwin began. "We've—"

Douglas sat up abruptly, his bellow of outrage so loud and unexpected that Baldwin almost dropped him. "Turn this goddamned stretcher around. I want Neacail of Glengalda's head, and I want it now."

"Then you'll have to go back to the village and dig up his body before the wolves and worms do their work," Willie said.

Douglas lowered back onto his elbows, blinking at the castle. "He's dead?"

The two men carrying him grinned at each other across the stretcher. "Ye dinna remember killin' him?" Baldwin said.

Douglas subsided onto the stretcher with a scowl. "That pleasant memory has apparently been denied me. Why does my head swim like a lagoon? Have you dolts drugged me to make me docile?"

"Docile?" The young man being borne across the bridge on the stretcher behind Douglas gave a weak hoot of laughter. "Douglas of Dunmoral does not know the meaning of the word."

"Douglas of Dunmoral." Douglas sighed. "I suppose I shall die as such. Docile Douglas. The Daisy of Dunmoral."

Baldwin shook his head. "'Twas the doctor who drugged ye and yon young warrior. To dull the pain."

"What pain?" Douglas said. "I am a man. I feel no pain."

"Douglas!" Rowena could be heard shouting from the gatehouse as the drawbridge was being lowered. "Dear God, he's on a stretcher."

"Are they dead?" Hildegarde demanded.

Gemma started to shout. "Is my brother dead? Answer me, Baldwin. I have a right to know!"

Frances joined in the women's wailing and weeping. 'Twas more than Douglas could bear. He lurched to his feet, swaying as if he would topple off the bridge.

Baldwin and Willie wheeled him around. Shandy and Phelps moved to his rear with Jerome's stretcher lest Douglas tumble backward off the bridge.

"Water," Douglas said, pointing down inanely at the loch. Then he looked at the drawbridge. "Gangplank."

Baldwin grinned ruefully. "Not exactly, Captain."

Douglas raised a heavy black eyebrow. "Remind me to have you flogged in the morning for insubordination."

"Oh, Douglas," Rowena said softly, startling him as she galloped across the drawbridge from behind.

He pivoted woodenly. He stared at her in wonder, endless seconds of silence elapsing. Tears of relief ran down her face until she giggled and

Douglas pulled her clumsily against his chest with his good arm. Then those tears fell on his chest, dampening his filthy shirt.

Still, he said nothing. He fingered her soft hair with reverence. He gazed down into her face, his eyes glazed, his expression bemused.

Rowena frowned in suspicion. "Do you not know who I am, my lord? You have a distant look that alarms me."

Douglas was offended. "Of course I know who you are," he said with swaggering arrogance. "You are my woman. You wait for me when I return from battle. You will bathe me, and I will bed you."

Baldwin cleared his throat. " 'Tis the *princess*, sir."

"Princess Rowena," Willie said in an undertone.

"That's my cousin you're talking about bathing and bedding," Jerome said from his stretcher. "The Heiress of Hartzburg."

Douglas gave her an addlebrained grin. "I know perfectly well who she is. She is Princess Rowena of the Pretty Hair. A princess is a good thing—" His grin brightened. "Am I a prince?"

Baldwin chuckled. "The Prince of Port Royal, sir."

"I think His Highness ought to lie down," Rowena said wistfully, peeling his clinging arms from her waist.

He nodded like a clodpate. "I think we ought to lie down, too. I have a stretcher for such a purpose."

Rowena shook her head sadly. "He does not know who I am. Get him on his back and carry him inside."

Douglas dropped down on the stretcher, groaning as if their conversation had drained the last of his strength. He folded his hands over his chest. He looked up with a thoughtful frown. "I know that you are the Princess Rowena, and I, apparently, am a prince. What I do not understand, however, is why we have not yet boarded my ship."

Chapter 27

"HOLD STILL, DOUGLAS, AND LET ME FINISH BIND-
ing your shoulder."

He reached up, chuckling, and caught her
finely boned wrist. "I would rather bind you to the
bed, Rowena. I would prove to you my virility
again. For political purposes."

"Political purposes, is it?"

"We will couple for your country," he said
lustily.

"Do I need to summon help?" she said.

"I wish to prove my patriotism, princess." He
winked at her with his blackened eye. "I shall be
your most loyal subject."

Rowena straddled him and forced him back
down onto the counterpane. For about two seconds he pretended to comply. Then he pulled her
between his legs, capturing her mouth in a deep

kiss that brought complete silence to the room. On his death bed, she thought, this man would be proving himself.

The fat tallow candle on the nightstand cast shadows between the green velvet bed curtains.

Douglas lowered his mouth to the creamy valley of her breasts. His free hand moved up to grip her bottom. This action caused him great pain. He was too much a man, however, to show it.

"The doctor will be here at any moment," Rowena whispered. "You are the worst patient I've ever seen, and Frederic and Jerome aren't any better."

He hooked his ankle around her stockinged calf, pinning her beneath him. She sighed in momentary surrender. Her hair had gotten wrapped around his muscular forearm. The weight of his groin, its warmth and vitality, pressed against hers. Delicious impulses sparked deep inside her.

"Pirates do not make good invalids," he said, his black gaze glittering. "We chase women around on our wooden legs and ogle them under our eye-patches. Once we get our hands on a genuine prize like a princess, our evil knows no end."

"You're dripping that vile poultice on my petticoats," Rowena said.

He brushed his unshaven jaw across the cleft of her breasts. "Take them off. And the poultice."

"Mrs. MacVittie is waiting for me to come

down to supper," Rowena said primly, suppressing a shiver of pleasure. "Your men have been working on their manners for the wedding feast, and want to show off."

"Why does the very prospect send a chill of terror down my spine?" Douglas said.

"I've no idea." Rowena smiled. "They're the most darling men. Now be a good pirate, and lie still. When we're done, you can wear the lace sling Hildegarde made for you."

Douglas sat up in horror, spilling Rowena to his side. "A lace sling? My men will laugh me into the loch."

"Not after the way you fought three days ago," Rowena said. "Are you certain you should not remain in bed another week, my lord?"

"I need to prepare myself to rescue your father, Rowena. Lying in a bed weakens a man."

Rowena compressed her lips. Douglas would not be rescuing anyone, but his pride probably was not ready to accept this sad fact. Still, her papa needed someone's help, and she could not remain in this castle much longer than it took for travel arrangements to be made.

Douglas fixed her with a baleful glare. "There is nothing wrong with me. Good God. I can most assuredly withstand a walk to the supper table."

"Do you want your crutches?"

"Crutches? I do not need crutches."

To prove this point he vaulted off the bed and executed a series of deep-knee bends. For a terrible moment he thought he might have to grab the bedpost for support. His head spun like a top. His heart pounded.

"There. I told you." He schooled his grimace of agony into a smile as every muscle and bone in his big body throbbed in rebellion. Lord, was there an inch of his flesh that did not ache? And his feet hurt, for the first time in his life. His blessed feet were killing him!

"I have conquered Spanish garrisons and captured galleons, Rowena. A little tussle won't stop me."

"You brought down seven men in that hut, my lord."

"Seven?" Was that all? he wondered. Hell, to judge by his groaning bones he would have sworn it had been at least fifty. Ah, well, he had won the fight. Neacail was dead, and Douglas did not look like such a daisy. He had kept his promise to Dunmoral, and to himself. He would heal, his desire for Rowena a potent medicine. He would marry her and concentrate on the happy business of begetting heirs. In a hurry.

"Now all we have to do is rescue Papa, reclaim his power, and round up the insurgents who threaten Hartzburg," Rowena said.

Douglas frowned. "Well, what are we waiting for?" He headed dizzily for his wardrobe. He would not lead a rescue in his nightshirt.

"You're in no condition to command an army, my lord." Rowena winced as he limped past her, banging his bandaged knee on the dressing table. "I must find another man to rescue Papa."

He skewered her with a dragon scowl. "Upon my corpse, woman."

"If you force that battered body of yours into another fight, then dropping dead at my feet is a distinct possibility."

"I conquered Spanish garrisons with a concussion, Rowena."

"Ten years ago, my lord."

"Ten?" Douglas said in astonishment. "How the devil do you know? 'Twas three at most."

"Ten, Douglas. I have memorized the date and place of most of your daring exploits."

He fought a wicked urge to push her down on the bed and throw himself upon her. Except that he suspected he might not have the strength for it. Had he broken his bloody kneecaps?

"My wounded warrior," Rowena said with a gentle smile. "My dragon in bruised scales. I shall pray that your body mends."

Douglas grunted, sinking down on the bed. "Stop that embarrassing prattle, Rowena. I need a mere day or two to heal before we travel to Hartzburg."

"Let us see if you can make it to the supper table first, my lord."

He pulled himself up by the bedpost. Then he drew her back against him, locking her arms in his hand without any effort at all. His other hand busily began to unbutton her gown. He untied her chemise and petticoats next. Rowena stared down in disbelief at the pool of silk and muslin that imprisoned her. With a wicked grin he removed his shirt.

His voice was a seductive whisper. "You cannot refuse me, Rowena."

It was, unfortunately, true.

Shivers ran down her spine as she felt his erection pressing against her bare buttocks. Then he began pinching her nipples between his callused fingertips. The muscles of her belly tightened. She felt a shameful dampness between her thighs.

"I love the way you respond to me," he said in a ragged voice.

She was too embarrassed to say anything. She just squeezed her eyes shut as he pulled her down on the bed, his big body looming over hers. He brushed his mouth back and forth across her distended nipples, and it felt so wickedly good, she wanted to die. He ran his hands over her naked curves. He probed her secret places with his fingertips until she couldn't hold still. She had to strain upward to feel him. She needed him deep inside.

He penetrated her slowly at first. He pressed inside, then withdrew in a rhythm that drove them both wild. But she was so tight and willing that he soon began to thrust, sliding his hands under her bare white bottom to bring her closer. Pleasure streaked through his groin as she stretched to accept his pulsing staff. He released a deep growl of domination.

He possessed her, not once but twice, proving his power and mastery.

He loved her so late into the night that Frances burned the haunch of venison and ended up making a stew from what she could salvage. He loved her with such abandon that Hildegarde, concerned by her mistress's absence, half-convinced Aidan that the water-horse had rea-wakened to spirit Rowena away.

He loved her until a cloaked silence fell around the castle, and Rowena, her supple body damp with perspiration, her veins bubbling, could barely heave a sigh of utter contentment.

"And now supper," he said cheerfully, springing out of bed, stretching his abused warrior's body this way and that to impress her with his prowess. 'Twas yet another deception (he felt like death), but Douglas would be damned before he'd sink exhausted back onto that bed. And as he helped his lady dress, he was too much in love, and pain, to hear the sentry's shout of surprise from the watchtower.

He was too engrossed in his princess to realize the threat he had most feared, and temporarily forgotten, was about to come true.

Chapter 28

DOUGLAS STARED WITH DISPLEASURE FROM THE doorway of the great hall. "What lackwit invited all these people here at this hour? I wished to celebrate our betrothal alone."

"I invited them," Rowena said. "These are our dearest friends."

"Friends? These men are pirates. I will not have my future bride subjected to an orgy. My crew cannot behave for five minutes."

The pirates rose respectfully from their benches as Rowena approached the dais. Dainty, Aidan, Shandy, Phelps, Gunther, Baldwin, Willie, Martin, Roy. They were no longer the servants of a Scottish castle. They were an assortment of the roughest, ugliest, raunchiest scoundrels to sail the Seven Seas. Brocaded hats, lace cuffs, knee-high boots, dirks and cutlasses. They had dressed for a royal occasion.

"This is going to be a disaster," Douglas said.

Mrs. MacVittie was present, presumably to orchestrate the debacle. So was the doctor, and Henry, as a representative from the village. Jerome and Frederic hobbled to the table, looking as miserable as Douglas felt.

Douglas sat with a sense of impending doom. In a quarter-hour it would be midnight. He was too much a pirate not to fear announcing his betrothal at the witching hour.

Even though his betrothed had indeed bewitched him.

He studied Rowena with a fierce pride he could not conceal. Candlelight glinted in her hair, drawn in a figure-eight from her face. Gentle amusement moved across her aristocratic features as she addressed his men as if they were her equals. How amazing that he, with his nefarious past and sin-tainted soul, had won her loving heart. There would be no more deception between them.

His smile hardened into a scowl. How could her brothers have allowed such an enchanting creature out into the world to raise an army? Douglas's blood near boiled at the thought of it, his princess leading unprincipled mercenaries into battle.

Of course, as her husband, he would have to

help rescue her papa. It looked to be a hell of a honeymoon.

"Ye're in fine shape tonight, sir," Baldwin lied.

Douglas fingered his blackened eye, staring down the table at his men in apprehension. No one had stabbed anybody yet, broken wind, or bellowed a bad word. This could not possibly last.

"What is the matter with you?" he asked Willie, who sat red-faced and looking tortured with a waterfall of lace frothing at his throat.

"Gemma's tied my cravat too tight." Willie sounded like a frog with a wheezy windbox. "I can't breathe."

Douglas's startled gaze stopped on Aidan. Aidan with his black shoulder-length hair tortured into lacquered ringlets. "What in God's name happened to your hair?"

"Frances took a pair of curling tongs to it," Aidan said through his teeth.

"Your men are behaving like perfect angels," Rowena whispered in his ear. "But why is your cook standing in the door with such a lost look?"

He reached for his goblet. "She is probably ashamed of what she was."

"Why?" Rowena asked. "Was she a murderer?"

"No. She kept a bawdyhouse on Tortuga. She cared for Gemma when I sailed." He took a deep drink of wine as he remembered those turbulent days. "We were the scum of the earth, princess."

"I want to speak with her," Rowena said. "Summon her here. The woman practically hides under the table when I visit her in the kitchen."

Douglas shrugged, then did as she asked. Frances turned pale, reluctantly trudging to the table with her eyes on the floor. She dropped Rowena a shy curtsy.

"Please sit with us, Frances," Rowena said. "I understand you were a nursemaid to his lordship's sister."

"A nursemaid?" Frances said in surprise. "Douglas said that?"

"Take a place at our table," Rowena said firmly. "In my palace, the nursemaid is an esteemed member of the family."

Frances stood there in an agony of longing. "Your Highness," she said, tears burning her eyes. "I can't. I'm a fallen woman."

Rowena smiled at her. "Well, I'm a fallen princess so that makes us a good match. Mayhap my lord and I will have a place for you in our nursery."

"You would trust me with your children?" Frances said in disbelief.

Douglas smiled. "You have a gentle hand and a loud bellow, Frances, both of which are needed skills for the raising of bairns."

"You need only learn to turn a deaf ear to Hildegarde's worries," Rowena added. "No doubt she will lord it over the nursery."

Douglas would have pursued this intriguing

interest Rowena had taken in their offspring, but a commotion from his other guests distracted him.

He sneaked a peek at his gold pocket-watch. He'd been wrong. The good behavior had not lasted even five minutes.

Trouble had erupted when Willie took a loud slurp of stew.

"Shut up, Willie," Baldwin said in an undertone. "Ye're offending the princess."

Willie lowered his spoon. "Well, your face is offending the poor woman. I've seen the backside of a baboon that was easier on the eye than your ugly mug."

"That wasn't a baboon's backside you were looking at," Dainty shouted. "'Twas a mirror."

Rowena rose to her feet to put a stop to this, but Frances, looking mortified, flung her back into her chair. "If you ruin her betrothal dinner, you weasels, I'll throttle the whole bloody lot of you! I've never sat next to a royal princess in my life."

Shandy emptied a pitcher of ale over Frances's head.

Frances picked up a knife.

Douglas leaned back in his chair with a deep sigh of resignation. Salty insults and eating utensils began to sail over his head.

"Is this going to be an orgy?" Rowena whispered as a boot landed in her bowl.

Hr grinned, wrenching her by the hand. He

hauled her out of her chair. They broke into a run as four men overturned a bench. "I'm not staying here to find out. Would you like a walk in the garden? Gemma's petticoats are still in bloom."

"Good idea." She stopped to hurl a loaf of bread at the man who'd thrown his boot into her bowl. "Thank you, my lord," she said, hurrying after him. "That was the best formal supper I've ever attended."

Their laughter didn't last long. The kisses Douglas planned to steal in the passageway were thwarted by the jingling of a horseman's spurs and a devastatingly cheerful voice, which Douglas had hoped he would never hear again in his life.

"Is anybody at castle?" the cheerful voice cried.

"My God, 'tis him." His face stark with fear, Douglas pulled away from Rowena as a jaunty figure in a white cloak rounded the corner.

Matthew, with his shaggy blond hair and angelic grin, the other side of Douglas's midnight soul.

"So there you are," Matthew said. "Cornering the kitchen help, are we, brother? Where is everyone? It took me nigh on a half-hour to stable my horse. This is not what one expects from an earl."

Rowena stepped out from behind the broad shadow of Douglas's back. "Kitchen help," she said indignantly. "I take exception to that."

"Rowena," Matthew said in shock, then chuckled as she launched herself into his arms.

Douglas's mouth tightened as he watched their warm reunion. He wanted to tear Rowena from his brother's embrace, but said instead, "You're the only person in the entire world who could travel from Sweden to Scotland in a white cloak without a speck of dirt upon it. This is unnatural."

Matthew winked at him over Rowena's head. "I changed in the stables. I would not appear before a princess in a disheveled state."

Douglas could not bear it any longer. He pried Rowena from Matthew's embrace, not even pretending to be subtle.

Matthew held out his arms to Douglas. "Congratulations on your newfound respectability, brother. Do you realize that you now outrank me?"

Douglas pointedly ignored the outstretched arms. "For a man with a broken leg you appear to have made an amazing recovery."

"Haven't I?" Matthew came a little closer, examining Douglas's face in the torchlight. "I cannot say the same for you though. Dear me, Douglas. Have we met the wrong end of a battering ram?"

"He rescued his village from raiders," Rowena said, gazing up at Douglas's forbidding face with a concerned smile. "And he refuses to rest abed for a proper recovery."

Matthew stared at them both for several moments, his gaze inscrutable. "I see. Well, perhaps I shall hear this stirring tale of heroism in the morning. For now I need to talk to you in private, Rowena. 'Tis most urgent."

Douglas folded his arms over his chest. He stared down at Matthew with a warning in his black eyes. "There are no secrets between us."

"Not that you know of," Matthew replied, giving Douglas a patronizing pat on the hand. "Do you have a private room that we may use, Rowena?"

"We can use Hildegarde's chamber," she said. "No spy or evil spirit could find entry there."

Matthew lowered his voice. "I have brought the ring."

Her eyes darkened in understanding. "Oh, Matthew, that means—"

The rest of her enigmatic reaction was lost to Douglas as she drew Matthew down the passageway, then up the winding stairs to Hildegarde's room. Douglas shadowed them like an intruder in his own castle, unsuccessfully trying to eavesdrop on their cryptic whisperings. He envied them their closeness, the bonds they shared.

". . . smuggled to me in Sweden."

". . . Erich escaped and is ready."

They reached the top of the stairs, glancing back at Douglas as if they had forgotten his presence.

"Make sure we aren't disturbed, brother," Matthew had the gall to shout over his shoulder.

"Make sure our friends don't hurt themselves in the hall," Rowena added as she bolted the door.

Douglas stared at that closed door, the demons of his piratical past rising in revolt. He swallowed over the lump in his throat. He felt alone, excluded, inadequate . . . afraid. He was the interloper.

He would not make a fool of himself.

He would not sprout horns of jealousy and use them to break his way inside.

He would be nonchalant and gallant about the fact that his brother had his future bride in her bedchamber with the door bolted. About the fact that she had belonged to Matthew to begin with.

He began pounding his fists at the door like a madman. He kicked the lock. "I demand to know what you are both doing in there. I will not be made to stand in the hallway like a lackey."

"'Tis all right, Douglas." Rowena's sweet voice floated out. "Your brother is just showing me his jewels."

"He's showing you—"

"Actually, they're her jewels." Matthew opened the door a crack, his handsome face annoyed. "For heaven's sake, Douglas, this is a meeting of political urgency. We cannot conduct it in secrecy with you yelling through the keyhole. These are the crown jewels of Hartzburg, smuggled out of the country by Rowena's loyalist faction to finance our rebellion."

"I care nothing for jewels. I only wish to know you will keep your clothes on." Douglas shouldered his way into the room, staring in anguish at Rowena on the bed in a sea of diamonds and sapphires.

"Our clothes on?" Matthew said in shock.

"You ought to apologize for that remark," Rowena said. "You have insulted your brother."

Matthew smiled warmly. "I understand. 'Tis his fierce seafaring temperament. I forgive you, Douglas."

"I don't want to be forgiven," Douglas retorted. "I want to kill you. I've wanted to kill you ever since you took Mama's body away from the place she belonged."

Matthew shook his head in genuine bewilderment. "After everything I've done to make amends between us? Why have you allowed your hatred to grow?"

Rowena moved between them to examine a necklace in the candlelight, murmuring, "I wonder why brothers must always quarrel. Can you not save your battle instincts for helping my father?"

Douglas was practically breathing fire. He stood over Matthew with a heaving chest and smoldering eyes. "You speak of amends. I still do not know where she is buried. You make me feel as if I am unworthy of standing at her grave."

Rowena looked up slowly. She had never heard such pain or depth of emotion in her Dragon's voice.

Matthew edged back a step. "You have made

yourself look like a demon, Douglas. Pirating is hardly a prelude to sainthood, and I shall take you to her grave whenever you like. Rowena, come and look at the bruise under his left eye. Is it festering, do you think? He has worked himself up into a feverish state."

"I hope not," she said, hurrying up to Douglas, bracelets dangling from wrist to elbow. "Yet I would not be surprised if he suffered a relapse. He's a terrible patient. Let me look at your eye, my lord."

Douglas pulled away from her hand. "'Tis a nervous twitch. It happens right before I want to kill someone."

Matthew frowned. "Don't talk to her that way, brother. She's only trying to help."

"I was talking to you, moron," Douglas said. "Rowena, take off that lurid jewelry. You look like a gypsy fortuneteller."

"You were talking to me that time," Rowena said accusingly.

"And he insulted the crown jewels of Hartzburg by saying you looked like a gypsy," Matthew pointed out.

Rowena put on another necklace in defiance. "I love gypsies. I may even have gypsy blood in my background. Does that bother you, Douglas, to learn that my blood might not be pure?"

"My blood isn't pure either," Douglas said in a nasty voice.

"'Tisn't?" Matthew said in surprise. Then, "Ah,

you are referring to your father. Well, do not fret
on that point. Humble origins are nothing to be
ashamed of."

Douglas walked Matthew back into the wardrobe. "I wasn't referring to my father, you trouble-
making nitwit. I meant that being related to you
tainted my bloodlines."

Rowena came to rescue Matthew just as he fell
back into the wardrobe. "Perhaps you don't wish
to marry me either, Douglas, now that you know I
might have gypsy blood in my veins."

"I never said that," Douglas shouted.

Matthew hauled himself out of a pile of Hildegarde's underwear, looking dazed at this turn of
events.

"Did he hurt you with his dragon's fury?" Rowena asked.

Matthew plucked a whalebone corset off his
chest. "I don't think so. Good heavens, Rowena,
this is the largest corset I've ever seen in my life.
You never took this size before. Hasn't Douglas
been giving you any exercise?"

"No, he hasn't," Rowena said. "I've been imprisoned in this castle under guard, wild gypsy with
impure blood that I am. That, however, is Hildegarde's corset, not mine. This is her room."

Douglas pushed Matthew back into the wardrobe. "How do you know what size corset Rowena
takes?"

"I allowed you to bully me the first time because I did not want to make you look stupid in

front of Rowena." Matthew struggled upward, coming at Douglas with his fists raised. "But enough is enough. I'm sorry I arranged this whole affair. Of all the woeful tales I've heard about you—which I defended, by the way—I never dreamed you enjoyed mistreating women."

"Arranged what whole affair?" Rowena wondered aloud.

Douglas took a punch and missed. Matthew jumped in the air with a menacing shout, which might have been a more impressive maneuver if he hadn't gotten one of Hildegarde's horsehair petticoats wrapped around his ankles.

Rowena heaved a sigh. "For heaven's sake, cease this senseless fighting. He is in no condition for fisticuffs."

Matthew grunted as Douglas hit him in the solar plexus. "Don't worry," he said between groans. "I won't hurt him . . . just teach him . . . a . . . less—*ooof.*"

Rowena placed herself between the two men, holding them apart at arm's length. "I meant that I did not want Douglas to hurt *you*, not with your leg just mended. He is twice your size."

"My leg?" Matthew stumbled back a step, breathless, staring down sheepishly at his satin breeches. "Oh, *that* leg. Well, it wasn't really broken, you see. 'Twas badly bruised. I told a tiny fib so that you two would have time together."

"A tiny fib?" Douglas said in a deadly voice.

Matthew looked anxiously from Douglas to

Rowena. "It worked, didn't it? You were embracing in the passageway when I arrived? Am I wrong in assuming that you have made a love match?"

"Matthew." Rowena had turned ghostly white. "What are you saying?"

Douglas straightened his shirt. "Never mind what the moron is saying. I want to know how he comes by the details of your undergarments."

"Do not tell him, Matthew," Rowena said.

Matthew nodded. "Never let it be said that I betrayed a princess's confidence. The secret of your corset will never leave my lips."

Douglas grabbed one of two ancient spears mounted above the bed. "I'm going to roast you over a spit, you scurvy dog."

Rowena gasped in surprise. "You sound just like a real pirate. Say that again, Douglas."

Matthew stared uneasily at the spear. "He *is* a real pirate. Perhaps we ought to tell him after all."

"Don't you dare," Rowena said. "We shall never hear the end of it."

"I cannot tell you, Douglas," Matthew said with a sigh.

Douglas gave him a chilling smile. Then he proceeded to slice the frog fastenings of Matthew's cloak with the tip of the spear. "Since we are half-brothers, I will give you the option of being roasted feet first or skewered through the gut."

Matthew blanched. "I'll tell you—"

"No, Matthew." Rowena pressed her index finger warningly to her lips. "If you tell him, I shall never be able to confide in you again."

Douglas jabbed the spear into Matthew's midsection. "Yes, but if I don't tell him, Rowena, he's going to skewer me."

"You wouldn't do that, would you?" Rowena asked Douglas.

He smiled at her. It was a menacing smile. "Yes, I would. Oh dear, brother, you've lost a button." And a row of pearls popped off Matthew's chest into the air.

"I'm telling him," Matthew said quickly. "Douglas, I borrowed Rowena's corset to wear to a masquerade ball when I visited Hartzburg. 'Twas an innocent act."

Douglas lowered the spear. "What?"

"I wore her corset to the Hartzburg ball."

"'Tis true," Rowena said reluctantly. "But he broke the laces, and Hildegarde had to fasten it together with leather thread. Fortunately, these repairs did not show beneath my dress."

Douglas glanced from Rowena to his brother, a rude snigger of disbelief escaping him. "My brother dresses as a woman."

"I told you not to tell him," Rowena said in irritation. "Now he shall think I have a mannish figure."

"No one would ever think that," Douglas and Matthew said in unison.

Douglas shook his head, looking Matthew over.

"I never took you for a lily, lacing yourself in corsets and such. I tortured myself comparing myself to your saintliness." A smirk settled on his face. "A saint in a corset."

Matthew's face reddened. "I don't dress in corsets! 'Twas for a masquerade. I was meant to be an empress."

"Only a man confident of his masculinity would dare dress as a woman." Rowena frowned at Matthew. "Don't say I didn't warn you. He'll never let either of us forget this."

"Well, obviously I am the biggest fool in the world," Matthew said indignantly.

Douglas sat down on the edge of the bed. He dropped the spear beside him. The excitement had tired him. He yawned. "You are a fool because you dress in ladies' garments?"

"No," Matthew retorted. "Because of the sacrifice I made for you and Rowena."

"Why do you keep prattling on about sacrifices and arrangements?" Rowena said in annoyance. "You do not make sense, Matthew."

Douglas leaned back on the bed, grinning insultingly. "Perhaps his corset is so tight it's stopped the circulation of blood to his brain."

"I have heard of such things happening," Rowena conceded with a chuckle. "Hildegarde often cannot breathe for lacing herself up like a sausage."

"'Vanity of vanities, all is vanity,'" Douglas quoted, folding his arms under his head.

"Was that Shakespeare again?" Rowena asked.

"I believe 'tis the Bible," Douglas said.

Rowena grinned at Matthew. "Would you like to borrow my petticoats tonight?"

"You are the most ungrateful pair I have ever met," Matthew said.

Douglas's grin faded. "Why did you write me that your leg was broken?"

"I was playing Cupid," Matthew said grumpily. "In my naiveté I envisioned you as a pair of potential lovers. I hoped that Rowena would inspire you to live up to the responsibilities of your newly acquired nobility."

"She certainly does inspire me," Douglas said. Then, "Rowena, what are you looking for?"

"The spear for you to skewer your brother," she answered. "I trusted him, and he deceived me. I will not be deceived again."

Douglas stood up abruptly. "He manipulated us. That is another reason why I should murder him."

Matthew backed toward the door. "I don't understand. I thought you two had fallen in love—"

"I've had a little rest." Douglas took the spear from Rowena, his face ominous. "Now I'm ready to skewer you in earnest."

"Not unless you catch me," Matthew shouted. He thumbed his nose. Then he made a mad dash through the door just as Douglas lunged at him.

* * *

Rowena shook her head, listening to them crash down the castle stairwell like a couple of wild boars. Curses rose into the air. Footfalls came running to investigate the commotion.

"Boys," she said.

Hildegarde poked her head into the room. "They are killing each other, Highness."

"I know." Rowena sighed.

"Shall I send for the physician?"

"'Twould not hurt," Rowena said.

"Has Sir Matthew asked to give you away at the wedding?" Hildegarde asked.

"The way Douglas is going at him, it does not seem either of them will live that long. Why is it that the men in my life are so prone to violence?"

"I couldn't answer that, Highness." Frowning, Hildegarde moved into the room to gaze at the fortune in jewels arrayed on the bed. "Good God. The crown jewels of Hartzburg—but this means—"

"My father is in grave trouble," Rowena said in a heavy voice. "He cannot hold out without reinforcements. Jerome was telling the truth. You may pack our belongings, Hildegarde. It looks as if I will be a warrior wife right after the wedding."

Chapter 29

Douglas couldn't sleep. For one thing he could not twitch a muscle without groaning in misery. For another, he would be married tomorrow, and if life got any sweeter than this, he simply could not imagine how.

His lady lay waiting for their wedding day within the tower. He grinned, anticipating the long nights ahead of loving his young wife, the chill winter mornings when he would snuggle into her body. When their bairns would bound into their bedchamber, disturbing them with shrieks of laughter and selfish demands. They would raise a family and grow old together, the years passing to make a potpourri of precious memories.

But did he deserve it? Did the little bit of good he'd done in the glen make up for years of greed and hurting people? Was he worthy of happiness? Guilt nagged at him for a life wasted, for the injustices he could not forget. 'Twould take a long time before he could live with the man he had been.

Or perhaps he would die having never made peace with himself. Something yet was lacking in his life. The love of a woman was a priceless blessing. Yet all was not well deep within his spirit. That last echo of darkness must be exorcised.

God help me, came the unvoiced cry from his heart, the human cry of countless hurting souls, the cry that Heaven waited so long to hear.

And to answer.

He got dressed and suddenly found himself in the castle chapel. Someone had left candles burning on the stone altar. Rowena most likely. His princess believed in the power of prayer.

"*She* deserves happiness," he said aloud.

"So do you."

He turned in astonishment and saw Dainty kneeling behind him.

"I never knew you were a praying man," Douglas said in accusation.

Dainty's deep laughter resounded against the stone walls. "How do you think we survived so many wild years together, Douglas?"

"I thought we had the Devil's own luck."

Dainty just smiled and stared at the stone

crucifix on the altar. *"That* is where we find our forgiveness and our purpose, Douglas."

He swallowed. "Not for men like me."

"Especially for men like you."

Aidan came in a few seconds later. He halted in his tracks when he saw he wasn't alone.

"Did you come to pray for me too?" Douglas demanded.

"Hell, no," Aidan said. "I was looking for the solar."

Gemma felt a strange quickening in her heart. She walked down the hall and saw a gentle light radiating from the chapel.

'Twas a light more powerful than the dawn, than the two candles that burned low on the altar. 'Twas a light that filled her with unspeakable joy and peace. The beauty of it brought tears to her eyes.

She gasped in wonder as she saw her brother kneeling between the stone slab pews. Her tears fell freely as she joined him. He put his arm around her waist, hugging her in a silence that neither of them could defile with words.

Afterward she said, "We were born poor, Douglas. Why do you suppose we're living in a castle now, and you're marrying someone as wonderful as Rowena?"

His voice was wry. "Certainly not because we've led an exemplary life."

"You've been a son of a swine," she said earnestly as they rose from the rough floor. "Why would God give you grace?"

"I don't have an answer."

They walked out into the hall. The castle was stirring, men singing, maids bustling to and fro to prepare for the great day ahead.

"But why should God give you all this when so many people suffer?" Gemma persisted. "Why doesn't he give it to them?"

He turned to her at the top of the stairs. "Perhaps that part is up to us."

On the morning of her wedding, Rowena covered her face, throat, and shoulders in a cold cream concocted of oatmeal, lard, whipped eggs and ground almonds. It was a popular receipt at court for the beautification of a noblewoman's skin. Mrs. MacVittie had passed it on to Rowena, claiming the notorious Countess of Castlemaine swore by it.

The princess wanted to look perfect for Douglas.

Douglas intended to give his princess a necklace of water pearls. He had purchased it many years ago on a whim on a Jamaican wharf for a woman he had not yet met.

He knocked now at that woman's door, the woman of his dreams. A monster answered him. He stifled a shout, backing into Aidan in the hall. The monster was probably a female—it had nice breasts and wore a nightgown.

" 'Tis bad luck to see the bride on her wedding day!" Hildegarde bellowed from the depths of the room.

The door slammed on the monster.

"Bride?" he said numbly. "*That* was my princess?"

Douglas and his princess bride were married a few hours later in the castle chapel, on a quiet afternoon in early December. Frederic and Jerome, as emergency members of the council, had granted permission for the ceremony. Pirates and village folk crowded the courtyard to admire the laird's wife in her lutestring-trimmed silver gown and tiara.

Douglas looked dashing in black velvet with a brocade hat and red sash on his shoulder that also served as a sling.

A band of pipers escorted the bride and groom on their ride into Dunmoral for the wedding feast. Father Gordon followed on his donkey.

Rowena looked radiant as she alit from the peat cart. "Humility before hierarchy," she had said when Douglas asked earlier if she wished to ride in a proper carriage.

It was a custom in this part of the Highlands to throw a shoe for luck at the newly married couple. Henry hurled an old brogue into the air.

Rowena ducked, and it hit Douglas on the side of the head, stunning him.

"Oh, Douglas," Rowena said, covering her face in her hands. "My goodness, are you hurt?"

"I don't know," he answered. "My body is too benumbed to feel any more pain."

There was a Highland wedding feast with oatcakes, cheese, cold mutton and a gigantic Bride's pie decorated with Cupids in the crust. The guests drank elderflower wine and heather ale.

The miniature pirate sloop *Delight* was floated in the loch with tiny candles glowing from its decks. Fire blazed from the miniature brass cannons.

Mrs. MacVittie gazed upon the celebration with a look of pride. "I have accomplished my dream. A shipload of pirates and they didn't drop a single spoon." She sighed deeply. "I call that a job well done."

"A shipload of pirates and they didn't murder anyone," Douglas said under his breath. "I call that a miracle."

Desire unfurled deep inside Rowena. Her breasts swelled as Douglas kissed each one in turn, blowing on her nipples until she twisted under him. His tongue circled her navel. He began branding her entire body with burning kisses. And with each he whispered, "Mine."

He seduced his wife in the winter shadows. A low fire burned in the hearth. Predator and pirate that he was, he plundered every ounce of sweetness from her body. Over and over.

She learned quickly how to please him. She slid her hands down his broad chest, to his belly, taking hold of his shaft. He gasped.

Shyly she explored his rugged body, the muscular ridges, the scars and healing bruises, the hard contours. His belly quivered. Her innocent touch aroused him so that it hurt to breathe. And when he felt her mouth at his manhood, his head fell back, and a low groan broke in his throat.

"I love you," he said, tangling his large hands in her hair.

"And I love you, my lord," she whispered.

Chapter 30

Two days passed. Hasty preparations were made for the long journey to Hartzburg. Snow fell softly on the hills. Herds of red deer foraged for food in the pine forest. A magical mist shimmered above the loch and wrapped the castle in dreamlike seclusion. The autumn days of what was called *Foghara* in Gaelic had yielded to the sleeping spell of *Geamhradh*.

The small army that Princess Rowena had raised was leaving Scotland before winter sank its teeth any deeper. She had found the perfect warriors to carry her father's campaign: The pirates of the *Delight*, and a more restless lot she had never envisioned.

The pirates had dreamed of the legendary city of gold. They had hoped to serve their dragon-captain in one final burst of greed and glory. Instead, they were serving Douglas and his sainted brother in a raid to strengthen Prince Randolph's stand against the rebels.

As Willie told Douglas, "Hartzburg needs us more than this castle does, sir. But don't you worry. We'll all be back together before long. The lads will never leave you."

"That's what I'm afraid of," Douglas said.

Douglas had awakened at dawn to see Dainty and Aidan off at the drawbridge. His two best friends had decided to help Matthew and Jerome liberate Rowena's uncle from the mountain rebels who held him hostage. Douglas, Frederic, and the pirates planned to join Prince Randolph in his fight. They would travel in separate parties.

Douglas joked for a few minutes with Dainty and Aidan as was their custom before a raid.

"Where will you go afterward?" Douglas asked them.

"I don't know," Aidan said, looking restless on his sturdy roan. "Maracaibo maybe."

Dainty said, "I have a friend in Marseilles who owns an inn. I might spend a year just fishing, building a ship."

They looked at one another for what they knew could well be the last time. These were men who wouldn't shed a tear if you tortured them on the rack.

"Go then," Douglas said as his brother Matthew, in white satin, emerged from the stables on his horse. "Be gone, you worthless dogs. I'm sick of your ugly faces if you want to know the truth."

Aidan nodded.

"The grace of God be upon you and your princess," Dainty said.

Douglas turned away, his voice low. "And on you both."

Baldwin looked at Douglas. A small crowd had gathered in the courtyard. "Well, Captain, I'm sorry to be leavin' ye, but Jerome has just asked me to be his man-at-arms, and I think the lad needs a good brain like mine on his side."

"'Parting is such sweet sorrow,'" Douglas said.

Baldwin stared at him. "Do ye mean that, sir?"

"No, but Shakespeare's Juliet apparently did," Douglas said.

Baldwin narrowed his eyes. "Is yer dragon's pride keepin' ye from askin' me to join your army?"

"Rowena's cousin needs that sharp brain of yours," Douglas said. "I have depended on it for too long."

"He's always welcome to come back to us later," Rowena said. "Douglas, you must remember your manners with our friends."

Douglas frowned at that, but not for long. He had captured his prize. He could afford to be gracious. He would, perhaps, persuade Rowena to move to another castle in an undisclosed location when they returned to Scotland. And he would, the minute he got her alone, remind his wife that a warrior must not be henpecked in public.

Epilogue

The Scottish Highlands
September, 1663

BLUEBELLS AND HEATHER COVERED THE HILLS SURrounding the castle. Children waded in the cool waters of the loch and played pirates on the peaceful shores with wooden swords.

The pagan flames of Needfire still burned hot and pure in the hearths of Dunmoral. With luck, and the Lord's grace, the ancient Celtic fire would never die out.

The castle had its protector, the eighth Earl of Dunmoral, even if he still didn't know Mary Queen of Scots from Queen Elizabeth, or a parapet from a pair of socks.

The princess also had her pirate, and she intended to keep him, even if she had to lock him up in the tower for the rest of his days.

In three months or so Dunmoral would have a genuine heir.

Hartzburg had been liberated from the rebels. Prince Randolph's banner flew high from his rocky castle where he ruled unchallenged. He had blessed his daughter's marriage to her dragon. After all, he told everyone who would listen, his son-in-law had saved him.

"What I want to know," Gemma said in the solar, "is did my brother turn Rowena into a royal hoyden, or did she reform him?"

Hildegarde chuckled as she dipped her quill into the inkwell to write out a list for the nursery. "I'm not certain that it matters. Perhaps we should worry more about what wicked children the pair of them will give this world."